IN THE HEAT OF PASSION

"I never hit anyone before in all my life!" Cara murmured.

"Did you like it?" Nick inquired.

Cara's horror began to fade, to be replaced by an awareness of her position. He held her so well imprisoned that she could barely squirm. "I did, rather. I think I'd like to do it again."

"Pray restrain yourself," he said, and dropped a kiss on the tip of her nose. Then he kissed her cheek, her temple, her eyebrows, and her ear, and pulled her cloak aside so that he might work his way down her fine slender throat. When she made no attempt to stop him, not that she *could* have stopped him, held prisoner as she was, or that he would allow it even if she tried, he drew back to look at her. Her lovely eyes had fluttered shut. Now they opened. Her luscious lips parted. She looked adorably dazed.

"Cara mia," he groaned, and claimed her mouth with his. Nick gave himself up to the moment. No woman he had ever known, and he had known many women, had ever fit so perfectly into his arms . . .

BOOKS BY MAGGIE MACKEEVER

CUPID'S DART

LOVE MATCH

LOVER'S KNOT

AN EXTRAORDINARY FLIRTATION

Published by Zebra Books

AN
EXTRAORDINARY
FLIRTATION

Maggie MacKeever

ZEBRA BOOKS
Kensington Publishing Corp.
http://www.kensingtonbooks.com

ZEBRA BOOKS are published by

Kensington Publishing Corp.
850 Third Avenue
New York, NY 10022

All Kensington titles, imprints and distributed lines are
available at special quantity discounts for bulk purchases
for sales promotion, premiums, fund-raising, educational
or institutional use.

Special book excerpts or customized printings can also be
created to fit specific needs. For details, write or phone
the office of the Kensington Special Sales Manager:
Kensington Publishing Corp., 850 Third Avenue, New
York, NY 10022. Attn. Special Sales Department. Phone:
1-800-221-2647.

First Printing: November 2004
10 9 8 7 6 5 4 3 2 1

Printed in the United States of America

1

Amidst the rural splendor of the Cotswolds, behind ornately scrolled ironwork gates, perched an immense residence made of honey-colored local stone, with a moss-covered slate roof. Surrounding it was undulating wooded country to the south, orchards and green hills where horses and cattle and sheep grazed, and extensive gardens all around. The house was embellished with a flagged courtyard and pedimented portico, windows of every description, a chapel, and more chimneys than a cat could count; the gardens with hothouses and forcing-beds, rock grottoes, mock Gothic ruins and a menagerie long fallen into disuse. Since the current mistress of those gardens believed in allowing the plants to enjoy themselves in unplanned ways, wisteria twined voluptuously along the old brick walls, and clematis scaled enchanting heights before tumbling drunkenly downward in sheets of graceful foliage and cataracts of pure white blooms, and the south terrace was an orgiastic blaze of lilacs in every imaginable hue.

On this particular overcast spring morning, Lady Norwood was strolling along the old stone paths with a basketful of sprigs and seedlings, which she paused occasionally to pop into all manner of odd nooks.

Trailing after her were two curious lambs, several clucking chickens, and an undergardener laden down with spade and shovel, rake and pruning knife, watering pot and shears and saw. The head gardener, a proponent of symmetry in all things, was hiding in the greenhouse, as he did whenever her ladyship set about wreaking disorder in his domain.

Lady Norwood knew that her servants thought her eccentric. Her deceased husband's servants, to be more precise. She spied a lonely spot in the underskirt of a hedge, and dropped to her knees to investigate. The sun burst through the clouds then, to caress her graceful back, kiss her perfect cheek, linger on her lovely (if somewhat untidy) hair. Master Sol could hardly be blamed for this sign of blatant preference. Lady Norwood—*née* Loversall—bloomed more brightly than any of her posies ever would. The Loversalls bred astonishing beauties. Chaucer had coined the phrase "fair as is the rose in May" while gazing on a Loversall.

It had been a nine days' wonder, this Loversall's decision to choose from among her countless suitors a gentleman at least thrice her age, for the women of Cara's family were notorious for their determination to love unwisely and too well, as the gentlemen were renowned for the number and quality of their mistresses. Both tendencies seemed to Lady Norwood excellent reasons for marrying as she had. She shooed a lamb out of the way, and pressed a marigold firmly into the ground, then sprinkled coal ash on the surrounding earth to insure that it would root well before she rose and brushed carelessly at her shabby skirts.

"There!" she said to the undergardener, who was squinting speculatively at a crack in the garden wall. Her smile dimmed as she glimpsed an approaching figure. "That's enough for now, Willie. Send word up to the house that we'll be wanting tea."

Willie eyed the newcomer. "Yes'm," he said. Squire Anderley owned the property adjoining the Norwood estate. 'Twas common knowledge that he'd also like to own Lady Norwood. So far the mistress was having none of it, bless her heart. Queer her ladyship might be, but Lord Norwood had doted on his wife, and his servants—excepting the head gardener—had gotten in the habit of doing likewise. Willie would send word to the house, right enough, and suggest to Cook that she might put some senna seed in the squire's tea cakes.

Squire Anderley strode briskly along the crushed stone path, his riding crop in hand. Paul would have been surprised to learn that an undergardener mistrusted him, not that he particularly cared what Lady Norwood's servants thought of him, or even his own. Servants existed to serve their masters, not to think. His own thoughts were for Lady Norwood as she stood among her flowers, awaiting him. Cara took his breath away, even in that outmoded dress, with dirt on her hands and cheek, her hair skewed in a careless coil atop her head, and chickens pecking at her feet. She was the most outrageously beautiful creature he had ever seen. Her features were as divine as any goddess's, her skin fair and fine as the most priceless porcelain; her eyes a rich sapphire blue and her hair a glorious mass of tousled red-gold ringlets; her figure so mouth-wateringly voluptuous that every gentleman who saw her wished to whisk her off to bed. Paul was no exception. That he had thus far refrained from slinging her over his shoulder like some love-starved Viking warrior spoke volumes for his self-discipline.

Lady Norwood absently plucked a posy as she watched her visitor approach. The squire was a tall, handsome man of five-and-thirty, with a sun-bronzed countenance, hazel eyes, and chestnut hair, broad shoulders and lean hips and strong thighs that showed to good advantage in his tight breeches and well-tailored coat. His stride was confident, his smile self-assured. As it should have been. Paul Anderley was master of the Gloucester Hunt, a person of no small importance in these parts, a leisured country gentleman blessed with no less than thirty thousand pounds a year. Ladies jostled for his attention, for he was currently without a wife. Men trembled to think the squire might learn of some half-drawn covert, or unstopped earth, or fox that shouldn't have escaped.

Cara wondered if she intended to escape, and if in that case he was prepared to pursue her through gorse, forest, and wood. Paul nudged the chickens aside with one booted foot and raised her hand to his lips. "Bat guano," she murmured.

Squire Anderley was accustomed to Lady Norwood's tendency to speak whatever thought was passing through her mind, which was admittedly a trifle queer in her; however, her astonishing good looks made a man willing to overlook what might in a less bedazzling female have been considered extremely annoying quirks. He drew her hand through his arm. "Yes, and I am pleased to see you, too, my dear."

Cara smiled, revealing an enchanting dimple at one corner of her mouth. Paul decided that it was long past time he took another wife. *This* wife, thereby attaching the considerable Norwood property to his own estate. Not to mention attaching Lady Norwood to himself. That lush mouth was made for kissing and nibbling and certain even more intimate pursuits.

Cara wondered why he was staring at her mouth, almost as if he was thinking about stealing a kiss, which was of course absurd. Paul Anderley was far too much the gentleman to go about stealing kisses from ladies in their gardens. At least from this lady in this garden, patently. "*Or* one may burn limestone to make lime. Whale bone is also said to be efficacious, though I've never had occasion to try it myself. My late husband had excellent results with seaweed. Some people keep dovecotes. You should know about these things, for the benefit of your estate."

She chose the oddest things to talk about. Ladies shouldn't know about fertilizer, surely. Paul eyed the lambs, currently chasing each other through the foliage. Or discuss it, at any rate. "I employ gardeners, a large number of them, to tend to such matters. As do you. I thought we might pass a pleasant half hour together. Come, walk around the gardens with me, and show me what you've most recently done."

The man didn't care a button for her gardens. Save to own them, that was. At which point he and the head gardener would doubtless set about restoring order to everything. However, Cara was always pleased to show off her latest horticultural endeavors. And while she was embarked upon an animated discussion Paul could hardly profess his great regard for her again. "I have been experimenting with hydroponics," she said, as she freed one of the lambs from a rosebush.

Cara thought she might distract him. The squire realized this, and was amused. Not that Cara wasn't herself a distraction, her lush body unfettered in her simple gown, and coal ash smudged on her perfect cheeks, and her glorious hair coming unpinned. Gravely, he listened, or pretended to, even entered into a discussion about a new variety of melon with which she was having some small success. Lambs and chickens trailed along behind as they strolled past a stone colossus, and along a fine yew hedge. At least Lady Norwood's favorite cow didn't accompany her today. The gardens were in an appalling state, as Paul already knew, due to some clandestine explorations of his own. He had assured the unhappy head gardener that the clematis would be the first to go, and then the wisteria. The lilac might stay, he thought, providing it was severely pruned.

Unless, that is, Cara begged on bended knee, and then she might do anything she pleased with the gardens, as well as with himself. With that tantalizing thought in mind, Paul maneuvered her beneath low-hanging tree branches, through a wooden archway covered with jasmine and roses, across a little footbridge, and into a cozy nook that featured a marble maiden pouring water from an urn, along with a sundial and a great oak bench designed in the shape of a shell.

He clasped her hands. She looked at him quizzically. Paul parted his lips to speak. An English setter bounded out of the shrubbery, plumed tail waving wildly, and knocked him smack off his feet.

"Naughty Daisy!" Cara knelt to give the dog a hug, and allowed her face to be licked. "Sit down and behave. Squire Anderley will think you are shockingly ill-trained."

Squire Anderley didn't think the beast was trained at all. He stood up, brushed dirt and twigs off his

jacket, and surveyed the setter with the critical eye of
a man who owned a pack of hunting hounds. The cur
looked well-bred enough, with her long, silky,
slightly wavy coat, white flecked liberally with orange, long fringed tail, orange ears, and speckled
mask. Better Daisy was off chasing partridges or
woodcocks, however—or perhaps the blasted chickens—instead of sprawling at Cara's feet, her tongue
lolling out of her mouth, which was curled in what
looked to him like the canine equivalent of a sneer, or
knocking innocent gentlemen down.

Cara disliked the stern way Paul was looking at her
dog. "I have been wondering," she murmured, "if the
grafting of a sweet onto a sharp-flavored apple would
produce a fruit of dual tang."

To be alone with him—well, almost alone, except
for the damned dog, the lambs, and the chickens—
seemed to make Cara nervous. This was a good sign.
Paul grasped her wrist again and pulled her down beside him on the bench. "Cut line, my dear! I've gone
to great lengths to speak privately with you. Not that
my words will come as any surprise."

Cara looked at the hand that clasped hers. Paul had
never tried to kiss her, for all his honeyed words.
Would he do so now? Or, as she suspected, was it
only her property he sought? Cara was no longer a
green girl. She had buried her innocence and youth in
these gardens, among the seedlings and bulbs. The
more curious of the chickens, a rooster, flapped its
way up onto the bench and into her lap.

Cara smoothed the bird's soft feathers. Not that she
truly wished to kiss Paul Anderley, or anybody else.
Firmly, she withdrew her hand from his. "I am very
much obliged to you, Paul, but pray spare your breath.

It is an oddity in me, I admit it, but I enjoy my single state."

God's teeth, but she was stubborn. Paul reminded himself again of how much he enjoyed the pleasure of the chase. Though she couldn't know it, he wished to kiss his quarry very much, even if she was clutching a damned rooster, but he was afraid that once he started he wouldn't be able to stop. "Blast it, Cara, it's unnatural for a woman to live alone."

Cara overlooked the profanity. "It's nothing of the sort. Moreover, I'm hardly alone, having something like three-score servants at last count. Norwood left me wanting for nothing, you know that. Be honest, Paul! You wouldn't truly wish to be married to so contumacious a female as myself."

No, but once he wed her, she wouldn't be contumacious long. He hoped. "You're a young woman still. Surely you must wish for a family of your own. Unthinkable that you should be content with only your servants and your plants and your hound for friends." Not to mention her bloody chickens and cows and lambs. Paul didn't dare reach out to touch her. The rooster looked as if it wished to give him a good peck.

Who said she was contented? At least Paul had called her young, even if it was a clanker, which was kind. "I thought *you* were my friend."

"Of course I'm your friend." Paul regarded her with exasperation. "You know very well that I wish to be more."

She knew that the squire wished to become master of the Norwood estate. Cara wondered if she would let him. She also wondered if he would try and kiss her then.

Mentally, she kicked herself. Kissing was entirely too much on her mind. "*You* should marry, my friend, but some lady other than myself. Someone who isn't unfashionable, and capricious, and years beyond her youth, which I am, no matter what you say." Absently, she brushed at a red-gold tendril that had escaped its moorings to tickle her cheek, as other ringlets had escaped from their pins to lie softly on one shoulder or tumble untidily down her back.

Paul itched to plunge his hands into that gleaming mass of hair. Beyond her first youth or no, Cara was the most desirable creature he had ever seen.

She was gazing curiously at him. Paul hoped he hadn't groaned. In an attempt to regain his composure, he plucked dog hairs off his breeches. "How absurd you are."

Perhaps she *was* absurd. Certainly most people would think so. Squire Anderley was wealthy, and personable, and a gentleman down to his toes; while she was not exactly beating away suitors from her door. Cara reminded herself that she did not wish for suitors. "You're not going to tell me, I hope, that you've tumbled violently in love," she said, and wasn't surprised to see him wince. "I think you wish to marry me simply because I've told you no."

There was some truth in her accusation: Paul was not accustomed to having his wishes ignored. Not that he doubted for a moment that those wishes would ultimately be fulfilled. Sooner rather than later, he hoped, lest he succumb to that Viking impulse.

He was too experienced a hunter to rush his fences, dammit. "I've made a mull of it. Again."

"Nonsense." Cara tucked the rooster under one arm, reclaimed her flower basket, and got up from the bench. "Why, here's Mortimer. Daisy, sit! You know you're not supposed to knock the servants down. Mortimer, you needn't have come all this way yourself to fetch us to tea."

"I didn't, milady!" The rotund butler huffed and puffed and panted to a stop. The lambs, who had been chasing after him, now chased each other around him instead.

Quite rightly, he ignored them. "That is, the tea *was* ready, but it's all drunk up. Hungry as a hog he was. Cook's fixing you another tray."

Paul reflected that Norwood House was as prodigiously ill-regulated as its gardens. "You're not making any sense. *Who* drank up all the tea? Speak up, man!"

Were Mortimer to speak up in the manner that he wished, he would advise Squire Anderley not to stick his nose into what was none of his affair. Since good manners dictated that a butler do no such thing, he also ignored Paul. "It's your brother, milady. Come all the way from Town."

"Beau? Here? Good gracious! Pray excuse me, Paul." Lady Norwood picked up her skirts and ran toward the house, affording Squire Anderley a tantalizing glimpse of trim ankles and muddy stockings. The setter gamboled in her wake, followed by the curious lambs, several squawking chickens, and the butler. Squire Anderley sighed, and brought up the rear.

2

The drawing room of Norwood House was a well-proportioned chamber with a lofty ceiling and tall windows, pretty paneled walls featuring oval plaques in relief, and a gleaming wooden floor; furnished with Hepplewhite sofas and chairs to match, pier tables and a commode, an ornate fire screen and a Wilton rug. The splendor of these items, however, was eclipsed by the gentleman who irritably paced the floor. He was of medium height and build, clad in dark green coat and buckskin breeches, double-breasted jacket with broad lapels, riding boots, and a rumpled cravat. His hair was rumpled also, as if he'd been running his hands through it, which he had.

He paused in his perambulations to gaze upon a painting of Lady Norwood that hung upon one wall. The resemblance between them was unmistakable. Beau also possessed the unmistakable Loversall features, the red-gold curls and sapphire eyes. He thanked his Creator daily that he didn't also have the damned Loversall dimples. Where the devil *was* his sister? He dropped into a wing chair. No sooner had he done so than there came a commotion in the hallway, and a great energetic orange-and-white bundle bounded into the room and smack into his lap.

"Down, Daisy!" said Cara, as she entered the room on the heels of her pet. "Beau, I am so sorry! You know she likes you of all things."

If Cara was a gem of the first water, her brother was quite top of the trees, and not at all unaccustomed to having females in his lap. He allowed Daisy to salute his cheek before pushing her to the floor and surveying his sister critically. Rather, Cara had once been a gem of the first water. "What have you been doing to yourself? You look the veriest drab. Why are you clutching that bird?"

Absently, Cara petted the rooster, which wasn't the least bit dismayed to find itself in the drawing room of Norwood House, although the kitchens would have been a different matter, the cook being renowned locally for her numerous inventive ways with a fowl. Reflecting that her older brother wasn't the least bit drab, even in all his travel dust, Cara dropped a kiss on the cheek Daisy hadn't yet licked. "Did you send word that you were coming? I thought not. Then you can hardly expect me to be dressed for company."

Beau glanced pointedly at the gentleman who had followed Cara into the room. Squire Anderley was attempting to control Daisy, who was responding to Beau's unexpected arrival with a great deal of tail wagging and licking and jumping about. "I see that you *have* company, all the same."

Paul caught Beau's gaze and returned it. "Lady Norwood and I were strolling through the gardens. She was startled by your arrival. I was concerned that something might be amiss."

Rather, the squire was concerned that something

might interfere with his determined courtship. Not that Beau had anything in particular against Paul. Still, he couldn't resist a little provocation. "I thought hunting season was over, Anderley. Yet here you are, complete with riding crop, as if you'd made up your mind to take the field."

Paul realized that he still held his riding crop. His hand twitched. "I reside in the area, in case you've forgotten. And since you aren't a hunting man, perhaps you don't know that it's unwise to get between the huntsman and his hounds."

Since he would not let her sit on him, Daisy dropped down at Beau's feet and flopped her head in his lap. He scratched one silky ear. "I wouldn't say I'm not a hunting man," he remarked.

Paul refused to be led into speculating about how many females Beau had brought to ground. If Cara was Venus and Aphrodite and Cleopatra mixed together, her brother was Adonis and Apollo and the Archangel Michael, seasoned with a liberal dash of Casanova and Don Juan. "There is a rhythm to the chase. Disrupt it, and the consequences may be severe."

"Such as the hunter giving up because the fox has gone to ground?" Beau moved his skillful fingers to Daisy's other ear. The dog sighed blissfully.

Paul gritted his teeth. Cara wouldn't like it if he flogged her brother. "Foxes are very obstinate. If a covert is deep enough, they often run an hour or more without an attempt at breaking. A skilled hunter learns to bide his time."

Beau raised a brow. Cara made an exasperated noise and took the rooster with her to stand by a tall window. Paul glanced over at her, and promptly lost his train of thought, because sunlight silhouetted Cara's lush body through the thin material of her gown, and glinted in her hair, and he was struck by a queer vision of himself bedding a fox. Not a *real* fox, of course, although there had been that red-haired vixen in Gloucester—

Beau's mocking gaze was fixed on him. Paul hadn't the slightest doubt that Cara's brother was aware of the lusty tenor of his thoughts. "The fox that goes to ground may still be dug out of its hole and killed," he snapped.

Did Paul truly think of her as vermin to be exterminated? Once they were married, would he set his hounds to tear her limb from limb? "Stop it, both of you! Beau, I'm pleased to see you, but I fear I wouldn't be seeing you if something wasn't amiss."

That might be, but Beau didn't care to speak of such things in front of strangers, which despite all his ambitions, Paul Anderley was. He gave the squire a pointed look.

Paul paused, but Cara didn't take the hint to ask him to remain. "You'll wish to speak alone together. I'll see myself out." Any intention he might have had to eavesdrop was foiled by Mortimer, who was overseeing the arrival of a fresh tray of biscuits and tea. There were no flies on Mortimer. He relieved his mistress of the rooster, which was also reluctant to leave the premises, and personally escorted both visitors to the front door.

Beau contemplated the tea tray, and wished for a glass of brandy. Unfortunately, his sister's suspicions would be roused if he asked for strong spirits so soon after setting foot in her house. "You must surely know that Anderley wants Norwood's land," he said.

Cara sat down behind the teapot. "Of course I

know it. I hope you don't expect me to thank you for pointing out that I am grown an antidote."

"Whose fault is that? Not that I'm saying you *are* an antidote, mind!" Beau looked at the dirt—he trusted it was only dirt—on his sister's face and skirts. "Norwood left you plenty of blunt. How long has it been since you had a new gown?"

True that her morning dress was several years out of fashion, but a lady hardly dressed up in all her finery to dig in the garden. True also that some of the garden dirt was lodged under her fingernails. Cara folded her hands.

"It's been two years since Norwood paid his debt to nature," Beau continued, as he slipped the hopeful Daisy a seed cake. "I'm amazed you haven't expired of boredom. Don't you think you've rusticated long enough?"

Though she didn't trust him for a minute, Cara was still glad to see her older brother. Due to the ten-year difference in their ages, they had never been especially close, but the hero worship she had felt for him as a child had evolved into a genuine fondness for the man, despite his myriad faults. "Stop feeding the dog! I'm no longer a girl, Beau. I don't crave excitement. It's quiet and restful in the country. I like it very well."

Beau didn't believe a word of it. Nor would he have, even had he not noticed how his sister's hands clenched in her lap. No matter how she might try and forget it, Cara was a Loversall. All the family craved excitement, whether they wished to or no. Their own Grandmother Sophie had likened her own turbulent desires to tornadoes sweeping across a burning desert. Not that Sophie had ever seen a desert herself, but she freely admitted to numerous adulterous affairs—there was hardly any point denying them, since she painted her lovers in the nude—and had even spent some time in a convent after a certain foreign dignitary was caught lacing up her stays. Her son, Cara and Beau's father, Kenelm, had vowed to pluck as many posies as possible before he shuffled off this mortal coil, and had utilized his charm, good looks, and unfailing panache to acquire a veritable fleet of paramours. The Loversalls combined bedazzling beauty with a voracious appetite for adventure. Had they a family motto, it would be: "Love fully, with complete abandon, and always with great style."

Yet here was Cara, hiding herself away in the country. In the past two years, she had resisted all efforts to dislodge her from the Cotswolds. Today Beau didn't mean to leave without her, even if it meant bearing her off bundled up in a burlap sack.

Cara watched the play of expression across her brother's handsome countenance. "Why are you so Friday-faced?"

Beau gazed at her over his teacup. "Zoë means to drive me into an early grave. You needn't tell me I may only blame myself, because even if it's true, it's quite beside the point."

Cara relaxed slightly. Beau's daughter was willful, and charming, and dreadfully spoiled. And beautiful, of course. "What has she done now?"

"It's not what she's done so much as what I fear she'll do." Absently, Beau stroked Daisy's soft fur. "I found a gray hair the other day. Flitwick plucked it out."

Cara sympathized. Was she not at the point in her own life when all that was left to her to hug was

Daisy and a kumquat tree? She reached for a cucumber sandwich. "You're only seven-and-thirty. Loversall men don't grow old. May I remind you of Great-Grandfather Gervase?"

Beau winced. The ancestor in question had possessed a voracious appetite for gentlemen and no more discretion than a cat in heat; had enjoyed dressing up and prancing about in lace ruffles, with long curls flowing from beneath a dainty cap, until one last *rapprochement* in a damp grotto had led to his demise from an inflammation of the lungs at the advanced age of ninety-three. Were that what he had to look forward to, Beau thought he might shoot himself. "Zoë's turned into a flirt."

Cara paused with her sandwich halfway to her mouth. "Zoë's a flirt? What did you expect! You're a flirt, I'm a flirt, the family has turned flirting into a fine art. And since when have you had anything against flirtation? Listen to yourself."

"I am, and you needn't think I like it." Beau sounded so melancholy that Daisy opened one brown eye and thumped her tail. "Anyway, I don't deny that *I'm* a flirt. It's quite a different thing when one's own daughter is batting her eyelashes at every man in town."

Cara tried unsuccessfully to repress a smile. "I have learned a great deal about chickens since I married Norwood. One cannot help but muse upon their tendency to come home to roost."

Beau nudged Daisy aside so that he might stretch out his legs. "What is it with you and chickens? And you needn't look so damned smug. This is your niece we're talking about. The little minx is running her *beaux* in circles. She says it is amusing to keep them dangling at the end of her string."

Cara remembered a time—oh, so long ago—when she'd done the same thing, and enjoyed it very much. "Admirers *are* amusing," she pointed out.

Beau shot her a darkling look. "Some may be. *Others* are as old as I am myself. God's bones, she's only seventeen!"

Cara refrained from inquiring whether Beau numbered among his own conquests any damsels of his daughter's age, because of course he did. Even Cook's eleven-year-old daughter had taken one look at Beau and professed herself love-struck. "If it's one of Zoë's swains that has you in such a fluster, why don't you simply forbid her seeing him?"

Beau snorted. "Would you have let yourself be warned off an unsuitable *tendre*? Cousin Ianthe is in a constant fret."

This didn't surprise Cara. Their cousin had highly developed sensibilities, and was easily hurt. "Zoë has been developing unsuitable attractions ever since she was in the cradle, most memorably for the butcher's boy. I doubt you have cause for real alarm."

"The deuce I don't!" said Beau, and snatched up a seedcake. Daisy looked hopeful, but this one he ate himself. "I tell you, Cara, I'm not going to let Zoë blot her copybook."

This from the greatest copybook-blotter of his generation? "Why not? The rest of us did."

Beau frowned at her. "You didn't."

Not for the lack of trying. Cara pushed away the memory of her own unsuitable attachments, and the days when admirers had still wished to kiss and hug her, before she'd grown so old and drab. "Zoë falls out of love as easily as she falls into it. She'll eventually grow bored with her new conquest, and order will be restored."

"Not this time it won't." Beau ran his hand through his rumpled hair. "She's made up her mind. I mean to see her safely settled while I still can. That's where I need your help."

Caught half-envying Zoë her infatuation, Cara sat bolt upright. "Beau—"

He raised his hand. "Let me finish. You're the only female in the entire history of the family who hasn't followed the tradition of loving unwisely but too well—'Just one more romance, one more throw of the dice,' wasn't that what Grandmother Sophie always said?—and though it seems very dull of you, things have worked out well enough. And if they haven't, I don't want to know! You have a good understanding, Cara. I've always said so."

Cara regarded her brother skeptically. "Next you'll mention that I have a strong sense of propriety."

"None of us do! There's the rub. But Zoë won't drive you to distraction like she does poor Ianthe. When she enacts you a Cheltenham tragedy, you'll just box her ears." Beau looked even gloomier. "And then she'll fly into a passion and drum her heels on the floor and hold her breath until she turns blue."

Cara set down her uneaten sandwich. "What an enchanting prospect! You exaggerate, I hope."

He didn't, not really; it seemed Zoë was either making kick-ups or shedding floods of tears and wailing that she wanted to Experience Life. Damned if Beau didn't feel like going on a repairing lease himself. "You wouldn't know if I was or wasn't, since you ain't seen the chit in so long. Shame on you! My poor Zoë needs an aunt's guiding hand. Anyway, you know you're tired of remaining cozily at home counting your sheep. Come to London and you may renovate *my* gardens. And visit the Horticultural Society, where they're doing experiments on strawberries and nectarines. Then there's the Herbarium at Kew." Cara looked intrigued, and he grinned at her. "Speaking of going to ground."

Cara had to admire her brother, shameless manipulator that he was. "Does Zoë know you've come to fetch me back to be her chaperone?"

"Zoë will enjoy spending time with her favorite aunt." Cara looked skeptical, and Beau sighed. "Hell and the devil confound it, you're my only hope. Whether you act on it or not, you know what's right. And for the most part you *have* acted on it, because the worst that's said of you is that you're An Original. Which when you think on it, is a damn queer thing for a Loversall." He eyed his silent sister. "I'll even stand the business for your new clothes."

Cara raised her eyebrows. Beau was notoriously tight-fisted. "You must be desperate."

Beau reached for the teapot. "I am."

Cara watched her brother pour tea into her cup as if it were the most natural thing in the world. Perhaps it was for him. She wondered how Squire Anderley would react were he to discover that his quarry had escaped, and whether he would set out in pursuit or simply look about for another fox. "Don't tease yourself. I can buy my own clothes."

If Beau lacked the family dimples, his smile was still dazzling. "Does that mean you'll come?"

As if there were any question. Dared she refuse, Beau would immediately remind her that loyalty had been a family tradition ever since the Battle of Hastings, when two Loversall brothers, after having done considerable damage with a homemade slingshot and a large Danish battle-ax, noted which way the wind was blowing and prudently removed themselves from the Saxon lines. "As you say, I know my duty, whether I abide by it or not. Although I don't know exactly what it is you think that I may do."

Nor did Beau. "Drop Zoë a hint or two. Set her a good example. Prevent her from tossing her bonnet over the windmill. Blast it, Cara, someone must do something and there is no one else but you!"

Now she was a good example. How very depressing. Cara rose and Daisy leapt to attention, as if hoping her mistress would throw her a stick. "No, Daisy! Sit down. Just who is this unsuitable *tendre* who has you in such a taking, Beau?"

Beau grabbed the setter's collar. "It's not only that he's unsuitable, he's also above her touch. The blasted man must have had as many *amours* as I have myself. You think I overstate the case? Zoë has set her cap at no less than Mannering himself."

Mannering! *Just one more romance, one more throw of the dice*—"I'll have Barrow pack."

3

"What in blazes," inquired Lord Mannering, "do you have wrapped around your neck?"

Baron Fitzrichard twisted on the carriage seat, the extreme dimensions of his shirt points and highly starched cravat making it impossible for him to properly turn his head. "D'you like it, Nicky? I ain't named it yet. I was thinking about the Coup du Foudue. Or perhaps the Preux Chevalier."

Nick eyed the neck-cloth. "The Faux Pas. The Mal-Apropos. The Imbécile. You see how I enter into the spirit of the thing."

"By Jove, that's unkind! After I canceled all my engagements this afternoon just to drive out with you. I'd meant to visit Lock's and order a new *chapeau* and then perhaps take a turn around Piccadilly and Pall Mall—Watch that donkey cart! Damned if you ain't making the flesh crawl on my bones."

Lord Mannering, who was an excellent whipster, deftly avoided the donkey cart, and charitably attributed his companion's mistrust of his driving to a well-known horror of heights. It was for that reason that the marquess had today bypassed his high-perch phaeton in favor of this somewhat less dashing curricle, drawn by a perfectly matched pair of bays, with a groom perched up behind.

All danger of donkey carts averted, he returned his attention to his companion, who in addition to his amazingly arranged cravat wore an exquisitely cut orange coat, ribbed kerseymere pantaloons, Hessian boots with heart-shaped top and tassel, a lavishly embroidered waistcoat, and a tall beaver hat perched atop carefully styled brown curls. "Anyone who drinks four bottles of champagne at one sitting deserves to have his flesh crawl on his bones, Fitz, not to mention a troop of devils banging cymbals in his head."

The baron winced at this reminder of his excesses of the night before. Still, a man had his reputation to maintain, an endeavor that in this instance had involved playing macao at Watier's late into the night. And then what must Nicky do but rouse him from his slumbers at the very crack of noon? Fitz blinked as the curricle turned into Berkeley Square. "Gunter's? Are you in your dotage? Because I can't think of any reason why you might want an ice. Unless—You ain't ordering a wedding cake!"

Lord Mannering maneuvered his curricle through the crush of carriages. "No, and not a turkey preserved in jelly, or a ham cunningly embalmed in rich wine and broth. You are here, Fitz, because your presence is required."

Fitz's brown eyes narrowed. "So you said, but you ain't said *why*."

Lord Mannering raised an eyebrow. "To lend me respectability, of course."

Fitz snorted. Nicky required no one's countenance to add to his own. Damned if Fitz knew how his friend did it, for the man was deuced careless of his appearance—

breeches and top boots, of course, and the jacket he wore so casually was by no less than Weston; but his cravat was tied in an ordinary manner, and his dark hair was worn in the simplest style, as if he didn't care how he looked. Despite this apparent disinterest, the marquess was tall, dark, and saturnine, immensely wealthy, and irresistibly handsome in the wicked way unmarried peers often were; and it hardly made a difference what he wore anyway, when so many ladies seemed intent on undressing him. "Respectability," Fitz muttered. "Now *there's* a fine bag of moonshine."

Berkeley Square, laid out in the 1730s, consisted of long ranges of stone-fronted terrace houses where various luminaries had dwelt, including Clive of India, who had resided at No. 45 on the west side from 1761 until his death in 1774 from an overdose of laudanum. In the center was an oval garden with long borders running parallel to the buildings on each side. Thirty plane maples grew there. In the center of the garden stood a little pump house with a Chinese roof.

A large number of carriages were gathered in the shade of the maple trees. Waiters from Gunter's hurried across the pavement with ices and sorbets, while gentlemen lounged against the railings and chatted with perfect propriety to the ladies in their carriages, no small feat in an era when a well-brought-up young lady wasn't allowed to be alone with a man for even a half hour lest her reputation, not to mention her sensibilities, be shredded beyond repair.

Fitz had no fear for his own reputation, and doubted that his spirits would be revived by an ice. He parted his lips to tell his friend so. Then he spied a certain carriage, and its occupants, and instead said, "Ha! Now I know why you begged me to come out with you."

"You have found me out, Fitz." Nick pulled his team to a halt and gracefully leapt down from the seat. "I begged you—as you put it, though I rather thought it was a polite invitation—not solely because I wished the pleasure of your company." He handed the reins to his groom. "But also because I felt myself in need of a chaperone."

Nicky in need of a chaperone? Not likely. Lord Mannering had proven himself so determined a bachelor that even matchmaking mamas no longer included him in their plans. "I suppose you think I'm bottle-headed, but I ain't. Even a blind man would notice the way the Loversall chit's been casting sheep's eyes at you. I have a bad feeling about this."

"It's all that champagne you drank." Nick turned away from his carriage. "Are you coming with me, or are you just going to sit there and sulk?"

Sulking, was he? Fitz's pride was stung. "Very well, have it your way. But don't expect me to eat an ice!"

Berkeley Square was crowded with ladies and gentlemen come out to enjoy the afternoon, the ladies in elegant equipages and morning dresses, the gentlemen moving among them like drunken bumblebees lurching from flower to flower. Or perhaps it was his own excesses of the previous evening that made Fitz think of the influence of the grape, not that he had allowed the cymbal-banging in his head to interfere with his toilette. Fitz knew he made a fine appearance—wasn't he wearing a fifteen-guinea embroidered waistcoat?—but he was plagued by the problem of persuading his pantaloons to keep their shape. Perhaps a strap under the arch of the foot. Although Brummel had already thought of that. Fitz disliked to be a follower. He aspired to be the Pinkest of the Pink.

The Loversall ladies were holding court in their carriage, which was not the most fashionable of the equipages present, a circumstance no one was likely to notice in light of the glorious creatures so gracefully displayed there. Ianthe attracted her own admirers, although she did not encourage them, and Zoë had so many swains that they were known to her family as Zoë's Zoo, among them a duke (married), an earl (not married, although he should have been), several viscounts, a baronet, and an elderly knight, as well as hopeful commoners from Abethell to Zike.

Fitz was one of the few gentlemen in London not struck noodle-headed by the beauty of the family. He had also thought his friend to be in that minority, but now he wondered, as Nicky bent over the older woman's hand. If a paler version of her cousin—Ianthe's hair was merely gold instead of tinged with red; her eyes robin's egg blue instead of sapphire, the skin around them taut with strain—she still remained beautiful at five-and-thirty, rather in the style of a great actress renowned for tragic roles.

At the moment, she also looked ready to sink. "Lord Mannering! I didn't realize—Or perhaps I mistake the matter and she didn't—Oh, if only I could assure myself of that!"

"Pray do not regard it," he murmured, as the young woman under discussion watched the exchange with wide-eyed innocence. When the marquess glanced at her, she fluttered her lashes and allowed a becoming flush to tinge her delicate cheeks.

Baggage, thought Fitz, without appreciation. Not that he could fault Zoë in appearance, for she wore a pale blue muslin pelisse over a white muslin walking dress, and a charming straw bonnet trimmed with wreaths of flowers, the strings fastened with a bow behind. Her red-gold hair was cut in a smart crop and arranged in close curls that crept out from beneath the bonnet to caress her perfect face. In addition to those lovely eyes, she had a charming little nose, lush lips, and dimples, two of them.

She was also short. Fitz didn't like short females. Or chits right out of the schoolroom who threatened to tumble gentlemen who should have known better smack heels over head. He watched Nick stroll around to the other side of the carriage and muttered, "Damned if I remember when I last had an ice."

"Oh! I am so sorry!" Ianthe practically wrung her hands. "Perhaps if we were to ask a waiter—I'm sure they would bring you something other than an ice— Perhaps a nice cup of tea!"

Fitz was ashamed of himself. It was hardly fair of him to take out his ill humor on Ianthe, who had borne the responsibility for her cousin square on her slender shoulders practically from the moment of that young woman's birth. No wonder she looked so drawn and pale. Not that anyone could look *other* than pale in that dreadful outfit. Spanish pelisse of shot sarcenet trimmed with Egyptian crepe and antique cuffs trimmed with Chinese binding; lemon-colored kid gloves and slippers; reticule of painted velvet; Gypsy hat of satin straw with edge *à la cheveux de fries*, tied with a colored handkerchief.

Ianthe interrupted his ruminations with a compliment concerning his waistcoat. Fitz beamed at her. "Guthrie's in Cork Street!" A discussion of embroidery stitches followed, from satin stitch to pearling, tambour stitch to herringbone.

If Lord Mannering was interested in this conversation, and he appeared to be, Zoë was not. "How providential," she murmured, with a practiced sideways glance, "that we should meet here today!"

The marquess looked pensive. "Apparently my memory isn't what it used to be. I seem to recall a missive requesting that I discover in myself an overwhelming desire for a sorbet."

Zoë regarded him reproachfully. "You're not *eating* a sorbet. It's an age since we've seen you, Lord Mannering. I was beginning to think myself forgot."

Nick studied the vivid little face turned so enchantingly toward his. "Impossible that anyone should forget you, Miss Loversall. You know that I am yours to command."

She dimpled. "Fiddle! I know that you're no such thing. Which is very odd in you, since everyone else admires me excessively." She glanced again at her cousin, deep in a conversation now—rather, Baron Fitzrichard was conversing—about the principles of female dress, which apparently had much to do with hostile colors and subordinate compounds. "Although Ianthe would scold dreadfully if she heard me say so! My cousin is positively Gothick. And so is Beau—he doesn't like me to call him 'Papa,' you see, because it makes him feel quite old. I'm never allowed to go anywhere. It's all a horrid bore!"

Lord Mannering didn't make the mistake of taking these complaints to heart. This lamentably mistreated young woman was not only currently at Gunter's enjoying an ice, but also frequently to be seen at fashionable gatherings everywhere. The sensation that Zoë had created upon her first appearance in Society showed no sign of abating yet. So charming was her manner, so irrepressible her spirits, that only the most coldhearted of critics whispered that she was *fast*, or recalled with anticipatory relish that her family tended to take things to excess. "How could I not admire the most beautiful damsel in London, if not all England? I await your pleasure, milady. Shall I slay a dragon for you? Or perhaps, if I may presume—" With a handkerchief, he wiped an errant drop of sorbet from the edge of her luscious mouth.

Her little tongue darted out to lick her lips. "You're teasing me," she said. "And I don't really want anyone slain, not even Cousin Ianthe, although I think she should be more *understanding*. After all, she suffered a romantic disappointment in her youth, and would have gone into a decline if it weren't for me. Is it true that older men like younger women because younger women rekindle their sense of romance, Lord Mannering?"

Cousin Ianthe was looking none too robust at the moment, and it wasn't difficult to imagine why. "I assume you are asking my opinion because of my advanced age. Alas, 'tis true that elderly gentlemen such as myself demonstrate their admiration differently than the young sprigs to whom you are accustomed. Rheumatism prevents us from getting down on our knees and spouting poetry to your eyebrows, although of course I long to do so." A slow smile curved the edges of his mouth. "Don't be so anxious to grow up, little one. You'll tumble violently in love ten times before you're twenty, mark my words."

Was Lord Mannering ravishing her with his eyes? No, he looked amused instead. Zoë couldn't help but admire his high cheekbones and chiseled jaw.

Not to mention the strong muscles of his thighs. She tilted her pretty head. "You make me sound a horrid flirt."

"The most hardened flirt in London," Nick said gravely. "Look at how you're flirting with me now, even though I am ancient enough to be your papa."

Zoë abandoned her posturing to giggle. "My papa is hardly ancient! And of course I'm flirting with you. Though I don't lack for admirers, or poetry, or all that, it's very dull stuff! I don't think *you* could be dull, milord, even if you tried."

Lord Mannering was far too fly to the time of day to make the mistake of paying any one young lady particular attentions, entice him as she might. Entertaining though this conversation might be, it had gone on long enough. "There are those who wouldn't agree with you," he murmured, and glanced at the annoyed gentlemen hovering about them, several of whom looked like they thirsted for his blood. "I must monopolize you no more."

"Wait!" The marquess was Zoë's latest conquest, or would be as soon as the stubborn creature could be made aware of his own mind. "Do you go to Lady Miller's rout?"

Nick could think of few things more insipid. However, the little imp looked absurdly hopeful. "Perhaps."

She beamed at him. "Then I shall save you the dinner dance!"

"I'm honored," Nick said gravely, and bowed politely, and took his leave.

Fitz broke off his own conversation and followed, with the result that Ianthe was left uncertain as to whether she should wear orange with green, or green with purple, or all three at once. "I don't like this, Nicky," Fitz said, as the gentlemen strolled out of earshot. "It ain't like you to amuse yourself with the infantry."

Lord Mannering questioned whether "amusement" was the proper term for what he was doing. "I was merely being polite. Would you rather I was not?"

Fitz looked exasperated. "Of course you're supposed to be polite, you're a marquess. But you *weren't* being polite just then! In fact, if you weren't getting up a flirtation, my name ain't Adolphus."

Alas, Adolphus was poor Fitz's given name, a fact known only to his closest friends. Nick glanced at him. "I'm not trying to get up a flirtation; *she* is. I daresay she finds it more exciting than practicing her scales upon the pianoforte."

Fitz blinked. "Is the girl mad?"

Nick reclaimed his reins from his groom and took his place on the curricle seat. "My dear Fitz, she is a Loversall. The entire family is mad. They are creatures of the senses, not of logic. It is a large part of their charm, as you would know if you had an interest in anything other than the latest furbelow."

Fitz climbed into the curricle. "I ain't a fribble!" he protested.

Nick lifted the reins. "I never said you were."

Fitz turned awkwardly toward him. "This is a fudge, ain't it, Nicky? Please tell me that it is!"

Nick smiled. "What if I were to tell you instead that I am quite *épris*?"

Fitz sniffed. "I'd say maybe *you* drank too much champagne."

4

It was late in the day when Lady Norwood's traveling carriage drew up in front of the Loversall town house in Brook Street, which if not among the most fashionable of London neighborhoods, was still respectable. From the carriage emerged Lady Norwood, her maidservant, Barrow, and Daisy, who at the last moment had refused to be left behind. Unfortunately, it had soon been discovered that the setter didn't travel well. Beau was grateful that he had ridden alongside the carriage, and not inside.

He dismounted, handed his reins to a groom, and strode toward the front door where the butler stood. Widdle had only recently come into the Loversall employ, following an unfortunate incident involving some missing silver plate. Servants did not last long in this household, but at his age—Widdle's hair was sparse, his posture bent—opportunities were scarce. He squinted at the women approaching in his new master's wake. One, a middle-aged female who looked as if butter wouldn't melt in her mouth, was evidently a servant. The other was unmistakably a member of the family. Widdle hoped she might be more conversant with the proprieties than the other residents of this household seemed to be. Except for Miss Ianthe, but of course no one listened to her. And was that orange-and-white-speckled creature a *canine?*

It was, and it knocked him over. From a prone position between lapping tongue and wagging tail, Widdle suggested that the lady might like some tea.

The lady first preferred to freshen up. Once safely inside her chamber—which had not changed a bit since she last saw it, from the canopy bed with blue silk hangings to the flowered china ewer on the corner basin stand, although she hoped dust and spiders had not been gathering all that time—Cara pulled off her bonnet and sank down in a chair. "I don't like this, mum," said Barrow, for what seemed the hundredth time since they'd set out from Norwood House. "What will Squire Anderley think, you running off like that?"

Paul would think, quite rightly, that Cara was playing least-in-sight, and he could make of it what he wished. Difficult, however, to reprimand a servant who'd been with her since she was a girl. Barrow only wished the best for her, in this case that Cara should marry Paul.

"Mortimer will tell him where we've gone." Cara wondered as she spoke if Mortimer would do any such thing; her abigail wondered also: Cara winced as Barrow's brush tangled in her hair. Order at length restored to her person as well as to her coiffure, Cara left Barrow unpacking and muttering darkly beneath her breath, with a subdued Daisy to keep her company, and descended the stair.

The house was as she remembered it, furnished in a gay rococo fashion grown somewhat shabby with use. The drawing room displayed an elaborate variety of carved shells and scrolls and fish scales, ribboned flowers and butterflies, ormolu and asymmetrical scrollwork. On either side of the chimney stood a sofa, and on the opposite end a confidante. An elegant narrow-waisted grandfather clock ticked away the hours in a somewhat eccentric fashion, its brass dial richly ornamented with cherubs in relief. The polished wooden floors were adorned by several small rugs, the walls covered with chinoiserie paper, the plaster ceiling enriched by simple ribs in low relief.

On a gilt bow-fronted table decorated with strings of bell flowers sat an oval japanned tea tray. Wrapped in a Chinese robe of puce silk, a lace cap, and a Norwich shawl, Ianthe stood by the fireplace.

She looked worn-down with fuss and worry. Cara felt a stab of guilt. Ianthe had lived with the family for as long as she could remember; had been like a second mama when Cara's own mother had decided she had exhausted all her maternal impulses (not to mention her patience with her husband's stable of mistresses) and had embarked with the widow of a Russia Company merchant on an extensive round of sightseeing, during the course of which she had published several volumes about her "Tours" in Scandinavia, Russia, and Poland, before succumbing to malaria in Madagascar.

Ianthe would no doubt have enjoyed a nice stay in the country. Cara had thought several times of suggesting that her cousin come to Norwood House, but had withheld the invitation because she hadn't wished her peace also invaded by her volatile niece. After all she owed Ianthe, to behave so shabbily!

Cara cleared her throat. "Oh! You came!" Ianthe hurried across the room to envelop Cara in a great hug. "I have so wished to see you. Everything is in such a muddle! I've been standing here teasing myself with thoughts of what to say to Beau." She burst into tears.

Cara drew her cousin to a sofa. "*He* should say 'thank you,' though it would never occur to him. You might have had a home of your own instead of staying here with Zoë." As she had herself had a home, Cara thought.

"Fiddle!" Ianthe pulled out a handkerchief, wiped her eyes, blew her nose, and picked up the teapot from a tray decorated with a huge chrysanthemum. "Someone had to look after the babe, and you were far too young. Beau, as we know, is useless in such matters. Zoë has him wrapped around her thumb." Ianthe's blue eyes brimmed with tears. "Still, I can't help but think I've done a dreadful job of it, for Zoë is—I needn't mince words with you, Cara: she's a horrid brat! Oh, she's sunny-tempered enough until her will is crossed. But since she's also highly capricious, it's next to impossible to guess what she wants from one moment to the next." She dabbed the handkerchief to her eye.

Cara accepted a cup of tea, and reminded herself that Ianthe had not been spared the family tendency for melodrama. "Perhaps Zoë is merely reacting to the strain of her come-out. You remember how it was. Everyone waiting and watching for the latest family scandal. We disappointed them, you and I."

"I sometimes wonder if we would have caused more gossip by behaving badly than we did by being circumspect." Ianthe gestured with her teacup. "As for Zoë, you are too generous. Easy enough for her to behave reasonably when you're around, because you haven't been around that much. No, I wasn't scolding! You have a life of your own, and I'm grateful that you do. But now that you're here, you'll soon enough see how things really are. When denied anything on which she's set her heart, Zoë screams and bites and kicks. You doubt me, I can tell. Look at this, if you please!" Ianthe drew aside her shawl to display bright scratches on one arm. "In her tantrums, she'll smash china, throw herself on the floor in paroxysms of rage, and worse. Do you recall that lovely vase that once sat on the mantelpiece?"

Cara surveyed the empty niche. "Oh, dear."

"Would that she had flung herself out the window instead! And all that Beau can say to me is that he wishes I would not enact the watering-pot. I swear I am almost out of patience with them both." Ianthe was one of those females whose looks were not diminished by tears, which was fortunate, considering the number of them she shed, as she was doing again at the moment, while she clasped her cousin's hand. "Cara, I'm so very glad you're here."

"As are we all!" Beau stepped into the drawing room, looking refreshed; his valet, Flitwick, had bathed and combed and powdered his master before bearing off his riding coat to treat it lovingly with spirits of hartshorn and a good stiff brush. Beau glanced unappreciatively at the tea tray, headed for the brandy decanter, and poured himself a glass. Then he glanced around the chamber. "Where's Zoë?"

Ianthe squeezed Cara's fingers. "She called me an addle-plot. Then she said it made her feel quite waspish to never have a moment to herself. I suggested that she take her dinner alone in her room. Yes, I know that you will say it was very *unfeeling* of me, and so she told me, but I could bear no more!"

"There, there!" Beau said hastily, for his cousin's

lips had begun to tremble. Ianthe must surely be the best weeper in all of England, at last count holding a record of twenty bouts of sobbing in one day. "No need to make a piece of work of it!"

Ianthe looked no less somber. "You may say that now, but it's you who'll fly into a pelter when you hear what she did while you were gone. At least I *think* she did it. We met Mannering at Gunter's. Don't glower, it was all perfectly correct. Except I think Zoë was responsible for him being there."

Beau could not help but scowl, despite his cousin's pleading. "That damned fellow! Things have come to a pretty pass when I can't even turn my back."

"Baron Fitzrichard was there also," Ianthe added. "He has designed a new way of tying a neck-cloth. I suggested that he call it the Dégringolade. I think he means to bring square-toed shoes back into style."

Beau couldn't have cared less about square-toed shoes and the foppish baron. "And while you talked to that man-milliner about shoes and cravats, Mannering no doubt took advantage of the opportunity to further his acquaintance with Zoë."

Ianthe stiffened. "Don't dare accuse me of being neglectful of my duties, Beau. *I'm* not the one who misbehaves."

"Don't get on your high ropes!" Beau strode restlessly around the room. He didn't blame Ianthe for Zoë's behavior—how could he? The child was a Loversall. But so was Ianthe a Loversall, and therefore should have had considerably more backbone than she had thus far displayed. "I'm not accusing you of anything. I just think you might discourage Mannering's attentions if you tried. You should have sent him about his business. I rely on you to check Zoë's starts."

Cara thought this judgment seemed severe. "Beau—"

Her protest went unheeded. Beau continued scowling, while Ianthe bit her lower lip. "I don't see why I should give Mannering a set-down when I quite like the man. *He* doesn't rip up at me for things I didn't do. And if you think *you* may stop Zoë acting like a little zany, then pray go ahead and try!"

Beau disliked hearing his daughter maligned, unless it was by himself. He said, "Zoë is but a girl."

"Zoë is a thorn in my flesh," Ianthe retorted. "I disremember when I last had a day's peace."

This bickering also was familiar. Ianthe and Beau could not be in a room for five minutes together without being at daggers drawn. Cara walked over to the French windows, drew aside the curtains, and looked outside. Although she could not see into the darkness, she knew the gardens were divided from the area at the back of the house by a simple stone colonnade. Two fine trees grew there, one a mulberry of noble growth, as well as roses of ancient lineage. Long neglected now, the flower borders had once been a blaze of tulips and jonquils, lilies and peonies and violets. Cara thought of her own gardens, and Paul Anderley. Were Lord Mannering to find himself alone in a garden with Zoë, would *he* steal a kiss?

She turned away from the window. "This squabbling accomplishes nothing! Has it occurred to anyone that Mannering might be serious? What if instead of merely engaging in a flirtation, he were to offer for Zoë?"

Beau regarded her with astonishment. "Are you mad?"

Cara frowned at her brother. "What I am is fagged to death! We have had a journey of some distance, and I dislike family brangles, as you may recall. From what Ianthe is saying, it sounds like the marquess may simply enjoy Zoë's company."

What was it about Mannering? Now even Cara defended him. "A gentleman may well enjoy a lady's company without wishing to marry her!" Beau snapped. "And if Mannering ain't married in all this time, he ain't going to marry Zoë. Besides, he's too old for her."

Ianthe looked thoughtful. "She's throwing her bonnet at him, and he's letting her. Perhaps that's a hopeful sign. Too, he told her that only his rheumatics prevented him going down on his knees and reciting poetry."

Beau choked on a swallow of brandy. "Rheumatics? *Mannering*? The man spars with Gentleman Jackson. You must have made a mistake."

"Why is it I who am always supposedly mistaken? Zoë informed me of that herself. Unless you think she's telling taradiddles, perhaps?" Ianthe paused. Beau didn't answer. "Whoever would have thought that Mannering was inclined to poetry!"

Beau didn't think so, certainly. Nor did Cara. They exchanged a startled glance. "Why are you both so surprised? It's not as if the marquess is a rakehell. No matter how Zoë has misbehaved, he's always acted the perfect gentleman toward her."

No gentleman himself, Beau may perhaps have been forgiven a certain skepticism. "So far," he said, and finished his brandy. "Perhaps. And so far as you know."

Ianthe stared. "You can't think he would offer her false coin!"

Beau thought his cousin surprisingly naïve. "No man can be blamed for playing fast and loose with a lass who hurls herself enough times at his head."

Cara leaned back against the window. "I believe we may be hearing the voice of experience speaking," she remarked.

Beau ignored this sisterly provocation. He was appalled by the notion of his daughter engaged in escapades, and didn't see that the matter had anything to do with how many escapades he'd indulged in of his own, an excellent example of the adage that what's good for the gander may not also be good for the goose. "I won't have Zoë plunged into the scandal-broth!"

Now it was the women who exchanged glances. Their family was notorious for the amount of dirty laundry it had aired in public, the exceptions being themselves. Ianthe mused upon Great-Aunt Amelia, who had eloped with her own groom and had wound up somewhere in Bavaria, where she attracted the attention of a princeling, and inspired a duel between that gentleman and a Greek. Cara was reminded of Third-Cousin Ermyntrude, who had eased her shattered heart by dressing as a man and fighting Red Indians in the Colonies.

Cara leaned her forehead against the cool window glass. What *would* Paul Anderley think when he discovered she'd gone to London? Probably that she was a coward. She was also flighty, because now she wished she might return home. Cara wished so all the harder when her niece walked into the room, looking like an angel with her big blue eyes and innocent expression and golden curls clustering around her face. "Hello, Beau. You came back. I wish you wouldn't go away like that. Ianthe is always *picking* at me and it makes me cross. Tell her she must stop!"

Beau gazed upon his daughter. He had fallen in love when he first glimpsed the red-faced shrieking infant, and felt no differently today. Indeed, he sometimes thought that Zoë was the only female he had ever truly loved, which was a sure sign of his basic faithlessness, considering how many females he'd had in his bed.

Zoë sank down on a footstool upholstered in striped horsehair and leaned against his knee. Beau stroked her gleaming curls. Impossible that he should deny her anything, which was precisely how they had gotten in the pickle they were in today. Knowing how a thing got broken didn't make it easier to mend, unfortunately. "I hear you met Mannering at Gunter's. What have you to say for yourself, puss?"

"One can meet any of one's acquaintance at Gunter's. You know that." Zoë peered up at her papa from beneath her long eyelashes. "Cousin Ianthe just wants to make trouble."

Beau glanced at his cousin, who pressed her lips together and said not a word in her own defense, primarily because she knew that if she spoke she'd call him a cabbage-head. "You misunderstand, poppet. Ianthe wants only the best for you."

Zoë drooped. Beau looked stricken. Cara realized with horror that Zoë reminded her of herself at that age. Zoë was smaller and more petite than she had ever been, however, and so vivid that she made Cara feel as if she had one foot already in the grave.

Hopefully, the resemblance was only superficial, and didn't extend to their personalities. Cara emerged out from among the draperies. "Hello, Zoë," she said.

Zoë spun round on her stool. Her fine eyes widened, then narrowed, and she turned a furious face on her father. "What the devil is *she* doing here?"

5

"I apologized, of course, although I didn't mean it!" said Zoë, as she bobbed gracefully on one foot. "I can't believe that Beau has been so duplicitous as to bring Aunt Cara to town to be my chaperone. She is to tell me how I am to go on, if you please! As if I needed a bear-leader. Or a governess! I already have Cousin Ianthe."

And Aunt Cara would perhaps be harder to bamboozle, reflected Lord Mannering, although he was prevented from making this comment by the movements of the gavotte in which they were engaged. When the dance brought them back together he said, "You don't appear particularly enamored of your aunt."

Zoë gave him her right hand, preparatory to the execution of the *moulinét*. "Cara is well enough, I suppose. But she is the only one of the family to marry *sensibly*, and I can't tell you how many people have already asked me why she chose Lord Norwood when she could have done so much better, for she was the darling of the *ton*. I'm sure I don't know what to tell them! I thought it was very queer myself. Although of course I was only a babe at the time!"

Lord Mannering relinquished Zoë's right hand, and took up her left. "Perhaps it was a love match."

"I think you must not have known Lord Norwood." Both hands now, and each couple turned round at their places. "He was quite old! If it weren't for her looks, one wouldn't think Cara was a Loversall at all."

The dance ended, to Zoë's regret, without her partner having said or done anything to raise a damsel's hopes, a reticence that she put down to his being fairly elderly himself, if still the most handsome gentleman in the room. "You *will* remember that we are engaged for the dinner dance," she said, with a flash of dimples. "Because if you don't remember, then I shan't eat at all!"

Nick released her hand, and bowed. "Inconceivable that I should forget, then."

Did he mock her? Impossible to determine, for no sooner had Zoë stepped off the dance floor than she was surrounded by her Zoo, in the forefront tonight the elderly knight, two viscounts, a Mr. Cuthbert, and a young gentleman freshly sent down from university for a caper including a trained bear. She laughed gaily, and loud enough for Lord Mannering to hear, and be stricken with regret.

The rooms were hot, and thronged with guests. Nick moved through the crowd, musing that Beau Loversall's worries about his daughter's conduct—or his tolerance for her displeasure—hadn't been sufficient to insure his presence here tonight. He found Fitz in the card room, gazing through his quizzing glass upon a singularly ineptly played hand. "I thought macao was your game. Have you discovered in yourself a burning desire to play whist?"

Fitz turned the glass on his friend and regarded him with an enlarged, ungrateful eye. "It's enough to turn a man's stomach. First Gunter's, and now this damned boring affair, and you *knew* it would be boring, and dragged me here anyway! You're in your dotage, that must be what it is. At least I *hope* that's what it is. Nicky, please tell me you ain't pining after the little Loversall."

"Do I look as though I'm pining?" The marquess tucked his hand in his friend's arm and led him out of the card room. "No? Then I must not be. You fail to grasp the significance of this occasion, Fitz. It is the first time in many years that three Loversall females have been together in one room. One cannot predict what may ensue. All the world is holding its breath to see if Lady Norwood will do something to amuse and entertain them now that she's returned to Town, Ianthe having been a sad disappointment along those lines, and Zoë—while showing promise!—is still too young to have hit her stride."

Fitz barely avoided being trampled by a plump matron in orange satin. "Your Zoë is a baggage," he said.

Nick removed a glass of champagne from a passing waiter's tray and presented it to his friend. "She is indeed a baggage. Yes, Fitz, I noticed your use of the possessive pronoun. I am choosing not to rise to the bait. You can hardly blame poor Zoë for wanting to make her mark in the world, the previous generation having failed to come up to snuff. Lady Norwood made a deadly dull marriage. Ianthe reacted to a mysterious romantic disappointment by simply not marrying at all, when the least she should have done was sink into a decline and wither dramatically away. Beau has no more mistresses than anyone else. Obviously it is up to Zoë to maintain the family tradition. Just how she's going to do this, she hasn't decided yet."

Fitz thought Lord Mannering knew more about the young woman's thought processes than he should. "I hope this decision doesn't include you."

Nick smiled wickedly. "My dear Fitz, of course it includes me."

Lord Mannering had not underestimated the effect of three Loversall women in one room together. That amount of female pulchritude was almost more than the senses could encompass, and the effect was to bring them more attention than at least two of the ladies wished. Despite the marked family resemblance, there were differences between them too: Zoë was petite and vivid, Ianthe elegantly tragic and pale; and Lady Norwood—Well. She had the face and figure of a goddess, was (in the words of one smitten and none-too-original gentleman) a veritable Venus come down to earth. She was blessed (as another admirer put it) with the face of an angel and the body of a Salome. And furthermore it was well known that Norwood had left her with pots of gold, in which case one might wonder why she wore a slightly outmoded evening dress, an unkind observation, considering how nobly Barrow had risen to the challenge of appropriately garbing her mistress so soon after their arrival in town.

Still, if Lady Norwood wasn't quite in the first stare of fashion, she was still very fine in a gown of sea green crepe that clung to her divine figure in all the places that it should, her hair arranged *à la grecque* in braids and coronets and adorned with flowers. Ianthe was dressed rather more fashionably in a dress of raw gold silk and a scarf of cream-colored sheer muslin embroidered with gold metal thread, a turban of white satin with yellow French knots, and long yellow gloves;

her hair was parted in the center and drawn up in ringlets behind. One who wished to find fault—and some did, for if the Loversall women were invariably stared at, they were not universally admired—might criticize the style as inappropriate for a woman of her years; it still suited her very well. The youngest member of the trio wore a charming dress of white gauze striped with blue, and an Austrian cap.

Zoë was all innocence. "Pray say that you have forgiven me, Aunt Cara, for my unseemly display of surprise. Beau should have informed me that he meant to fetch you to town. Of course I understand why he did so! You know so much more of the world than Cousin Ianthe. It is so *generous* of you to take me in hand."

Cara glanced at Ianthe, who was looking somewhat martyred, and having application to her fan; and wondered how she was supposed to have obtained this knowledge of the world while secluded peacefully in the Cotswolds. Before she could inquire where her niece had come by her odd notions, Zoë added, "Although it's surely a little late to wrap me in lamb's wool, with Beau having a new *petite amie* every other week, and Ianthe scolding him for his licentious behavior while I'm trying to sleep!" And then, fortuitously, she was swept off by one of her admirers—this one an admiral in the Royal Navy—to get a glass of lemonade.

Cara took a deep breath and relaxed her hands, which she had clasped together in an effort not to grasp her niece's shoulders and give her a good shake. If Zoë was oblivious to such things, Cara was all too aware of the barbed tongues that hid behind the smiles of Polite Society.

Once she had not been. Once she had believed that people were what they seemed. She had been young then, and the belle of her own Season, as Ianthe also had been. Now Cara was a widow, consigned to the sidelines, while Ianthe was a confirmed spinster. Although Ianthe had still enjoyed several country dances, grown long in the tooth or no, and Cara a Scotch reel.

In truth, Ianthe had already been a spinster when Cara made her own come-out. Cara was one of the few people who knew why. She thought of what Paul Anderley had said to her. "Ianthe, have you never longed for children of your own?"

Ianthe turned a face of perfect horror on her. "After Zoë?"

"I take your point," Cara said wryly. "But you know what I meant."

Ianthe shrugged. "I made my bed and I've slept in it, as they say. It was my choice."

Before Cara could say more, Zoë returned to them, having procured her lemonade and got rid of her swain by hinting that she might later be persuaded into a tête-à-tête. Zoë had perfected the art of allowing each of her admirers to think she might misbehave a little bit with him, when she didn't mean to misbehave at all, or not really, until she tumbled into love. And then—Well, she was a Loversall! "Gentlemen are infinitely curious and interesting, don't you think? Of course *you* wouldn't wish for suitors, Aunt Cara, being so many years beyond your youth! And Cousin Ianthe is even older! Oh, have I said something I should not?"

Cara cut her a sharp look. "Yes, and well you know it. Licentious behavior, indeed. For an unmarried damsel to even know such words is beyond outrageous. You may also give up trying to provoke me, and mind your manners, please."

It was very shabby of her aunt to scold when Zoë

had behaved herself quite well this evening thus far. She hadn't spun around the floor for two successive dances with any gentleman, or granted three dances to any of her beaux; hadn't done anything without being told she might; hadn't screamed with boredom until she was purple in the face.

She thrust out her lower lip. "I hope you don't mean to load me with reproaches, Aunt Cara. It would be far too great a bore. 'Shocking,' 'imprudent,' 'displeasing'—I've heard it all before. Since I haven't a grain of proper feeling, you might as well save your breath. Anyway, I don't plan to make a byword of myself. And what would it matter if I did?"

"I thought you had a partiality for Lord Mannering," Ianthe interrupted, faintly. "Don't you wish to be a marchioness?"

"Of course I have a partiality," retorted Zoë. "Lord Mannering is so very *manly*, don't you think? He may even turn out to be my True Love. But Beau says I am too young to marry, and he should know, for he married young himself." Although Zoë did not rule out an elopement. Perhaps she would run off to Gretna Green with Lord Mannering, and then leave him languishing somewhere pale and brokenhearted, which would be a feather in any maiden's cap. "I mean to Experience Life before I marry. If I've learned anything from Beau, it is that one should try on the shoe to see if it fits before purchasing it." She snickered. "Look at the two of you, gasping like a pair of fish!"

No wonder Ianthe had turned into a wet-goose. Cara felt somewhat whimpery herself. "Because you are behaving badly!" she retorted. "Strive for a little conduct, or I shall take you home." Zoë's lip protruded further.

"And if you pout at me much longer, your face will freeze that way!"

Zoë didn't wish to be forever pouting. She nibbled on her lower lip instead. Nor did she care to leave the rout so early. She had not yet contrived to waltz with Lord Mannering, standing face-to-face with him, with her hand on his shoulder, and his hand on her waist, at which point the feeling of her in his arms would doubtless tempt him to yearn to take liberties.

The evening was not over yet. Nor was dinner. Perhaps during dinner Lord Mannering might be so bewitched by the pulse fluttering daintily in her throat that he would lose his appetite, or at the very least drop his fork on the floor.

"But I don't *want* to have dinner with that little baggage!" protested Baron Fitzrichard, as Nick steered him inexorably through the crowd. Reluctant as he may have been to attend Lady Miller's rout, Fitz had risen sartorially to the occasion, the highlight of his costume a pale pink waistcoat patterned all over in roses, worn over a second of plain rose, with a corbeau-colored coat boasting exaggerated shoulders and gilt buttons, Florentine silk breeches, white stockings, and buttoned shoes. He had additionally contemplated a patch at one corner of his mouth until his valet persuaded him that so dramatic a fashion statement should be preserved for a more important affair. Instead, he had settled for the quizzing glass, which he wielded frequently to good effect. In contrast, Lord Mannering was almost somber in a dark blue evening coat, white waistcoat, black pantaloons buttoned tight to the ankle and strapped over varnished black shoes.

Fitz glimpsed the Loversall ladies then, and stared. Granted, they were all three lovely, but his attention was primarily for Ianthe, not because of her overwhelming beauty, but because she had taken too much to heart Fitz's instruction that there should be one predominating color in a lady's costume to which the rest should be subordinate, as in a piece of music there was a relation between the successive sounds or notes. Fitz wouldn't go so far as to say Ianthe looked jaundiced, but in all those varying shades of yellow she did bear more than a passing resemblance to a primrose.

He hurried forward. Too late to repair tonight's damage, alas, but it was clearly incumbent upon him to offer several words to the wise. How most diplomatically to phrase it? "Delicate colors require to be supported and enlivened, and therefore are best relieved by contrast," perhaps. No, Ianthe had already demonstrated herself entirely *too* susceptible to contrast. Perhaps a reference to the relationship of the fundamental keynote to the series of other sounds constituting a musical chord.

Zoë placed herself in Lord Mannering's path, cutting him off as neatly from the others as an American cowboy with a steer. He looked at her quizzically. Very much a creature of impulse, Zoë dimpled and went straight to the point. "I know I shouldn't ask you this, Lord Mannering, but why haven't you married? Aren't you concerned that you should get yourself an heir while you still can?"

The chit really was appallingly rag-mannered, as well as highly conceited to think she would be forgiven anything in a society where all other hopeful misses behaved just *so*. "Young ladies aren't supposed to talk about such things," said Nick. "As you know very well. But to satisfy your curiosity, since you *did* go so far as to ask: I already have an heir, my nephew Colin, with whom I'm quite content. He is at Oxford now. Perhaps you would like to meet him? Colin is an amiable fellow, and agile enough to get down on his knees and spout all sorts of nonsense."

Zoë chose to overlook this unchivalrous attitude. He *had* called her "untouchable." "I've shocked you," she said.

Had she known what it would take to truly shock him, Miss Loversall might have been shocked herself. She really was the most outrageous child, fluttering those long lashes at him, her lips drawn into a luscious pout.

Her voice had dropped almost an entire octave. Nick said solicitously, "Are you taking a chill? Such a pity. I was going to ask if you wished to accompany me onto the balcony for a breath of fresh air."

Zoë wished very much to go out onto the balcony with Lord Mannering. Perhaps he would attempt to seduce her there. "'Tis nothing!" she said hastily, in her normal voice. "I merely had a lump in my throat. And yes, I would like a breath of fresh air, for it is so very close in here!"

Lord Mannering was all solicitude. "No, no, my dear Miss Loversall. You must not be so reckless. Just because I have *my* heir doesn't mean that you should take chances with your health."

Dubiously, Zoë regarded him. Was the marquess making fun of her? Perhaps it was time for a change of subject. "I thought perhaps you would not—" And then she broke off and very nearly stamped her foot.

Instead of paying attention to her, Lord Mannering was intent on her family and his friend.

Ianthe was twinkling at Fitz. "I've disappointed you, Baron. I fear I'm not in the habit of thinking much about my dress. But now I shall remember what you've told me, and when next we meet you will see that I am a veritable symphony."

Fitz flushed. "I didn't mean—"

"Nor did I!" Ianthe said quickly. "I was just teasing you a little bit. Allow me to make you known to my family. My niece, you have already met. This is my cousin Cara, Lady Norwood."

Fitz tried hard not to stare. Lady Norwood was even more goddess-like at close range, tall and lush and glorious, with a bosom that beggared description, and a pair of sparkling sapphire eyes in which a man might happily drown. Somewhat jerkily, he bowed. When he straightened up, she was still studying him, with an expression that was both amused and oddly kind. "Peonies," she said.

He blinked. She laughed. "Forgive me, Baron Fitzrichard. I have been so long out of Society that I've gotten in the habit of saying what I think. Your waistcoat reminded me of my garden. I miss it very much. Are you aware of the color-changing properties of the hydrangea? Could you work that into a waistcoat, it would be a masterpiece indeed. Not that I mean to infer that this waistcoat isn't, because of course it is!"

Fitz beamed at her. Ianthe also smiled, revealing her own version of the family dimples, which were very fine. Zoë wished that she might poison both her cousin and her aunt. Not fatally, of course, just enough to make them ill enough that she might slip away. Not that she wished to slip away alone. Was Mannering ravishing her with his eyes? He was not.

"Have you noticed the baron's neck-cloth?" said Ianthe. "It is of his own design. He is pondering a name for it. I had another notion, Baron. Perhaps, the Amourette?"

Cara eyed the neck-cloth, which Fitz's long-suffering valet hadn't been able to prevent him from tying himself. "The Coup de Grâce," she said.

Fitz, who had been demonstrating his unique left-handed style of manipulating his snuffbox—that damned Byron had taken the credit for it away from him, alas—inhaled abruptly, and sneezed. Nick chuckled and moved forward. "I think your creation has been christened, Fitz."

Zoë trailed after him. "This is my aunt," she said, so gracelessly that Ianthe's brief good humor fled.

"No introductions are necessary." Nick bent over Cara's hand. "Your niece has told me all about you, Lady Norwood. You're the pattern-card of propriety who is to show her how she must go on."

6

A pattern-card of propriety! Cara ground her teeth.
She would go down in the family annals as the only
member of the family to have never blotted her copybook. Even Ianthe would be remembered as having had
her youthful disappointment, as a result of which she
had foresworn all other *amours* and devoted herself to
Zoë, although she would have been better advised to go
into a nunnery, like their ancestor Francesca, who had
still ended up being captured by corsairs and flung into
the harem of the Grand Turk. Since the world didn't
know about them, Cara's own romantic disappoint-
ments didn't count.

Surely she was not now regretting that she had not
acted like a Loversall! Cara sighed, and tried to instill
order upon her chaotic thoughts. Conflicting emo-
tions assaulted her at each turn she took in London.
Mocking memories lurked around every corner. It
was far from comfortable to recall her younger self.

If only she hadn't allowed Beau to persuade her to
accompany him. Cara had been happy where she was,
or if not happy, certainly not discontented. She leaned
against a sadly weathered classical maiden who re-
tained possession of only one breast and wondered
if Beau's garden would benefit from a Gothic ruin.

In truth, Beau's garden *was* a Gothic ruin. Wide and overgrown stone paths led through what had at one time been lovely beds of plants and flowers surrounded by circles of white, blue, and red sand. Cara remembered the posies that had bloomed here in her mother's day. Now the pool was dry, and the garden dominated by nature in so profusely weedy a manner that even her enthusiasm faltered. Cornflower, broad-leafed spurge, fingered speedwell, pheasant's eye—she frowned at an especially fine example of groundsel. Between Beau's garden and Beau's daughter, Cara foresaw that she would be expected to stay in town far longer than she wished. Wistfully she recalled her clematis and wisteria, her lilacs and her yew tree; her cows and chickens and sheep. She dreaded to think what mischief the head gardener was getting up to behind her back.

Cara walked along the crushed stone path, pushing aside branches and vines. At least the roses still flourished, many of them grown six feet high. Later in the summer they would erupt in glorious bursts of white and pink and yellow. More than one of the bushes was already in bud, which according to the French, was a sign of ill luck. She touched a bird of paradise flower that had miraculously managed to survive alongside a maidenhair tree. Daisy burst through the undergrowth, a stout stick in her mouth.

After a brief tussle for possession, Cara threw the branch. Daisy raced happily in pursuit. The setter would need a good brushing after this adventure. Already her silky coat was tangled with twigs and burrs. Cara wouldn't be surprised if she'd acquired some vegetation in her own hair.

Along a weathered garden wall—stone, with niches

for statues that had either disappeared altogether or deteriorated sadly with time and neglect—bloomed a lone pink peony. Cara smiled, remembering Baron Fitzrichard's waistcoat. Thought of Fitz reminded her in turn of Lord Mannering, and Zoë. As well as of her sudden role as the family expert on propriety, which was a sad comment on her life. Cara grabbed a handful of weeds, and yanked.

A pattern-card of propriety! The odious man had *laughed* at her. Zoë could hardly be blamed for setting her cap at Mannering, for the marquess was handsome as the devil, with his dark hair that gleamed gold and russet in the candlelight, his high cheekbones and chiseled jaw; the lines of laughter and sensuality around his dark eyes and wicked mouth; that muscular body that wasn't camouflaged a whit by finely tailored clothes. Cara decimated a passion flower. Daisy burst out of the bushes, stick clenched between her teeth. Cara reached out to throw the stick, but Daisy was off and barking before she had the chance.

Beau, who was making his wary way along one of the stone paths, heard the barking and flinched. Like Baron Fitzrichard before him, Beau had the devil of a head. His excesses of the previous evening had naught to do, however, with macao and champagne, but rather resulted from a romantic tryst. What had happened there—or rather, *didn't* happen—had led him to drown his disappointment, and the lady's, in drink. Beau supposed he should not be surprised that his amatory skills had begun to fail him, though in all the history of the family such a thing had never happened before. It was just another part of the general misery that seemed determined to assail him from all sides at this stage of his life.

As Daisy seemed determined to assail him. "Down! Quiet!" he said. Daisy dashed off and returned, tail eagerly wagging, with her stick in her mouth. Gingerly he grasped the sodden thing and threw it a good distance. Daisy dashed off in pursuit.

Beau continued along the path. Widdle had informed him that "the lady" was in the garden. Beau assumed that "the lady" was Cara, since Widdle referred to Zoë as "the demoiselle" and Ianthe as "the mistress," despite all attempts to gently persuade him to do otherwise. Even Zoë hesitated to distress Widdle lest he take umbrage, because Lord knew what sort of butler they might end up with next.

Beau found Cara contemplating a dense and spiny evergreen shrub with clusters of golden yellow flowers. "Why are you here?" he said irritably. "Why didn't you go with Zoë and Ianthe to visit the shops?"

Cara brushed dirt off her hands. Beau's legendary tight-fistedness didn't extend to his daughter, who had vowed she would expire if denied a new dress. "I sent Barrow in my place. She knows my measurements. And I suspect her tastes are more refined than mine."

Widdle's tastes were more refined than Cara's. Beau eyed her ancient morning dress. "Bad enough that you went about like a dowd in the country, but you're in London now."

Cara, as has been established, was in no good mood herself. She plopped her hands on her hips and glared. "Perhaps I shall introduce a haystack or a woodpile to your garden. Since my preferences are of so rustic a bent! Or perhaps I shall just take my provincial self back home."

"Perhaps you should." With his lower lip thrust out, Beau looked remarkably like his daughter in a pet. "You're here to look after Zoë, are you not? A trifle difficult to do while hiding in the garden, don't you think?"

There was truth in his accusation. Cara reined in her temper. "Please try and understand. It is very difficult for me to present myself in public when I am constantly being recognized and quizzed. People ask the rudest questions, and what they think is no doubt even worse than what they say."

There was truth in her words also, but Beau chose to overlook it. "If you hadn't secluded yourself in the country with your sheep and your kumquats and your blasted chickens, Zoë might not have turned into such a strong-willed minx."

"And perhaps she would have, with you indulging her every whim!" But Cara didn't wish to war with her brother, and so she changed the subject. "Did you know that Mannering was at Lady Miller's rout?"

Beau didn't wish to quarrel either, not with his last hope. "Mannering was at *Lady Miller's?* Good God, where will he show up next?" He looked around the garden as if expecting the marquess to pop out from beneath a bush.

Daisy returned, panting, minus her stick. Both Beau and Cara ignored her. The setter dropped down on her haunches and watched them curiously.

"He also took her down to dinner. The rest of us accompanied them." Cara hadn't enjoyed a spoonful of the repast, even though it had included rib of lamb and mayonnaise of salmon, boiled fowl and Béchamel sauce, collared eel and lobster salad and boar's head; charlotte russe à la vanilla; veal-and-ham pie; jellies, compotes of fruit, cheesecakes, dishes of small pastry, and blancmange, all arranged tastefully up and down the table, interspersed with flowers and epergnes; and additionally a joint of cold roast and boiled beef placed on the buffet, something substantial for the gentlemen to partake of to keep up their strength. Instead she had sat quietly, and listened to Baron Fitzrichard's explanation that delicate colors required to be supported and enlivened, and therefore were best relieved by contrast; though the contrast should not be so strong as to equal the color it was intended to relieve, for it then became opposition, which should be avoided at all costs; while Ianthe responded with flattered interest, and Zoë fluttered and flirted and struck her attitudes.

The girl truly was shameless. Cara didn't know what Beau expected *she* might do. Warn Zoë against coming under the gravest censure, so that Zoë might fairly say, so what? A Loversall wasn't dissuaded by such considerations in the ordinary way of things, let alone when in pursuit of his or her True Love.

True Love! Cara wasn't sure that there was such a thing. If she'd once had such youthful fancies herself, she'd long since set them forcibly aside. And if such fancies sometimes crept into her dreams—Vigorously, she uprooted a nettle. Perhaps Cara had scant control over her dreams, but she didn't have to dwell upon such nonsense in the daylight hours. Then why was she sitting here, brooding about it, all the same?

If Beau had suspected that Mannering would appear at Lady Miller's, he would have attended the damned rout himself, and consequently was glad he hadn't suspected, for he disliked such events.

Thoughtfully, he brushed dog hair off his breeches. "Perhaps I've been a trifle hasty. Maybe Mannering's interest *has* been piqued."

Cara flung down the nettle. "You're as mutton-headed as Ianthe if you think Zoë may bring such a man to heel."

Mutton-headed, was he? Exposure to the sunlight, and his unusually short-tempered sister, had not helped Beau's headache one bit. "I'll tell you what *I* think! You're jealous of your own niece." Before Cara could recover sufficiently from her astonishment to reply, or box his ears, he set out in search of his valet, and a soothing tisane.

Cara scowled at her brother's retreating back, then turned away and wandered farther along the path until she came to the neatly arranged vegetable garden, which lay near the kitchen door. This area, at least, had been tended, most likely by the cook. Potatoes, Jerusalem artichokes, French beans, and spinach and carrots grew in neat rows, the beds bordered by tidy ranks of herbs. Cara knelt down and ran her fingers over slender stalks of barge and lavender, hyssop and rosemary and chervil, parsley and rosemary and sage. Marjoram, which when made into an oil warmed joints that were stiff. Lovage, when fried with a little hog's lard, encouraged the breaking of a boil. Chamomile, "the doctor," good for almost every ailment known to man.

Almost any ailment. Cara spied some lurking fennel, and gave it a good yank. Daisy stopped digging in the garden to plop down beside her mistress and give her cheek a companionable slurp.

Could she be jealous of Zoë? Cara plunged her fingers into the rich earth. Once it had been she who admirers flocked around like bees to the honey pot. Now any flocking done would be around Norwood's fortune. His fortune, and all that lovely property. Flocking there would be, Cara knew, for she was hardly a naïf. She slapped her fist on the dirt, startling Daisy. "Damn, damn, damn!"

Only then did Cara become aware that she had an audience, because Widdle cleared his throat. The butler didn't know what to make of the lady kneeling, cursing, in the garden dirt. Not that he knew what to make of any of this household, except that he didn't think highly of the quality of their silver plate.

Energized by the sight of the butler, Daisy leapt up and knocked him down. "Squire Anderley come to see you, Lady Norwood," Widdle announced from his bed among the herbs. "He *said* you wouldn't mind if I brought him into the gardens, though I thought I should ask you first."

Cara scrambled hastily to her feet and discouraged Daisy from bathing Widdle's face. Then she pulled the butler upright, and brushed him free of dirt. "It's all right, Widdle. Squire Anderley and I are old friends." Widdle looked uncertain. "You may leave us alone together, you know."

Widdle was uncertain. The lady didn't look happy to see her visitor, and he disliked the expression in the gentleman's eye. However, it wasn't Widdle's place to argue with his employers. Not that the lady *was* his employer, precisely, but he didn't think he should argue with her either. Struggling with his indecision, Widdle walked back down the path toward the house.

Cara studied her visitor, who appeared travel-weary and cross. "Sit!" he snapped. Daisy sank down, panting, at his feet. Cara assumed he had been talking only to the dog. "Business has brought you to town?"

"Unfinished business." Paul moved toward her. "I've brought your mare with me. I assumed you would wish to ride."

"How kind of you." How presumptuous. Cara took a prudent step backward. "Mortimer told you where we'd gone?"

Mortimer had not, despite threats, bribes, and all other manner of persuasion. "I am perfectly capable of adding two and two together and arriving at four." Paul was further irritated to see that Cara's hands were again grimed and her hair awry. She looked so impossibly lovely that he wanted to shake or kiss her. Since he could do neither, he looked around the garden instead.

If Norwood House was a prime example of the noble art of picturesque gardening run amok, this place was a horticulturist's version of the nether regions. "Your gardener would succumb to an apoplexy on the spot."

Barrow would be pleased, thought Cara, that Paul had followed her to town. She was uncertain how she felt about the matter herself. "I'll grant that Beau's gardens are a somewhat overwhelming task."

Daisy reappeared, with her stick. Absently Paul took the thing and flung it. He doubted that the condition of her brother's gardens, deplorable as they were, had brought Cara here. He doubted also that he would accomplish anything by shaking—or kissing—her.

Rather, he might accomplish something, but nothing that would advance his suit. "I know you a little too well to stand on ceremony with you. Won't you tell me what's amiss?"

Cara plucked an especially frothy dandelion. She

understood that Paul was feeling outmaneuvered, which made him cross and out of charity with her. However, were she to reveal family problems, then Beau would be cross and out of sorts.

Beau was already cross and out of sorts, and Cara felt in need of a confidante. "You've come a considerable distance to become embroiled in our difficulties. I warn you that you'd be better advised to return home."

Paul might have grasped her hands, were they not so grubby. He settled for a smile. "What fustian you are talking! You know I consider myself part of your family. What can I do to help?" He looked critically around him. "Perhaps arrange to have some bat guano brought to town?"

Cara sighed. "If I had some bat guano with me, I'd put it in my niece's bed. Zoë has been spoilt all her life, and expects admiration from all the world, which for the most part she receives, for she is truly lovely as well as impetuous, spontaneous and gay." She gave the dandelion an absentminded puff, scattering it to the wind. "Now Zoë has taken a fancy to a gentleman of whom her father can't approve. At least he couldn't approve yesterday! I can't help but wonder if any gentleman will prove worthy enough to satisfy Beau, not that it will make the slightest difference when my niece falls madly and passionately in love."

If only Cara would fall madly and passionately in love with *him*. Paul reached out and plucked a piece of vegetation from her hair, which led Cara to wonder if the squire felt freer in Beau's wilderness of a garden than he did at Norwood House, and why; and if he would try and kiss her now, and if she wished him to.

"So there it is!" she said brightly, and stepped away

a little farther, lest the squire decide he felt freer than she liked. "My trouble is Zoë, and I don't see how you can help with that."

Zoë sounded like a typical Loversall. Thank God Cara didn't fit the mold. Surely it wouldn't be difficult to find the chit a husband if she was the nonpareil that Cara claimed. And then Cara would return to the country where she belonged.

Before he could comment, footsteps sounded on the gravel path, accompanied by a volley of wild barking, and female voices raised in argument. For all the privacy afforded her in this ruined jungle of a garden, Cara reflected, she might as well have been at the Royal Botanic Gardens at Kew.

Zoë tripped into view, looking especially enchanting in a muslin dress with full sleeves and a high neck and a hem of colored ribbon headed by a broad lace border, its low neck filled in with a blond fichu. She eyed Paul with frank interest. "Widdle said you were here with a gentleman, Aunt Cara. Now we know why you didn't come shopping with us, you sly thing! Barrow picked out the nicest gown for you, not that *I* would wish to wear purple, but it should do quite nicely for a person of your age. We have come to act as your chaperones, because you know it isn't proper for you to be out here alone."

Zoë knew how to make her presence felt. As well as how to make her aunt feel so ancient that it was miraculous she could get around without a cane. Cara performed introductions, reluctantly.

"Charmed," said Paul, insincerely. This young woman was no more charming than an ill-mannered pup. Interpreting his expression as one of admiration—after all, what else could it be?—Zoë went on to entertain him with a description of a dinner dress that was being made for her, with a worked muslin body, half-high, and a sarcenet skirt trimmed with patent net and ribbon disposed in draperies.

How Paul must dislike this chatter, thought Cara. To have to listen to it served him right. Another time he would perhaps think twice before he burst uninvited in on her. And perhaps he wouldn't, for he was a man who knew what he wanted and pursued it with assurance. Cara might admire his singleness of purpose more if only it were not directed at herself.

Daisy bounded into the clearing, tail wagging ecstatically, a snapdragon trailing from her mouth, and one ear turned inside out. Ianthe followed, sadly out of breath. She was even more than usually eye-catching today, wrapped in a bright green and gold Indian shawl that had been made into a dress, its wide border forming the hemline. Around her shoulders was draped a large shawl of muslin worked at the border and ends with embroidery, looped down the back with a ribbon bow. Her hair was pinned up in a large chignon, atop which she had placed a frivolous straw hat.

Another member of the family, decided Paul. Hopefully the intrepid Barrow had chosen new clothes for her as well. She greeted him with a brief nod before drawing Cara aside.

"I'm so sorry!" Zoë twitched her skirts fastidiously away from a trailing runner-bean. "I've never known my cousin to be so impolite. Not that anyone will scold *her* for it. Considering how she and Cara are always ringing peals over me, it seems monstrous unjust!"

Ianthe clutched at Cara's hand, distracting her from the interesting spectacle of Paul's expression growing more and more appalled. Ianthe's own expression was even more than usually anxious. Cara patted her hand. "Has Beau ripped up at you again, Ianthe?"

"No! Although surely he would, if he found out about it, but, Cara, Beau must never know!" Ianthe bit her lip. "There is no telling what he might do! Fight a duel, perhaps—or worse!"

Whatever had put her cousin in such a fidget? "Don't fret. I won't tell Beau if you think I shouldn't. Whatever it is!"

Ianthe pressed the handkerchief to her reddened nose. "You think I'm being a goose, and perhaps it's true, but what if I'm not? Aggravating as Beau is, I don't wish to see him killed! Because of course he *would* be killed in an affair of honor: you know as well as I that he has no ability whatsoever with weapons of any sort. Oh, I cannot bear it! This was given to me in error." She thrust a note into Cara's hand.

7

"Smitten, that's what he is!" said Barrow, and tugged the brush through Cara's hair. Daisy, who had already endured her own brushing, lay sprawled before the fire. "To come all the way to London after you! I told you his affections had become fixed."

Lady Norwood was seated at her dressing table, across which marched silver-topped jars and bottles. Barrow stood behind her, watching her mistress in the oval looking glass. "Hunting season is over in the country," Cara retorted. "Therefore, the squire has followed the spoor to town. A man can hardly ride to hounds if the fox isn't there."

Barrow brandished the hairbrush. "You and your foxes! The squire is a fine man. What if someone else should catch his eye while you're shilly-shallying, miss?"

Only to Barrow was Cara still a miss. "Can you be a little less vigorous? Should the squire's fancy stray, I wouldn't care a fig."

"Poppycock!" retorted Barrow. "You'd care more than a fig if you saw the squire dangling after someone else. You like the attention of the gentlemen every bit as much as your flibbertigibbet of a niece."

Cara had already been treated, several times, to Barrow's opinion of Zoë. The gentlest of the abigail's comments had been "hell-born babe." "Gentlemen don't dangle after me anymore. Or if they do, it's Norwood's fortune they want. Just as it's Norwood's fortune Paul Anderley wants, and the Norwood property. I don't know why you refuse to see that for yourself."

Barrow saw many things, among them that it was unnatural for a woman to hold property, her mistress being a perfect example, for no sooner had Miss Cara become a widow than she'd begun behaving with pertinacious obstinacy. Although to say the truth, she'd been pig-headed before, but not to this degree. Barrow set down the brush and began to braid the long red-gold hair, muttering dire warnings about being at one's last prayers and left on the shelf.

If Cara was praying for anything, it was that Barrow would leave her alone so that she could get on with what must be done. "I'm a widow, remember? I'm already *off* the shelf. But if it's on the shelf you'll have me, I am quite happy there."

Barrow didn't believe a word of it. Her mistress hadn't been happy for a long time. She tied a neat green ribbon at the end of the thick braid. "Squire Anderley has a decided partiality for you. You're an ungrateful girl if you don't appreciate what a singular stroke of good fortune that is for you."

Cara picked up a silver jar, and unscrewed the lid. "A good mount must be serviceably sound as well as good-mannered. Beauty being in the eye of the beholder, those are the qualities at the top of a prospective buyer's list. And if she turns out to be a kicker, then he must put a red ribbon in her tail."

Barrow eyed the ribbon she had just tied, which

apparently should have been red. "Take care lest you bungle it, my fine lady! The squire is a prize."

"The squire is a man!" Cara retorted in exasperation. "Much like any other, as near as I can see. Enough, Barrow! Leave me in peace."

"Hoity-toity!" muttered Barrow, under her breath. Aloud, she suggested various remedies for the headache that had kept her mistress at home.

"No!" protested Cara. "I don't want water of white poppies, or a poultice of violets, or to have my temples and forehead anointed with oil of roses and juice of sickle-wort! Nor do I wish to endure any more lectures. Do go away, Barrow, and leave me to my bed."

Barrow narrowed her eyes. She knew her mistress well. Appearances to the contrary, Lady Norwood had as queer a kick in her gallop as any other Loversall.

A mere servant, however, could hardly voice her misgivings. Or she *could*, but it would only put her mistress further out of temper. Wearing a martyred expression, the abigail left the room.

Blessed silence. Cara put down the little pot she had been holding, and rubbed her temples. Daisy ambled over from the hearth to drop down at her feet. Cara stroked the setter's silky back with one bare foot.

Outside, darkness had fallen. Candlelight flickered on the satinwood dressing table, and firelight on the hearth. At this very moment, Beau and Ianthe and Zoë were displaying themselves at Covent Garden during a performance of *Macbeth*. Cara had pleaded a headache to avoid accompanying them. Beau thought she was sulking. Ianthe thought her very brave. Zoë patently thought of nothing but herself.

Brave? She was an utter coward. But Ianthe had been correct in predicting Beau would do something dashing and dramatic and foolhardy if he knew his precious daughter had been offered an insult. Cara stared moodily at her reflection, then got up from the bench. Daisy rose also. "No!" said Cara. "You're not going with me." Not especially disappointed—it *was* dark outside—the setter stretched out on the hearth and went back to sleep.

Cara dressed quickly and simply in one of her old gardening gowns, and for the difficulty of lacing them, left off her stays; twisted up her long braid atop her head and secured it there with pins. Then she wrapped herself in a dark cloak. No one would mistake her long for Zoë, for she was taller and more fully formed, but she should pass briefly in the dark, at least long enough to deliver a crushing rejection, a denunciation of ignoble motives, and a demand that paths should never again cross.

And if the deception were discovered, then what? Cara didn't know. Ianthe's suggestions had been vague on that point. Before she left the room, Cara rearranged her pillows, pulled the coverlet over them, and extinguished the candles. Anyone who checked on her—Cara knew well that Barrow's suspicions had been aroused—would think that she slept.

She opened the door and glanced out into the hallway. This was not the first time Cara had crept out of her brother's house. His servants would not dare try and stop her, but she wanted no report of her strange behavior to get back to Beau, who might fairly ask where she had gone, and why, after vowing that she wished to stay indoors. Cara made her way unchallenged down the dark back staircase, and almost to the little-used side door. There, however, luck abandoned her, not because she was rusty in the practice of sneaking about, which naturally she was, but because Widdle had taken to keeping a jealous eye on the silver plate, inferior though it might be.

The butler squealed as if he'd tripped over a ghost, then peered fearfully about, and relaxed to find Daisy nowhere in sight. "I thought you was a housebreaker, my lady!" he gasped.

"So I see." Cara eyed the candlestick that the butler held poised above his head. "I'm going out, Widdle. I wish that no one should know about this but ourselves."

Widdle lowered the candlestick, which to his knowledgeable eye was of significantly higher value than the silver plate. A person might rightly wonder why he was carrying about a candlestick at such an hour. He suspected the lady *did* wonder, from the shrewd look she gave him. Tit for tat, as they said. Widdle announced that he would be as quiet as the grave.

Cara slipped out the side door, and into the street. The night was dark, foggy, and quiet, save for the occasional night-coach and carriage and watchman calling out periodic descriptions of the weather to anyone who hadn't the eyes to see it for himself. Cara drew her cloak more tightly about her and stayed as close to the houses as she dared.

A scrawny dog darted out from a dark alleyway, startling her so badly that she almost stumbled. Men's voices echoed out of the fog. Cara ducked between the buildings as two drunken bucks staggered out of the mist. She should have brought Daisy along for company.

No, on second thought she shouldn't have, because Daisy would have been even more skitterish than she was. To bolster her flagging courage, Cara recited a litany of various past Loversalls. Gwyneth, who had run off with Gypsies and dwelt among them in their encampments in the woods, quite happily from all reports. Leda, who had been seduced by a Russian ambassador, went at length to Moscow, and became a favorite of the Tsar. Ariadne, who had consumed young lovers with an appetite that shocked even the members of her own family, among them a shepherd, a strolling musician, and the son of a coppersmith. In comparison, it seemed extremely poor-spirited of Cara to be starting at the merest sound while merely out, unaccompanied on a late-night stroll. Instead of imagining a bogeyman, a true Loversall would go and investigate, for the creature lurking in the shadows might be one's own True Love.

Cara already knew that she was not among the more adventurous of the Loversalls. There would be no corsairs for her, no harems, no coppersmiths' sons or seraglios. The only bed she wished to be in was her own, and now.

Sounds echoed eerily. Street lamps cast only a dim glow into the gloom. What was Zoë thinking, to consider going out so late? Cara couldn't help but remember every tale she'd ever heard of footpads and murderers, not to mention press gangs and other creatures of the night.

A hackney coach waited at the designated corner, the driver muffled in a heavy coat on his high seat, the horses standing patiently in the fog. Cara's footsteps slowed. Surely she had not come so far to turn craven now.

Cautiously, she approached the cab. The vehicle appeared to be empty. The driver turned his head to peer down at her. "'E said as ye'd be a looker. Bein' as ye've already kept me horses waitin' overlong, missy, mebbe ye'd get in."

Did the man think she was a woman of easy virtue? Cara didn't know whether to be appalled or amused. To hesitate was to be lost, and so she climbed into the cab.

The interior was dark, which was perhaps fortunate, because from every indication it was also none too clean. Unknown substances gritted on the floor beneath her half boots. The air stank of spoiled fish.

The cab rattled through dark streets, around corners, in such a tangle of contrary directions that Cara soon lost all sense of where she was. By the time the cab drew to a stop, she was well and truly lost.

The cabby opened the carriage door and held out his hand. Gingerly, Cara took it and let the man help her down. Impossible to make out his features, between his hat and the muffler wrapped around the lower part of his face, but she sensed that he was young. "'E said as ye was to go the front door," the cabby said, and climbed back up onto his seat. The cobbled street was close to the river, judging from the thickness of the fog.

Before her stood a tall house built in an older style, its top stories rising into gables and jutting out in shallow bays, its lower windows tiny jeweled squares set in designs of ornamental lead, its rooftop adorned with clusters of chimneys with protruding stacks. At least Cara knew she wasn't in Westminster or Whitehall: this building had survived the Great Fire. Behind her, the hackney clattered off into the night.

What the *devil* was she doing? Cara stared up at the house. Light glowed from several of the old windows. She reminded herself of her family, and the Battle of Hastings, and reluctantly climbed the front steps.

The door was opened by a maidservant in a neat dark gown, white apron, and starched cap. The girl didn't react to the sight of a lone female on her doorstep with so much as an eyelid's blink. "If you'll follow me, please, mum," she said, and led Cara through a vestibule paved with black marble, past a delicately carved wooden staircase that led to the upper floors, down a hallway inlaid with different colors of wood, to a parlor at the back of the house. There, the girl curtsied and withdrew. The servant had clearly expected her, as had the hackney driver. Cara wondered how she—or Zoë—had been described.

She glanced curiously around the parlor. Wainscotted walls once painted a brilliant red with touches of blue and green were faded now, their colors echoed in the carpet on the floor. Bookshelves lined two of the walls, displaying volumes bound in velvet of different colors, especially red, with ornamental gold clasps. On a third wall hung a tapestry depicting a somewhat brutal hunting scene. Beautifully embroidered draperies softened windows fashioned with horizontal mullions and diamond-shaped leaded panes in between. Inviting pillows of crimson satin graced the window seat. Two walnut wing chairs covered in embroidery were drawn up to the fire. A book lay open on a small table of red marble streaked with white. Cara picked it up. Lily's *Eupheus: The Anatomy of Wit.*

A long oak table used for informal dining, fancifully embellished with intricately carved animals and flowers. A cabinet four feet high, with two shelves inside that held curiosities. Old maps of England, Scotland,

France, and the Low Countries. A counting table with a chequered top. A perpetual almanac in a frame.

A brandy decanter decorated with all-over diamond cutting. Ladies didn't drink brandy. Cara poured herself a glass. Whatever she had expected, it wasn't to have been brought to such a place as this.

If only she had never returned to London. If only Beau had never had a child. If only she had a pistol, or something with which to defend herself. For all its treasures—and this was a room filled with treasures—the parlor lacked a fireplace poker or anything else she might use as a weapon. Cara wondered if she might defend her virtue with a wooden chair. Not that it was *her* virtue that was in need of defending. She walked to the fireplace, which was embellished with a rear opening of brick laid herringbone-wise, a mantel frieze carved with monkeys and birds and fruits, and a scene of Diana bathing carved in the chimneypiece. A cozy fire burned in the hearth.

Moments passed, then half an hour. By the time the doorknob turned, Cara was in such a state of nerves that she had consumed not one glass of brandy, but two, and was contemplating a third. She stared at the door. Then, remembering that she was supposed to be her niece, Cara quickly turned her back. Her disguise wouldn't pass for a moment in this bright candlelight. No use now trying to persuade the man that Zoë wanted no more to do with him. She supposed she'd have to beg.

The door opened, closed. A key turned in the lock. Footsteps crossed the floor. Nearer, ever nearer, wood to carpet . . . Cara clenched her hands. The feet stopped just short of touching her. "Well met, Lady Norwood," drawled an amused masculine voice.

A pattern-card of propriety, was she? Cara spun around. "Damn you, Nicky!" she snapped, and raised her fist, and punched the marquess smack in the jaw.

8

She'd punched him. The blasted woman had punched him. Which, when all was said and done, was hardly the worst she'd done to him over the years.

Nick touched his battered jaw. Cara looked almost as startled as he felt. Before she could recover sufficiently from her shock to abuse him again, he unceremoniously picked her up, plopped her down on the table, and held her prisoner there with arms on either side of her body, his legs pressed against hers.

They were practically nose to nose. They were definitely thigh to thigh. Nick's blood stirred. Not to mention other portions of his person. If she hadn't noticed yet, it was a matter of mere time. Lord, how could she *not* notice? Or perhaps she had. There was a horrified expression in her beautiful eyes as she stared at him. Curious, he waited for her to speak. She murmured, "I never hit anyone before in all my life!"

And of course he had to be the first. Nick could not help but smile. "Did you like it?" he inquired.

Cara's horror began to fade, to be replaced by an awareness of her position. He held her so well imprisoned that she could barely squirm. "I did, rather. I think I'd like to do it again."

At least she wished to do something again. Before

she could become enamored of the notion of further violence, Nick leaned closer still. "Pray restrain yourself," he said, and dropped a kiss on the tip of her nose. Then he kissed her cheek, her temple, her eyebrows and her ear, and pulled her cloak aside so that he might work his way down her fine slender throat. When she made no attempt to stop him, not that she *could* have stopped him, held prisoner as she was, or that he would allow it even if she tried, he drew back to look at her. Her lovely eyes had fluttered shut. Now they opened. Her luscious lips parted. She looked adorably dazed.

"Cara mia," he groaned, and claimed her mouth with his. The taste of her was as intoxicating as he had remembered it all these years. He plunged his tongue into her eager mouth, and his fingers in her hair, scattering hairpins everywhere. Her hand moved to his chest, tugged at his cravat. Nick gave himself up to the moment. No woman he had ever known, and he had known many women, had ever fit so perfectly into his arms.

The moment, or moments. Perhaps even hours. When Nick at last regained his senses, Cara's cloak was on the floor, her hair not only unpinned but unbraided and tangled around her shoulders, her gown in a state of shocking disarray; while his cravat had been untied, and his shirt yanked open. Her hands were splayed on his bare chest. His hands rested on her bare skin also, one on her shoulder, and the other on her knee.

She was disheveled, bemused, and bewitching. Impossible for either of them to deny how much he wanted her now. In case she *did* mistake it, he moved slightly against her. She flushed. Now perhaps she would cease being such a termagant and listen to what he had brought her here to say. He leaned his forehead against hers. "Cara," he sighed.

"Satyr! Goat!" She pushed at his chest. "Luring innocent young women to your lair!"

It would seem the moment—or moments—had ended. Nick didn't feel like releasing her just yet. He placed his hand atop hers and captured them against his chest. "I don't think that goats have lairs. And you're hardly innocent, my love."

Her fingers twitched, as if she wished to claw him. The expression in her sapphire eyes was not so blissful now. "No, nor am I young, and well I know it, so you needn't harp on the subject. The fact remains that no gentleman would invite a well-brought-up young woman to misbehave like this."

She was glorious, even in a temper. Nick raised her hands to his lips and kissed them. "Misbehave how? Pray be more precise." He turned one hand over, ran his tongue along her palm, took a finger in his mouth.

"Um," she said, distracted, and then snatched her hand away. "Release me at once, you toad, or I shall make you sorry that you did not!"

First a goat, and now a toad. This reunion wasn't going exactly as Nick had hoped it would. However, it *was* going as he had expected, which was why the door was locked. He eyed her with amused curiosity. "How do you propose to do that?"

Cara glowered. She looked unutterably desirable, her lips swollen from kissing, her cheeks flushed, and her hair tumbling down her back. "I don't know. But I promise you won't like it one little bit."

There would be no more kisses now, at least not willing ones. Nick wanted desperately to pick Cara up and carry her off to his bed, there to indulge in deliciously delirious paroxysms of passions that lasted for hours. After which, she'd doubtless run off to her country fortress, where long-fanged monsters lurked in the moat, and servants waited to douse him with boiling oil. Nick released her and moved away.

Cara watched him walk toward the fireplace. Absurd, to feel bereft. He moved like some sleek dark jungle beast, all sleek muscle and coiled strength, ready in an instant to pounce and bring down his prey. She swallowed as Nick took off his jacket and tossed it onto a chair, then bent to build up the fire. So there *was* a poker in the room. The firelight gleamed russet in his hair.

Damnation! This was what came from kissing. Yet Cara had wanted to be kissed. Well, hadn't she? She'd even left off her stays. And now that she'd been kissed, want it or not, she wished very much for more. As if she didn't already know what madness came from kissing Nicky! He stood up and smiled at her. Cara scooped up her scattered hairpins and ducked behind a box chair.

She was ridiculous. And enchanting. Not to mention voluptuous, her breasts thrust into fine relief as she raised her arms above her head to pin up her wayward curls. Nick could not help but think of peaches. Large, luscious, ripe peaches, so delicious for the tasting that a man didn't care if the juice ran down his chin. And if he didn't get control of his wayward thoughts, he was going to have to leave the room.

Having achieved a coiffure remarkably similar to a haystack, Cara lowered her arms. "You look absurd," Nick remarked. "Cowering behind that chair. Surely you don't think that I would do you harm?"

The frown returned. Her nose twitched. She said, "Lucasta Clitheroe."

Lord Mannering wasn't fool enough to be drawn into a conversation about Lucasta Clitheroe in this particular moment. "She's the Countess Fenton now. You're likely to encounter her at some point. It would probably be best if you didn't try to snatch out her hair."

Lady Norwood crossed her arms beneath her sumptuous bosom. "Whyever should I wish to do that?"

"You seem to dislike the lady."

"I hope you don't mean to tell me I should not!"

She looked both belligerent and wary, and so she should have been, because if Nick made up his mind to take her, that chair would not long stand in his way. Despite Cara's opinion of him, he was a gentleman, however. More or less. Most of the time. "How do you like my house?"

She looked startled. "This isn't your house."

"But it is. You're remembering the place in Bedford Square. This is also a family dwelling. Since few people associate the place with me, I can be private here. But I'm forgetting my duties as a host. Are you hungry? Would you care for some tea?" Nick eyed the lowered level in the diamond-cut decanter. "Some brandy perhaps?"

Cara had already had sufficient brandy. The sweet taste lingered in her mouth. Or perhaps that was the taste of Nicky. "Your house is beautiful," she said. "I assume you use it for your trysts, since you were so intent on bringing Zoë here."

"Actually, I wasn't." Nick watched her with some amusement. "Intent on bringing Zoë here. Your niece is terrifying. She puts me in mind of a young she-wolf."

Cara tried hard not to chuckle, and failed. Since the

marquess had apparently lost his interest in kissing her, she came out from behind the chair. "Do you deny you sent the note that brought me here?"

Nick was glad to see she'd relaxed sufficiently in his presence to be seated, although she'd find soon enough that carved mythological figures entwined with flowers didn't make an especially comfortable perch. "True enough, I sent the note. However, Zoë's presence here was never my intention. My servant was instructed on pain of disembowelment to deliver it to Ianthe."

Cara stared blankly at him. "I don't understand. You wished for an assignation with *Ianthe*?"

Of course he hadn't wished for an assignation with Ianthe. Where Zoë was too young, too short, too dazzling to suit his taste, Ianthe was too tragic and water-logged. Cara, however—He said, "Don't be absurd."

Cara bit her lower lip and set to ruminating. Nick was silent, watching her. The ancient gown she wore was a faded blue in color, and clung to her magnificent body like he wished he might. Her hair made a brilliant, if somewhat untidy, coronet around her head. She looked like some pagan priestess about to engage in a fertility rite.

She had always looked that way. When he'd first glimpsed Zoë, during that first incredible second before he realized she wasn't the female who had long haunted his sleep, Nick had experienced an appalling flash of *déjà vu*, as if the years had reversed themselves for him, and he was again seeing Cara for the first time, a moment he would never forget, for it had literally affected all the rest of his life. Now that Cara was with him again, so many years later, he found her much more captivating than she had been as a girl. Definitely she was more captivating than her niece.

And considerably more sensible. She said, "You don't want Ianthe."

It was a rare pleasure to watch a fine mind function. Cara's mind was working at such a furious pace that smoke would at any moment puff out of her ears. "I do not."

She grasped the carved chair arms. "Let me make sure I understand this. You expected *me* to come here."

"I did."

"You encouraged Zoë to set her cap at you so that Beau would persuade me to return to London."

"I did."

"You never wanted my niece."

"I most emphatically do not want her." Nick moved away from the table. "The devil, Cara, give me credit for a little common sense."

Cara would give him credit, all right, for being a conniving scoundrel. And even more handsome than when she had seen him last. The lines of experience around his eyes and mouth suited him, as did his short hair. His shirt remained open, for she had torn off his buttons in her haste to touch his skin.

She didn't regret it for an instant. Considerable time had passed since she'd enjoyed the sight of a man's chest. Few chests, she suspected, were as handsome as Nicky's. And as great a pleasure to rest against. "You are considerably better," she said, "than a kumquat tree."

Lord Mannering sincerely hoped that he might be. "Obfuscation," he observed, as he poured brandy into a glass. "To confuse, and make obscure. I knew that if Beau grew worried enough about his daughter, he'd persuade you to return. Although I will confess to wondering at times if I'd bit off more than I could chew."

He stood too close for comfort. Prudently, Cara removed herself from the chair. "You were right to wonder. Zoë throws things out of windows. She also scratches and bites. Beau is afraid you'll play fast and loose with her."

Nick remembered when Cara had bit and scratched, though not in a rage. Apparently she was remembering also, because she glanced at him. "Zoë says that you are very *manly,*" she added. "She notices these things because she means to have several *affaires de coeur* before she settles down to become some poor man's wife. But she means to sample even those goods before she makes her purchase. You can see why she's driving Beau to distraction." Nick looked dismayed, and Cara could not stop herself from smiling. "How is your rheumatism, pray?"

Lord, those dimples. Her smile was like a blow to the belly. Or maybe to the heart. "I'll get down on my knees for you if you wish it. I did so once, as I recall. And then you married Norwood. I have never understood why."

His voice had turned husky. Cara was stricken briefly mute by a vision of Nicky on his knees before her, and what he might do there. She reminded herself that even her own brother had said she was grown drab and dull. "Don't try and claim you wore the willow longer than a sennight. I know otherwise."

He was not so foolish as to claim anything of the sort. "I never said I was a monk."

Anyone less monkish, Cara could not imagine. The memory of his kiss still tingled on her lips. "Why haven't you married, Nicky? You need to get yourself an heir."

Nick was running out of patience. If Cara backed any farther away from him, she'd end up in the fire. "Why is everyone so concerned with my progeny? I have an heir, my nephew Colin, who will someday be a fine man, even if at the moment he's driving my sister to distraction with his pranks. He's already been sent down from university once this term. Speaking of heirs, you didn't give Norwood one, I hear."

To talk of heirs with Nicky was to open doors of memory best left closed. Cara looked away. "That was a different matter. Norwood didn't require an heir. His title died with him. It is unkind of you to use me like this. I would never have thought you'd go so far to get your revenge."

Nick wasn't feeling kind, nor did he know why he should be expected to, when all was said and done. He placed his hand on Cara's cheek, and turned her face to his. "Revenge is not a luxury in which gentlemen indulge."

Her eyes narrowed. "No? Yet you brought me out in the streets of London alone at night. Anything could have happened. Had you thought of that?"

Her skin was cool against his hand, and soft and smooth as silk. Perhaps he *had* been base enough to wish her frightened a little bit, but never would he see her harmed. "You weren't alone for a moment. My servants think I'm quite mad."

"And the hackney driver?"

"He thinks I'm mad also, but it matters naught to him, because I'm also rich."

Cara wasn't certain she didn't agree with them. Not

that her own processes of reasoning were above reproach. "But, Nicky, why?"

His hand slid down her cheek to cup her jaw. "Because you showed no signs of returning to London on your own."

How she wished to turn her head and press her lips against his palm. Cara stared at Nick instead. "And of course it would never occur to you to come to me."

His thumb brushed across her lower lip. "Did you want me to?"

Difficult to remember, with him touching her like that. "I think," Cara said unsteadily, "that I never wanted to see you again."

Nick raised his other hand and framed her face between them. "You made that fairly clear. We have unfinished business between us, Cara. Frown at me all you will, but admit that you wouldn't have let me in if I'd come knocking at your door."

Could she have turned him away? Cara didn't know. "Very well. I've come to London. Now will you discourage my niece?"

He bent his head and brushed his lips against hers. "No. Not unless you encourage me instead."

Not unless she *what?* The scoundrel! Cara jerked away from him and raised her hand. Easily, Nick caught it. "Why are you so determined to do violence to my person?" he asked, in exasperated tones.

"I'm feeling violent." Cara tried to twist free. Perhaps Nick hadn't meant what she'd thought he did. Surely he hadn't meant what she'd thought he did!

On the other hand, Cara wasn't altogether certain she didn't want Nick to mean what she'd thought. He had the most appalling effect on her. "What the devil are you up to, Nick?"

How cross she looked. How troubled. Nick touched a fingertip to her furrowed brow. "I'm flirting with you, *cara*. Has it been so long that you've forgotten how it's done? And if you run off again to the country, I swear I'll elope with your wretched niece."

9

Ianthe sat alone at the table of carved mahogany, in front of her a teapot which greatly resembled a cauliflower glazed yellow and green, and a single muffin on a plate. It was the family habit to breakfast informally, from dishes placed on the mahogany sideboard. Rather, the family *would* be breakfasting informally, if they ever crawled out of bed. Ianthe picked up a piece of muffin and crumbled it on her plate.

Cara walked into the room, dressed for riding in a habit fashioned from a shade of blue that matched her eyes, around her throat a froth of white lace. Daisy trailed hopefully after her. "Good morning," Cara said. She dropped her plumed hat, gloves, and riding crop on a side table, and moved to inspect the dishes on the sideboard. Daisy followed. "No! Bad dog. You have already been fed."

Muffins were hardly all the sideboard had to offer. Among the choices there were fan-shaped dishes and octagonal and square, an oval egg stand with twelve cups, a Chelsea tureen in the shape of a rabbit, and a burnished copper coffeepot. In those dishes were, among other delicacies, broiled mackerel and dried haddock, mutton chops and cold tongue and a veal-and-ham pie. Cara wrinkled her nose at broiled sheep's kidneys—although Daisy looked hopeful—and chose a plain boiled egg.

Cara sat down at the table. Daisy flopped down by her chair. Ianthe poured tea from the cauliflower pot into a fresh cup. "You missed a treat by not joining us last night. Zoë was very disappointed by Lord Mannering's absence. It appears that she has no interest in callow youths. Beau read her a dreadful scold and then chucked her under her chin and called her his precious puss. I thought I would cast up my accounts."

Cara wondered if she might cast up her own accounts. She picked up a spoon and poked at her boiled egg. She was not used to drinking brandy. Nor was she used to kissing Nicky. Although she once had been.

She glanced up to find Ianthe looking at her oddly. "What did Zoë do to cause Beau to scold?"

Ianthe contemplated the ruin of her muffin and reached for the marmalade pot. "Beau has apparently decided that flirting is the eighth deadly sin. Not that I noticed him giving it up himself."

Of course Ianthe would have noticed. Cara wondered if her cousin still cared for Beau in the way she once had. Unfortunately, first cousins were forbidden to wed. Or perhaps fortunately, because Ianthe would have been even more miserable if she had married the faithless Beau.

Although, *had* she married him, they would not be having this conversation about Zoë. Cara pushed aside her boiled egg. "Who did she flirt with?"

Ianthe spread marmalade on her muffin. "Who *didn't* she flirt with? She has added a lieutenant in Prinny's own regiment to her Zoo. Baron Fitzrichard was also at the theater. During intermission, he came to speak with us. He has decided to use your name for his neck-cloth."

Cara stared. "Zoë flirted with Baron Fitzrichard?"

"No." Ianthe smiled. "Although she might have tried to, had he not quelled her with his quizzing glass." Her anxious look returned. "I don't mean to appear vulgarly inquisitive, Cara, but—*Does* Mannering want her, do you think?"

Heaven only knew what Nicky wanted. Cara wasn't altogether convinced, despite his words, that he didn't crave revenge. However, as for Zoë—

Cara picked up her teacup. "He does not."

"Oh, and I had so hoped he did!" Ianthe's tears welled. Having come prepared for the occasion, Cara handed her a handkerchief.

Ianthe dabbed at her damp eyes. "You mustn't think I *like* being a watering pot—oh yes, I know that's what Zoë calls me!—because I don't! But it seems like everything has passed beyond my control. If only—no, you mustn't look like that! Don't think for an instant Beau is being truthful when he says that if you'd exerted a properly auntly influence, instead of staying in the country with sheep and your kumquats, Zoë wouldn't have turned into an *enfant terrible*. Zoë was beastly even in the cradle, and he knows it as well as I." Ianthe paused for breath, and frowned. "It seems very odd. If Mannering doesn't care for Zoë, why does he encourage her, do you think? Because he *does* encourage her, I've seen it for myself."

Cara contemplated the damask tablecloth, and supposed she shouldn't be surprised to discover that the white-on-white design was a hunting scene. How to explain to Ianthe what Nicky truly wanted? If indeed he *did* want her, and wasn't running some sort of rig, though the evidence certainly had seemed to point that way. His touch had been so ardent, his embrace so impassioned, his hand upon her knee so warm—

Cara picked up her napkin, and fanned herself. Zoë wouldn't take kindly to the intelligence that Lord Mannering preferred her elderly aunt to herself, which was also odd of him, because Cara had inspected herself in the looking glass that morning, and her doubts had not been assuaged. "I don't know what Nicky's up to," she said, truthfully. Daisy inched closer to her chair.

Just how Machiavellian *was* the marquess? Cara had asked herself that question countless times during her long and sleepless night—or not so long, by the time she'd snuck back into the house and climbed into her bed, but sleepless all the same. She wished she might trust Nicky, but knew she dared not.

Cara drew patterns with her fork on the tablecloth. Ianthe watched her silently. Daisy looked back and forth between them. Ianthe fed the setter a muffin crumb.

" 'Methought I heard a voice cry, Sleep no more!' " Zoë swept into the room, snatched up a table knife, and held it before her nose. " 'Is this a dagger which I see before me, The handle toward my hand?' " Having secured her family's startled attention, as well as Daisy's, she dropped the knife back onto the table and approached the sideboard. "The theater last night was splendid, Aunt Cara. A pity you had to miss it. How's your poor head?"

Her headache looked irritatingly young this morning, in a demure white muslin dress. Any more angelic, and the chit would need a harp. "My head hurts like the deuce. I hear you had a good time last night."

Zoë deposited a plate filled to overflowing upon the

table, and herself upon a chair. " 'Art thou but a dagger of the mind, a false creation, Proceeding from the heat-oppressed brain?' Of course I had a good time. I always have a good time. Although I would have had a *better* time if Beau hadn't started scolding me." She popped a forkful of veal pie into her mouth. "And if Lord Mannering had been there."

"Don't talk with your mouth full!" Ianthe said automatically, as Cara ruminated on where Lord Mannering *had* been, and what he'd been doing. "However," Zoë added, "it doesn't signify."

It didn't? Cara blinked. Lord Mannering had been engaged in a most improper—and quite delightful—midnight tryst with none other than herself, and it didn't signify? Would that she were so blasé!

Zoë had been a little too generous slathering marmalade on her muffin. She scooped up a wayward dollop from the tablecloth and stuck it in her mouth. "I have decided to fall in love with Lord Mannering. He cannot be my True Love, because he will soon be too old to sire children, and I do want to have children someday. However, he is the perfect person with whom to have my first *affaire de coeur,* for he has had enough of them to know what he's about!"

If Cara had choked at the notion of Nicky being too old to sire children, which she had, Ianthe blanched at mention of *affaires de coeur.* "Bless my soul!" she murmured, and cast Cara an anguished glance.

'Twas clearly the moment to take up the mantle of aunt1y duty. Cara had never wished to do anything less. "Young ladies don't think about such things, Zoë," she said. "Let alone mention them out loud. Has it occurred to you that perhaps Lord Mannering might not wish to have an *affaire de coeur?*"

Zoë waved her knife. " 'If it were done when 'tis done, then 'twere well it were done quickly.' " She noticed a bit of veal pie stuck on the knife and licked it off. "Whyever should I think that? The marquess is out of his senses over me. When I abandon him, he will be quite shattered. However, I must follow my heart! It is the way of Loversalls."

"*Certain* Loversalls are prone to flights of fancy," snapped Cara, as an aghast Ianthe fed the last of her muffin to the dog. "And to speak more highly of themselves than is nice. You still have not explained what makes you so certain Lord Mannering has formed this great attachment to you."

Blithely, Zoë embarked on a broiled kidney. "How could he not?"

Cara watched, somewhat queasily, as Zoë made short work of the kidney; told herself sternly that she should be tolerant, because the girl was so very young. Did the wretched child truly fall in love with Nicky, he surely would break her heart.

If, that was, Zoë possessed the capacity to love anyone other than herself. If, indeed, she had a heart. Cara might have been more concerned for her niece had she not suspected that what Zoë intended to fall in love with was not Lord Mannering himself but the notion of having London's most determined bachelor dangling at her apron strings.

Cara wondered if Nicky might be persuaded to dangle. Then she also wondered if he might be persuaded to be Zoë's first *affaire de coeur,* which inspired her with a strong desire to empty the marmalade pot over her niece's stylishly cropped head.

Beneath the table, Ianthe nudged her. Cara cleared her throat. "My dear, you wouldn't wish to be accused of boldness, or of making an ungainly exhibition of yourself. Society will tolerate a good deal, but there are limits, especially for a young woman of good breeding." Lord, what a prude she sounded. *Do as I say, not as I do.* Even Ianthe glanced at her askance.

As did Zoë. "Piffle! As if I cared for such stuff." She waved her fork, thereby casting a piece of dried haddock onto the floor. Daisy moved immediately to investigate.

"Daisy, no!" said Cara, but it was too late. Guiltily, the setter licked her chops. "Your manners are as bad as Zoë's."

"'Cabin'd, cribb'd, confined!'" observed that young woman. "I know what that's like. I never realized before, Aunt Cara, that you're so high in the instep."

"I'm not!" said Cara, stung, then recalled that she was supposed to be. "That is, I merely meant to warn you that you might wish to impose a check upon your natural high spirits lest they lead you to disagreeable consequences."

"What fustian!" Zoë reached again for the marmalade. "As if you've never done anything you should not."

Such as kissing Nicky? Cara opened and closed her mouth.

"I knew it!" crowed Zoë. "Tell us all. Ianthe will also like to know."

Ianthe already had more to think about than she wished, as result of Cara's casually uttered "Nicky." She murmured, "No, I don't!"

Cara sought to regain control of the situation. Not that she'd ever *had* control of the situation. She rapped her fork on the table. "Never mind what I might have done! We were talking about you."

"It probably wouldn't be all that interesting anyway. Seeing as it happened so long ago." Zoë lifted a knife laden with marmalade to her mouth. Ianthe protested, "Knives are for cutting, not licking, Zoë!"

'Twas like dining in Bedlam. Cara bit back the temptation to retort that the latest thing she'd done that she shouldn't had been just the previous night. Zoë thought her too old and stodgy to have an *affaire de coeur* of her own? Well, they'd just see about that!

Gracious! What was she thinking? Sternly, Cara banished all memory of the previous evening from her mind. "What do you think you will gain from an *affaire?*"

What an absurd question. Zoë looked pityingly at her aunt. "Experience, of course. As well as considerable pleasure, if what Beau says is true." She giggled at Cara's startled expression. "Goose! He didn't say it to *me*. And then, after I've had all the experience I want, I shall settle down and live Happily Ever After with my own True Love."

Her niece was an innocent, Cara reminded herself, while Ianthe sighed. So innocent—or arrogant—that she thought she might arrange her life as she wished. "I'm not sure that Happily Ever After exists outside of books."

"You have to marry the right person." Zoë eyed her aunt. "Why did *you* marry Norwood? Everyone is asking me. It does seem a trifle queer."

Ianthe also looked curious. Cara was about to either confess all, or tell them to mind their own business, when Beau walked into the room. "Good morning, everybody. How's your headache, Cara? You missed an excellent play. Kemble was splendidly tortured, and Mrs. Siddons very affecting as well. Ianthe went through four pocket handkerchiefs."

Beau looked clear-eyed and rested, as if he'd enjoyed an excellent night's sleep, which doubtless he had, now that he'd cozened his sister into coming to London to give pointless advice to his brat. Perhaps she would empty the marmalade pot over *his* head. Cara pushed back her chair.

For the first time, Zoë noticed how her aunt was dressed. "Where are you going?" she inquired.

Cara glanced at the tall windows. If sunlight didn't stream through the glass, it had at least made a long enough appearance to assume the absence of rain. "Squire Anderley and I are riding in Hyde Park." She picked up her feathered hat and placed it on her head.

Looking speculative, Zoë propped her elbows on the table and dropped her chin into her hands. "Squire Anderley is very handsome. Are you going to have an *affaire* with him?"

"Tsk!" said Beau, from the sideboard where he was loading up his plate. "Your aunt isn't going to do anything of the sort. And you shouldn't know about such things, puss."

Zoë fluttered her eyelashes at him. "I don't know how I *couldn't* know about *affaires* when you have them all the time. I think Aunt Cara *should* have one. It might make her less priggish. However, you're right, she is probably too old."

Cara bit her tongue and wished the marmalade pot were handier. Daisy whined. Ianthe looked at her cousin sympathetically and murmured, " 'When shall we three meet again in thunder, lightning, or in rain?' Remove your elbows from the table, Zoë."

10

The morning was gray, overcast, and chill, which while not an unusual event in London, was still responsible for the paucity of riders in Hyde Park. Baron Fitzrichard regretted that he found himself among them. "Are you sure," he said to his companion, "that there ain't insanity in your family? Some ancestor who went off his noodle? It would explain a great deal."

"I don't think so, although one can never be sure about these matters." Lord Mannering refrained from quizzing Fitz about his own ancestors, although he might well have done so, for the baron had chosen to combat the morning's gloom with a waistcoat striped vertically in bright yellow, and a jacket of equally bright green, as well as the Coup de Grâce, although now that the cravat had been officially named, he was thinking of creating a different style. "What's that on your face? I'd get my valet a pair of spectacles if I was you."

Fitz ignored this slur upon the growth of hair that he was carefully cultivating on his upper lip. "You needn't try and change the subject. I ain't asked *you* about that bruise on your chin. We were talking about this damned nasty habit you're developing of dragging me places I don't want to be. I warn you, I'm riding in the opposite direction if I see the little Loversall! If you don't watch your step, Nicky, that one will lead you smack into parson's mousetrap, which would be a great pity, since you've managed to avoid the altar all these years." Awkwardly, he turned his neck. "Unless—You ain't *wanting* to get yoked?"

Gray, chill morning though it might have been, Lord Mannering's mood was sunny. "I intend to avoid getting leg-shackled awhile longer yet. That's where I need you, my friend. Should anyone impugn my reputation, you will swear that I behaved at all times like a perfect gentleman."

Fitz snorted. Still, there was some truth in his friend's raillery. 'Twas a sad day indeed when a fellow dared go nowhere without a chaperone lest he be compromised.

If riders were scarce in Hyde Park this morning, wildlife was not. Ducks and geese and swans swam in the Serpentine, rabbits and squirrels rustled in the bushes, cows and deer grazed on the grass, and birds twittered in the trees. Nick glimpsed a pair of rabbits doing what rabbits did best. What he had wished very much to do himself just the night before, when he hadn't behaved like a gentleman at all, and didn't regret his misconduct a bit. Nature was a splendid thing, indeed. He wondered how his companion in debauchery fared this morning, and if she'd managed to get any more sleep than he had. And if her sleep, like his, what little there had been of it, was filled with delicious dreams. Dreams of Cara with her cheeks flushed, her hair spilling loose down her back. Her bare back, as her front was also bare, plump, ripe fruit to savor to his heart's content. . . .

Nick saw her then, as if he had conjured her, riding

toward them on a dappled mare, some distance away. She was dressed today in sapphire blue.

Not peaches today, but blueberries. Plump luscious blueberries just bursting with juice. Although blueberries had never been so buxom. He groaned.

Fitz eyed him with concern. "Are you all right, Nicky? Because I don't mind telling you that you look damned queer!"

Nick didn't hear him, or if he did, Fitz's comments were of no more significance than the buzzing of a bee. Cara looked superb on horseback, perfectly balanced in her saddle, her hands held in a natural position, with her elbows close to her side.

Not that Cara didn't look superb in everything she did. In any position she chose to assume. Such as in Nick's bed when he managed to get her there. And if he *didn't* get her there, Fitz would be correct in anticipating lunacy in the Mannering family, because it would be his.

Since the marquess clearly wasn't going to answer, Fitz looked around to see what might have inspired his friend's strange behavior. "By George, there's Lady Norwood! Who's that with her, do you know?"

Nick frowned. So bemused had he been by the unexpected sight of Cara that he hadn't realized the charmer of his heart and soul was in the company of another man. A well-mounted, sun-bronzed, handsome man who wasn't old enough to be her grandfather, like Norwood had been.

Hell and the devil confound it! Nick hadn't expected competition, which this man clearly was, which just showed that he wasn't thinking with his brain, because any man with even half his wits about him would have anticipated that Lady Norwood would have admirers, for she was both beautiful and rich.

As well as voluptuous. Her riding habit fitted too damned well. Whoever he was, that blasted man was practically drooling on her chest. Nick urged his horse forward. Fitz trailed after him down the bridle path.

Paul Anderley scowled at a squirrel chittering upon a low-hanging branch. The squirrel twitched his tail and scampered up the trunk, as if he knew the squire was thinking of putting him in a stew. And well Paul might have done so, were he still in the country. Along with several of the rascal's fellows, who were making an ungodly racket in the treetops.

Paul didn't care for London. Nor did he like Hyde Park, and didn't give a damn if kings had once hunted there for deer, or that William of Orange's asthma had prompted him to move from St. James's Palace to Kensington and build the Route de Roi across the wild and lawless space between the two palaces, so dangerous an area that George II was robbed there a century later of his purse, buckles, and watch.

Of all this, Lady Norwood had already informed the squire, and furthermore gave every indication of enlightening him more. Paul reminded himself that the hunt frequently lasted several hours, over challenging terrain. He had every intention of making Cara a formal declaration again this morning, as soon as she let him get a word in edgewise.

Cara knew what the squire intended. This required no especial prescience on her part: Paul made a formal declaration at every opportunity. However, she was in no mood for it today. "The Serpentine was created by Queen Caroline. As well as the Long Water and Round Pond, and the Royal Botanic Gardens at Kew. A vast collection of plants from every corner of the world is displayed there, set in an attractive historic landscape with splendid architectural features, even including the wizard Merlin in his cave. Did you know that Merlin is said to have predicted the Hanoverian dynasty?"

Merlin could have predicted the collapse of the monarchy for all Paul cared. Finally, she paused for breath. "My dear Lady Norwood—"

Nick had drawn close enough to overhear their conversation. "The menagerie at Kew is also very fine," he ruthlessly broke in. "Exotic animals from Africa, Australia, and India. I would be pleased to escort you to Kew, Lady Norwood. From time to time the gardens are open to the public. I'll speak to Prinny if you'd like."

Paul had no great fondness for his regent. At the rate Prinny was eating and drinking and fornicating, he would soon need a crane to get on his horse. Nor did Paul care much for the intruder, who looked every inch the haughty gentleman, mounted on a coal black horse that stood quite sixteen hands. He especially didn't care for the way Cara smiled at him.

Paul summoned up the air of authority that served him so well in the country. "And *you* are, sir?"

"Nicholas Anston, the Marquess of Mannering," Cara said quickly, before Nicky could utter the crushing set-down which clearly hovered on the tip of his tongue. "And here is Baron Fitzrichard. Gentlemen, this is Squire Anderley, a neighbor of mine. You are very *visual* today, Baron. That is an especially fine waistcoat."

At last, someone with taste sufficiently refined to appreciate his efforts. The baron beamed at her. "And you are fine as fivepence, Lady Norwood! A spot of sunshine on a gloomy day."

Fitz was not usually so fulsome. Nick wondered what had inspired his friend. Although Cara *was* a spot of sunshine, for not even the grayest of days could diminish her glowing hair, or her sparkling eyes, or—

Was *Fitz* gaping at her bosom? Nicky checked. The baron was not. Lord, but he was in a swivet, to be suspecting poor Fitz of lechery.

Paul stared at the baron's waistcoat. What sort of man would adorn himself in a garment the color of ripe lemons, a gigantic bunch of seals dangling from his fob? Not to mention adding tassels to his riding boots, along with garters which attached to the boot behind and passed around the knee in front. And then there was that abominably tied neck-cloth. The sorrel horse was well enough, if a little docile-looking for Paul's taste.

This antipathy was mutual. While Paul gawked at his costume, Fitz raised his quizzing glass and subjected the squire to a critical inspection. Blue coat with brass buttons, leather breeches, top boots, and a Belcher neckerchief—How very unimaginative. Fitz sniffed.

As the two men sneered at one another, Nick deftly maneuvered his horse next to Cara's dappled mare. Just the night before he'd kissed her, and run his hands over her fine body, and threatened to elope with her niece. He didn't know if she would turn away from him, or box his ears. "I've been reading the results of some interesting investigations made by de Saussure. He believes that plants require mineral substances to achieve satisfactory growth."

Cara glanced over her shoulder. Paul was looking like a thundercloud. Fitz winked at her and embarked upon a lecture about costume, which in ancient Greece, had been elevated to the rank of a fine art, its principles defined, its influence appreciated, and public officers appointed to prevent the violation of its fundamental laws.

Cara could have kissed him. "How do you feel about fox-hunting?" she inquired, as she returned her attention to Nick.

Ah, the familiar obfuscation. "My sympathies are generally with the fox. Why do you ask?"

Because Cara felt like a fox that had broken from the covert and was running upwind as far as she could. "If a fox clearly didn't wish to be caught, would you let her go?"

The marquess didn't think they were talking about foxes. "That would depend on the fox, I suppose," he replied, a trifle absentmindedly, as he decided that his companion must be wearing stays today, because her habit fit her like a glove. If only he might unwrap the lace from around her throat and press his mouth to the pulse beating sweetly at its base. Then he'd unbutton her jacket and unlace her stays. . . .

Nick shifted in the saddle. Soon *he'd* be drooling on her chest. "Lovely day," he said.

Cara eyed him. It was nothing of the sort. Nicky looked older in the gloomy light. And not one bit less handsome. So did she, no doubt. Look older, that was, not more handsome. "And your opinion of women owning property?"

Norwood had left her with property, a great deal of it. "Why not?"

"And gardening?"

"Gardens are very nice. I have several myself."

"Are they orderly?"

"I have no idea." Nick remembered her fondness

for green growing things. "Perhaps you would like to take them in hand."

It wasn't the marquess's gardens that Cara wished to take in hand. She scolded herself. "I've been experimenting with hydroponics. What is your opinion of whale bone?"

He grinned at her. "I dislike it of all things."

Cara could not suppress her dimple. "I was referring to the use of whale bone as fertilizer," she protested.

Nick longed to kiss that dimple, to fling her silly hat to the breeze; to pull Cara off her horse and onto his and have his wicked way with her in the middle of Hyde Park. *Was* it possible to make love on horseback? Given sufficient ingenuity, he mused, it was probably possible to make love anywhere.

Behind them, Fitz was still pontificating. "I am reminded of a maxim of De Fresnoy's, which applies as well to the arrangement of colors in dress as in painting. 'For bid two hostile colors close to meet, and win with middle tints their union sweet.'" What Paul Anderley replied was impossible to make out, but it wasn't uttered in admiring tones.

Cara had set Nicky a harsh catechism. All his answers had been correct, leaving her uncertain whether she was vindicated or dismayed. Time enough to ponder that later. She urged her horse to a quicker gait, so that they might not be overheard. "Zoë went to the theater last night. She was very sorry that you weren't there."

Easily, Nick's horse kept pace with hers. "Were you? Sorry that I wasn't there?"

Did the man expect her to thank him for attempting to seduce her? Or perhaps that wasn't the right word, because if Nicky had *truly* tried to seduce her, then seduced she would have been. "I am reminded of Great-Great-Great-Great Uncle John, who dropped down choking after eating fruit in the middle of a play at the Theater Royal, and was only revived by a prostitute known as Orange Moll, who thrust her finger down his throat and brought him back to life."

Nick interpreted this remark to mean that Cara *was* uncomfortable seeing him again so soon after he'd done what he did, which wasn't half of what he'd wished to do. "Is this the same ancestor who appeared naked upon the balcony of Oxford Kate's tavern in Covent Garden and preached to the crowd gathered below?"

The mare shied at a chipmunk. Cara controlled the horse easily. "It is. He was also responsible for the careers of several actresses, for he was in the habit of seducing a woman by informing her that she was so beautiful and so talented that she should take a career upon the stage. After, of course, he gave her careful instruction on how to play her love scenes."

"And this reminded you of me?" Nick was startled. He'd never said such a thing to a woman in all his life.

Cara ignored this silly question. Nicky could seduce a woman with a single wicked glance. "John wished to wed an heiress. He discovered that a suitable young woman was on offer for sale in Somerset. Not being foremost in the running—probably not being in the running at all, I suspect, for he didn't have a good reputation in Society, not that that seems to have slowed his amorous progress one whit—he snatched her by force from her coach at Charing Cross. As result of which, her family being no little bit annoyed by his presumption, he languished in the

Tower while the rest of London was visited by the plague."

"The choice," droned Fitz, as he and the squire rode up behind them, "of the predominating color will be indicated by the situation, age, form, and complexion of the wearer. Your complexion, sir, would indicate a certain excess of spleen. I would suggest you wear a red jacket so that a comparative fairness might be produced."

Nick smiled. Fitz had clearly set out to be as annoying as possible, which was very annoying indeed. "Did he marry his heiress, this ancestor of yours?"

Again, Cara urged her horse forward. "He did. Although there was a tricky moment when one of his mistresses draped her undergarments out of his bedroom window. In later years they sat down peaceably to breakfast together, surrounded by their children, his children from his various mistresses, and hers from her various paramours."

Nick was stricken by the notion of sitting down to breakfast with Cara. "And the point is?"

Cara turned her head to study him. "Never underestimate a Loversall."

Nick quirked a brow. "I doubt I could."

Fitz and Paul had fallen some distance behind them. Cara drew her horse to a halt in a copse of trees. "This is serious, Nicky. Zoë informed us over the breakfast cups today that she wants you to be her first *amour*. Because of your vast experience. I assume, though she didn't say it, that a daughter of Beau Loversall can settle for nothing else. However, she doesn't wish for you to father her children, because she doesn't want any children just yet, and by the time she does want them, you will be too old."

Nicky had been thinking of stealing a quick kiss before they were interrupted. "The devil I'm too old!" he said.

"*I* don't think you're too old!" said Cara; the look in Nicky's eye suggested he might try and persuade her otherwise. "When Zoë abandons you, as she intends to, your heart will be quite shattered, you poor thing."

The marquess looked sardonic. Doubtful that he would ever be as shattered as when Cara had abandoned him. Or rather, ran away. Fitz's voice could be heard coming closer. He was now explaining the circumstances of his neck-cloth, which was all the rage; to wit, that the creation had been named by no less than the divine Lady Norwood, for whom he had formed a lasting passion, not that he expected her to return his regard. Still, a gentleman in such a situation wished to rise to the occasion sartorially, so to speak, which was why he decided to drop a hint. "Don't go getting your hackles up! I mention it for your own good. Fine feathers make fine birds!"

Would Nicky heed her warning? Cara was distracted by the sight of his hands on the reins. Those same hands that had been on her body last night. Although then he hadn't worn gloves. She wished that his hands were on her now, at this very moment, gloves and all. Not that a person could make love on horseback in Hyde Park. Or could they? Cara wished she might find out.

Nick was charmed by her wistful look. "It seems I'm destined to have an *amour,*" he murmured, at the same moment Paul Anderley was heard to utter, "Curst man-milliner!" Cara looked beleaguered. Nick added, "I've told you my terms."

At any second their tête-à-tête would be interrupted.

Cara looked at him reproachfully. "Do I find myself a victim of blackmail?"

Nick lifted her hand to his lips. "You do, indeed."

Fitz was first into the copse. "By Jove, I believe my honor has been impugned! I should demand satisfaction, don't you think? After all, m'father did insist on all those fencing lessons. *He'd* wish for me to defend my honor. If I fight a duel, will you second me, Nicky?"

"Mercy!" said Cara, eyes alight with amusement. "Surely not a duel! With wicked sharp swords that slash and cut? My dear baron, you can't truly wish to spill blood!"

If Nicky wanted this Loversall, Fitz couldn't blame him. Fitz half wanted her himself. "Oh, but I do!" he said, as Paul Anderley rode up to them. "This *person* compared me to a cow turd stuck with daisies! And after I'd been so kind as to point out the various means by which he might improve his own appearance! I think—I *know!*—there is nothing for it but that honor must be satisfied. And do pray call me Fitz!"

Fitz was wringing every possible ounce of drama from the moment. Paul longed to throttle him, along with the damned marquess, who looked every bit as entertained as if he were watching a play.

Cara bit back laughter. "Surely you didn't say such an unkind thing, Squire Anderley. Perhaps the baron misunderstood?

The baron had misunderstood nothing. Paul had tolerated the mincing jack-a-dandy's prittle-prattle until he could stomach no more. Not that the popinjay could mince on horseback, but there *was* something suspicious about his sorrel's gait. Or there had seemed to be, because they'd dawdled along at an old lady's pace, falling farther and farther behind, until the fribble had touched his heels to the horse's flanks and left Paul blinking at his dust.

And then he'd ridden into the copse to see Cara flirting—*flirting!*—with that blasted Mannering. "I said it and I meant it! And there'll be no bloody duel. If you've had enough entertainment for this morning, Lady Norwood, I will see you home."

"Now there's an interesting point!" mused Fitz. "If one fellow demands honor be satisfied, and the second fellow refuses, does that mean the second fellow is a cad?"

"It means the second fellow is all out of patience!" Paul glowered at Cara, whose hand Lord Mannering still held. "Lady Norwood, if you please!"

Cara didn't please, not with Nicky holding on to her as if he owned her, which she hadn't realized until Paul pointed out the fact. She snatched her hand away. "I'll be expecting you," the marquess murmured, for her ears alone, "at ten o'clock tonight."

11

Among the many social festivities favored by the *ton*, musical evenings were much enjoyed, where young ladies of the best families showed off to hopefully good advantage the result of expensive lessons from imported teachers who, even if they couldn't speak the English language without mangling it, perfectly understood the complexities of forte and adagio. Because this particular evening's entertainment included not only Handel's *Water Music* performed on the glass harmonica, but also a pair of Italian opera singers hired for the occasion, in addition to the young ladies whose relatives had made known their severe displeasure should any of the invitees fail to attend, Lady Clement's rooms were filled. They were not quite so filled as they might have been, however, for Lady Norwood was not present, a circumstance upon which her brother was brooding as a nervous Miss Carruthers recited Mrs. Barbour's stirring lines, "Still the loud death drums, the thundering from afar. . . ."

Cara was supposed to chaperone Zoë, was she not? She could hardly chaperone anyone from her bed-chamber, where once again she'd secluded herself, claiming an aching head. Damned if Beau could see that his sister had done a single useful thing since she'd returned to town. So here he was, accompanying Ianthe and Zoë to this dull affair, and listening to a whey-faced chit blather on about freedom being prostrate, and fallen blossoms strewn on a foreign strand.

Beau would have much rather been at one of his clubs. Or with one of his own fallen blossoms, although that garden was also in disarray. He had visited one of those lovelies just this afternoon, and matters had been progressing nicely, when the lady was moved to announce that she didn't think she cared to be one of several anymore, even if it *was* traditional for a male Loversall to keep a stable of sweethearts, at which point both ardor and Beau had fled out the door. First he'd disappointed Lavinia, and now he'd fled from Sidoney. Beau dreaded to think what would happen when he visited Celest.

Ianthe, at least, was intent on the young performer, perhaps because the girl had mentioned heart wither-ings. She dabbed a pretty lace handkerchief to the corner of her eye. Zoë was off in another room, escorted there by her young lieutenant and several of his fellow officers, enjoying a glass of punch. Beau wondered if his love life might improve when his daughter was safely settled. Perhaps he should start interviewing prospective candidates for her hand. Separate the wheat from the chaff, so to speak. Although all he'd seen thus far was chaff. And hopefully, in the interim, none of his own blossoms would spread word of his failure to perform all about the town. Reference to throbbing bosoms caught his attention. He eyed the young performer critically. Her hands were clasped to her own bosom as if it were thus afflicted. It was a nice bosom, Beau decided. Ægypt's virgins, indeed.

If Ianthe was not similarly affected by mention of

bosoms, she was very moved by Miss Carruthers' stirring delivery, and the fact that the damsel had stumbled over only a few lines; and when London began exulting, thus signifying that the interminable verse was coming finally to an end, she prepared herself to enthusiastically clap.

Fitz also awaited that moment, in the hallway outside the drawing room, which he already knew to be the most elegant of chambers, with pretty blue-and-white foliate-striped wallpaper, rosewood furniture inlaid with lacquered gilded brass, a beautiful plaster ceiling with moldings of musical instruments, large windows, and a fine marble chimneypiece. He cast a last critical glance at his reflection in an exquisitely gilt-framed wall mirror alive with carved moving animals and birds, foliage, and twisting candle brackets; and assured himself again that he looked especially fine tonight in a midnight blue coat and white satin breeches, with frilled linen on his shirtfront, and shiny buckled shoes with daringly square toes. All of this splendor was secondary, however, to his masterfully tied cravat, a variation on the Coup de Grâce, which incorporated elements of the Mathematical, with two horizontal dents as in the latter, and two collateral dents as in the former, as well as a Gordian knot, in a lovely shade of cerulean blue, which was complemented by the clocks in his stockings and the stripes in his waistcoat. Where Brummell believed that the severest mortification a gentleman could incur was to attract attention in the street by his appearance, Fitz believed the opposite, and had spent two hours scrubbing himself with a pig-bristle brush, then tweezing his eyebrows and whiskers with the aid of a dentist's mirror, before beginning the serious business of putting on his clothes.

The recitation ended to polite applause. Next on the program was the glass harmonica, which Fitz had already decided his eardrums could tolerate. He strolled into the drawing room and glanced about for a vantage point from which to best display himself. Ianthe Loversall caught his eye. She was dressed with unusual restraint in a dress fashioned from rose Italian crepe, lavishly trimmed with floss silk and blond lace, her hair dressed in the antique Roman style, confined at the back of the head in two light knots, and adorned with a bandeau of polished steel. If at her age she should more properly have been wearing toques and turbans and French caps, she was hardly mutton dressed as lamb.

He made his way toward her. Zoë had also returned to her family, a glass of punch in her hand, a viscount, the aged knight, and her Hussars trailing in her wake; and although the latter gentlemen did indeed sport an impressive amount of gold braid on their blue uniforms, to compare them to performing monkeys was unkind. Fitz grudgingly conceded that the young woman looked unexceptionable in a gown of clear lawn with a cherry-colored sash and edging around the skirt, her hair dressed in irregular curls and decked with flowers.

Unfortunately, she didn't act it. "Hello, Baron Fitzrichard!" she chirped. "Is Lord Mannering also here?"

Fitz looked down his nose at her. "Don't know why he should be. For that matter, don't know why anyone should be! Only reason I'm here is because m'cousin is making her appearance. I'd be drummed out of the family if I hadn't come. I *like* my family." He also liked his cousin, and had twisted several arms to insure that several people who might have liked to be otherwise were here. Nicky had pleaded a previous engagement. Blandly, Fitz remarked, "Lady Norwood ain't here?"

Ianthe smiled at Fitz. "Poor Cara has the headache. Allow me to present to you my brother. Beau, this is Baron Fitzrichard. He has been kind enough to instruct me in the principles of female dress."

"You are the epitome of harmonic progressions this evening, Miss Loversall!" Fitz said gallantly. He then turned his attention on her brother. Corbeau-colored coat with covered buttons, white Marcella waistcoat, light sage green breeches, hair fashionably tousled, cravat tied in the elegantly austere Trone d'Amour— No gentleman so striking in appearance could *not* have taken a considerable amount of time with his toilette, which was a charming thing in one known to be a regular Trojan, a noted Corinthian, and at home to a peg.

"Delighted," said Fitz, and bowed.

"Likewise." Beau returned the salute. "We're here because Ianthe is too tender-hearted to fail to lend her support to any budding musical endeavor. Your cravat is very fine. And I cannot help but admire your moustache."

Fitz beamed in response to the compliments. "Your cousin is going to sing?" inquired Ianthe.

"Lord, I hope not!" Fitz shuddered. "She has a voice like a bullfrog. But she plays the harp prodigious well." Conversation ceased then, because a young woman seated herself at the keyboard of the glass harmonica, a curious device with a set of glasses nestled inside each other and mounted on a spindle which was turned by a foot pedal, and began to play.

Paul Anderley paused on the threshold of the drawing room, and gazed into the crowd. No arm-twisting relative of one of the performers had brought him here tonight—Paul didn't care for music, and even less for women, young or otherwise, who chose to make themselves a public display—but some arm-twisting of his own had secured him an invitation to the event. Arm-twisting and a hefty bribe to a certain elderly butler, who had refused to speak of his employer's business for less than ten pounds. A gleam of red-gold caught Paul's eye, and he made his way toward it, earning several annoyed glances, about which he didn't care the least. Then he grew annoyed himself, because that red-gold hair didn't belong to the member of the family he sought. Beau grinned at him. "Hello, Anderley. Misplace your fox?"

Paul chose to overlook this provocation. "Lady Norwood didn't accompany you?"

"Poor Aunt Cara has the headache," offered Zoë, eyelashes aflutter. "She seems to be the sickly sort, poor thing."

Here was no potential suitor. "Zoë," Beau said sternly, "behave yourself!" Unaccustomed to being rebuked by her papa, Zoë stared at him in astonishment.

Paul took up a stance behind the ladies. If Cara was in a fragile state of health, it was easily understood. Her family would leave anyone terminally vexed. And as for headaches, he might soon have one himself, due to the warmth of the crowded room, and the mingled odors of candle wax and a hundred different perfumes. An "Ahem!" caught Paul's attention. He turned to see Baron Fitzrichard peering at him through a quizzing glass.

A *blue* cravat? It was enough to make a man ill. "Dandified jackanapes," muttered Paul.

Fitz raised his quizzing glass in a salute. "Country yokel," he retorted, for if the squire was correct enough in brown coat and cream-colored breeches, his cravat was tied in the Irish, which Fitz considered very dull indeed.

Damned if the baron wasn't brandishing his glass as if it were a sabre. "Impudent coxcomb."

Fitz set about distracting his opponent with a bit of slashing about. "Padgroom!" he observed.

To accuse him of poor horse-handling ability! Paul bared his teeth. "Curst dandy!" he retorted, somewhat unoriginally.

Fitz executed an artful combination of the Vertex strike, delivered from above, against his opponent's scalp; then followed with the Wrathful, executed from the right shoulder upon the opponent's left ear. "Turnip sucker! Honors to me, I think."

"Quiet!" snapped a lady seated in front of them, who happened to be related to the harmonium player. "*Some* of us would like to hear the entertainment, if you please!"

Paul didn't please, particularly, but it was beneath him to get into a brangle with a fribble. He couldn't understand why Cara and her cousins encouraged the man. He crossed his arms and looked severe.

The harmonium recital ended. Next on the program were the Italian opera singers. Paul disliked opera. He scowled all the harder. Observing this reaction, Fitz immediately waxed enthusiastic. "The Italian manner of singing is refined and full of art. It moves us and at the same time excites our admiration; it is the very spirit of music; pleasant, charming, expressive, rich in taste and feeling; and it carries the hearer agreeably from one passion to another. The French manner of singing, on the other hand, is more plain than full of art, more speaking than singing, the expression of the passions and the voice more strange than natural. Although one cannot disregard Rameau's treatise on musical theory, which provides musicians with a well-organized, enduring concept of harmonic progressions and tonality!"

Fitz's opinion to the contrary (which wasn't really his opinion, and voiced only to further aggravate the squire), a significant number of the guests agreed with Paul concerning the opera, or sufficient of them that low conversations continued as the male mezzo-soprano, pretending to be in a Persian garden, sang to a tree; and a female soprano compared the victims of love to a little stream that loved its freedom.

Ianthe felt sorry for Paul Anderley, who clearly was out of his depth. "You are Cara's neighbor, I believe? The Cotswolds are very fine. All those lovely rolling hills."

"All those sheep," interjected Beau.

Ianthe cast her cousin a chiding glance. "Sheep are also very nice! All that lovely wool. Tell me, Squire Anderley, do you ride to hounds?"

Paul immediately brightened and embarked upon a paean to the hunt. Batteaus, when hunters were preceded into the field by beaters, began the first Wednesday in November and continued twice a day for the rest of the three-month season. There was surely nothing so beautiful and stirring a sight as the hunters assembled for the start of the day's hunt, as could be attested to by the ladies who rode out to the meet to see their menfolk off, although it was not considered respectable for them to actually follow the hounds.

Fortunately, because the mere thought of slaying living creatures revolted Ianthe, the squire's conversation wasn't entirely limited to the hunt. He could also talk quite knowledgeably about fly-fishing or yachting or pugilism, and could even describe in great detail the most recent occasion on which Tom Molineaux had challenged the champion Tom Cribb, not that he would speak to Miss Loversall of such masculine topics. The elder Miss Loversall, that was. He didn't wish to speak to the younger Miss Loversall at all.

Zoë had been too long ignored. Her aunt and Squire Anderley were deep in conversation, and Beau was deep in the dumps, while Baron Fitzrichard contemplated the opera singers through his quizzing glass. Her admirers had departed en masse when the male mezzo-soprano first opened his mouth. Instead of paying attention to the singers, Zoë chose to eavesdrop on her cousin's conversation. "Tally ho!" she said.

Impertinent chit! thought Paul, and Fitz also, although the two gentlemen were unlikely to realize that on this one point they agreed. Ianthe said gently, "Zoë, it is impolite to interrupt."

Zoë ignored her and fluttered her eyelashes at the squire. "Are you in *amours* with my aunt, sir?"

Paul waited for someone to remonstrate with the abominable chit for her boldness, but Beau and Ianthe—and Fitz—were regarding him with as much curiosity as Zoë. "I have a great regard for Lady Norwood," he said stiffly.

"You poor man." Zoë sighed. "Loversalls give their all for romance. *Just one more romance, one more throw of the dice.* And when they are through with dicing, they fling themselves off the battlements like Romola; or drink a fatal dose of poison, like Odo; or visit the menagerie in the Tower, like Casimir, and get eaten by a bear. We are victims of our tumultuous passions." She slanted a glance sideways at Fitz. "Where *is* Lord Mannering, do you know?"

Fitz knew that Nicky should stay as far away as possible from this little vixen. "I'm sure I couldn't say. M'cousin is performing next. 'Passacalles de primero tono' from Diego Fernandez de Huete's *Compendio numeroso,* volume two, 1704."

Zoë turned back to her father, who was still lost in contemplation of the astonishing discovery that he had passed his prime. Could it be possible that there was truly no life left in the old fellow? Or that a man was limited to a finite number of *amours*? Surely he had not exceeded his quota at only seven-and-thirty years of age! True, he had been profligate, but he didn't think he'd been so wasteful as that.

Zoë poked him with her elbow. "You are not paying attention to me, Beau. I should think that you would be interested to learn that I have fallen in love. It is quite serious! I have all the symptoms of someone who is lovesick."

Beau eyed his vivid daughter with a degree of trepidation. "And what might those symptoms be?"

Prettily, she drooped. "I can think of nothing else. My spirits are very low. I cannot sleep, or eat. I daresay I may even succumb to the vapors soon."

Beau might have been more concerned had he not seen Zoë make a good meal that very evening. Not to mention coquetting with the members of her Zoo, who were hovering in the hall outside, waiting for the

Italian caterwauling to cease so that they could again converge on her. Encouraged by his silence, Zoë languished all the harder. "Am I not grown pale and wan?"

Beau admired the roses in her cheeks. "Indeed you are," he said gravely.

Zoë tilted her head and looked woeful. "If I cannot have him, I shall wither away on the vine like Cousin Ianthe." That maligned lady, who with her companions had been listening to this fascinating conversation, closed her mouth with a snap.

Fitz was astonished to hear such nonsense. "I'll tell you what it is: the chit needs spectacles! Forgive my boldness, Miss Ianthe, but you ain't withered the least bit."

Ianthe twisted her handkerchief. "Thank you, Baron, for assuring me that I am not yet turned into a prune."

So chagrined did she look that Paul was also moved to comment, "Miss Loversall, you look little more than a girl." Ianthe gave him a grateful look.

Beau remembered what Ianthe *had* looked like as a girl, before she had become so unhappy. He regarded his daughter with disfavor. "Your aunt is far from an antidote. You will apologize to her."

Apologize? Zoë had never been asked to do such a thing in all her life. However, Beau was looking stern. So were Squire Anderley and Baron Fitzrichard. Even Ianthe was looking less watery than was her wont. "I'm sorry, Cousin Ianthe. I didn't mean to compare you to a dried fruit."

As apologies went, this one was substandard. Fitz surveyed Ianthe thoughtfully through his quizzing glass. "Patches and powder and paint, Indian satin and Flanders lace would suit you. Or perhaps I am recalling a portrait of some earlier Loversall."

"Drusilla," Ianthe said gloomily. "She stabbed herself with her lover's sword."

Fitz refused to let his own spirits be deflated. "I've often wished I had lived in a previous age. How I would have enjoyed, for example, a Spanish drugget coat lined with Persian silk or a scarlet cloth suit laced with gold; diamond buckles and purple feathers and a full curled wig." He contemplated Paul, who was looking revolted. "I wonder what era might have suited Squire Anderley. I think—Yes, a corsair. He seems prone to a certain bloodthirst."

Paul snarled an answer. Fitz embarked upon a dissertation regarding the proper tying of a neck-cloth. Ianthe smoothed her handkerchief on her knee. Zoë sulked.

Beau felt guilty. It was hardly for him to censure his daughter's conduct; Cara was supposed to do that. Although he could hardly expect Cara to protect his precious lamb from wicked Lord Mannering. Beau knew what a man of that ilk was after. He *should* know, being a man of that ilk himself. Or he had once been. For all the pleasure he was deriving from his own excesses of late, he might as well remain at home. This reflection put him in no better charity with his fellow profligate.

However, due to all that profligacy, Beau well knew how female minds worked. "Very well, you may have Mannering," he said, in tones so low that the others couldn't hear.

Zoë was instantly all smiles. "Oh, Beau, you are so good to me!"

Beau held up his hand. "You may have him *if* you can bring him up to scratch."

Zoë's smile vanished. "I don't want to bring him up to scratch!" she snapped. Ianthe looked at her with approbation, and she lowered her voice. "I want him to seduce me, which is quite a different thing, and it is quite absurd of you to look so shocked, considering how many damsels you have no doubt seduced yourself."

Shocked? He was horrified. If Cara had done what she was supposed to, Beau wouldn't be having this embarrassing conversation with his daughter. "That's different!" he said.

Zoë fixed him with a look known universally to parents. "*How* is it different?"

Beau could hardly explain to his daughter that he'd never seduced a maiden, for although such a declaration probably wouldn't shock her, either, it would certainly discompose him. He narrowed his eyes. Could it be—

No it couldn't! Zoë was a maiden, or she wouldn't be going on about wanting to *not* be one, which was an appalling thing for a papa to have to hear. "It just is! And I'll hear no more of this nonsense, miss!"

The opera singers retired then, and Zoë's swains hurried back into the room. A young woman dressed in white muslin approached the harp that sat in one corner of the room. The harp had a beautifully carved Egyptian figurehead forming part of an elaborate beech and satinwood frame. The young woman wore a resolute, if somewhat terrified, expression on her face. "There!" Fitz said proudly. "M'cousin is about to perform."

12

While Fitz's young cousin was embarked upon "Passacalles de primero tono," with an expression of intense concentration and a very polished style, Lady Norwood was seated with Lord Mannering in front of his cozy fire. On a table between them lay an Elizabethan backgammon board, the game markings and decorations inset with mother of pearl, the shakers and counters fashioned of red-and-white ivory. Cara was a ruthless player, as Nick should have remembered. She had immediately waged an all-out attack on the blots on his home board, and with a clever bit of hit and cover, and a hara-kiri play, had maneuvered him into a position in which he was trapped on her ace point trying to get a shot.

"Do you accept a double?" she asked. Nick shook his head. He would not resign the game tonight, no matter how high the stakes grew.

Play continued until Cara had three checkers remaining on her two point against his single checker bravely doing battle on his one. Nick rolled the dice, and looked, and laughed. "The *coup classique*," he said.

Cara looked down at the board. "Odious man."

Nick rang for his maidservant. Cara had contrived

somehow to let him win, and now she was hiding a smile. "Would you like some tea?"

Tea was hardly a fitting a drink for a lady engaged in an assignation. "Some sherry, perhaps."

Nick gave the order, and stretched out his long legs toward the fire. He was wearing neither a jacket nor a cravat—why should he not be comfortable in his own home, or one of them?—as a result of which Cara longed to touch him, and smooth the hair back from his brow, and slide her hands inside his shirt. Idly, she toyed with a doubling cube.

She was nervous, and Nick knew it, and was even perhaps a little pleased to see her so; as well as amused that she had dressed herself in a severely high-necked long-sleeved gown and a corset so rigid she could barely breathe. "I trust your journey here was uneventful," he said.

"Yes, thank you." Uneventful, but oddly exhilarating. The dark streets had not been frightening but familiar, for Nicky had said she would be safe, and in this Cara trusted him, if in little else. The hackney driver had greeted her with a tip of his hat and a wink, as the little maidservant had met her with a smile at the front door.

The girl returned with a sherry decanter and a plate of biscuits, which she set down on the table before bobbing a curtsy and backing out of the room.

Cara nibbled on a biscuit and watched as Nick poured sherry into a glass. "You keep a small staff here," she said.

Nick handed her the sherry, then touched her cheek. "I can be alone here or not, as I wish. Despite your accusations, this isn't a trysting place. I've brought no woman here but you."

Cara froze. Nick trailed his finger along the line of her jaw, then moved away. She took an unladylike gulp of her sherry, which he pretended not to see. "This house came into the family along with the daughter of a scrivener, and has since served as residence of choice for my more reclusive relatives, most recently a dowager great-aunt."

"Who doted on you," Cara guessed.

"No. But she didn't loathe me, like she did the others."

"You visited her? Brought her posies?"

"No. I couldn't abide the old witch."

"Ah. But the others did. Brought posies, that is."

"They did, and that reminds me—" Nick rang again for the maidservant. She appeared as quickly as if she had been waiting, or eavesdropping, right outside the door. "Fetch the Sophora japonica from the conversatory, Mary. Jacob will help you." The girl looked doubtful. "The tall brown thing. With leaves. Jacob will know."

Cara looked intrigued. "You have a Sophora japonica?"

Nick smiled. "I thought it might content you until I can arrange to visit Kew."

Mary returned, with a grizzled manservant who bobbed his head shyly at the sight of his master's guest. Between them they carried a slender and somewhat bedraggled seedling stuck in a small tub. Nick eyed it doubtfully. "It is—or I'm promised it *will* be—a Japanese pagoda tree."

Cara set down her sherry glass and knelt beside the tub. Gently, she touched a leaf. "It's beautiful. No one has ever given me so nice a present before."

Surely she jested? Nick wondered if Norwood had

not realized that Cara would prefer a living thing to the finest jewel. And then he wondered what she would do if he reached out this moment and drew her into his arms. Her lips reminded him of plump strawberries tonight. Damned if he didn't want to lick, nibble, and taste the woman from the crown of her head to the soles of her feet.

As if she knew what he was thinking, Cara rose, pink cheeked. "Surely no victim of blackmail has ever been so cosseted before."

"I would like to cosset you ever more," said Nick, but prudently refrained from saying how. Instead, he showed her some of the treasures in his parlor, demonstrated the use of the perpetual almanac, pointed out the more curious of the volumes on his shelves. *Culpeper's Complete Herbal* and *The English Housewife* only mildly intrigued her, but *New Principles of Gardening*, written by a Mr. Langley, who espoused rural gardening in the spirit of old Roman ruins, caught her interest. Cara leafed through the old pages, and mused that perhaps her brother's garden might benefit from an obelisk. She suspected that it already had at least one rabbit warren, another garden embellishment of which Mr. Langley approved, for reasons known only to himself, for the creatures munched ceaselessly on growing things. Nick suggested that Cara take the book home with her to peruse at her leisure, and then set out to amuse her with gossip, from Corn Laws and the National Debt and Select Committees to elopements, infidelities, bankruptcies, and suits for breach of promise, and a certain gentleman who had become so besotted with his mistress that he cut his wife and family in public. By the end of this disarming recitation, he had gotten her settled once more in her chair, her slippers abandoned on the floor, and her feet propped in his lap, where he was lazily massaging them with an expertise that made her want to purr.

The sound of his voice both soothed and stirred her senses. Cara chuckled. "Can all that be true?"

Nick smiled at her. "Most of it. I like to hear you laugh."

He was talking now about Lord Byron and his half sister, two people Cara had never met and about whose misbehavior she didn't care in the least. Nick's touch warmed her to her toes.

His head was bent. Cara studied his profile, the high cheekbones and strong jaw. The bruise where she had hit him. She wished she might kiss it well. And then perhaps she'd kiss his neck, his throat, open his shirt even further and press her lips to his chest.

Once she had known those features by heart. Now Cara wished that she might learn them all anew. Nicky was even more handsome now than he had been when—Well. Each time they met, the memories grew stronger, and her desire to know how much—or how little—he had changed.

Nick looked up to see her regarding him thoughtfully. Perhaps she was wondering about his intentions, which must surely be as obvious as her reasons for wearing that graceless dress. Cara looked as prim tonight as was possible for her, which wasn't very, considering that her stockinged feet were in his lap, and her glorious hair was already coming unpinned. He moved his hand to her ankle, and waited to see what she would do.

Blissfully, she wiggled her toes. "Will you truly take me to the Royal Botanic Gardens at Kew?"

Yes, and make love to her there in the Herbarium and the Orangery and at last in Merlin's Cave. "I will take you anywhere you wish."

Cara watched his hand move lazily on her ankle. The marquess didn't appear in the least like a man out of his senses over Zoë or anybody else. Or like a man who could be shattered by the loss of a mere ladylove. Cara wondered if he *had* a ladylove. She longed to scratch the trollop's eyes right out. "Why did you never marry, Nicky?"

His lips curled. "I was waiting for you."

"But I was already married."

"To a man three times your age. Chances were that you would outlast him." Nick didn't mention how many times he had wished to assist Norwood to shuffle off this mortal coil.

Did she believe him? Cara didn't know. His touch was like a drug, lulling her to imprudence, and an almost overwhelming sense of intimacy. "Perhaps you have noticed that I am encouraging you," she murmured. "Now will you *dis*courage Zoë?"

Nick knew the moment her mood softened. Her whole body relaxed. Her prodigious fine body, which he itched to release from those damned stays. As he longed to release her hair from its pins. How splendid she had looked mounted on horseback. He dragged his thoughts away from different types of mounting, lest he go too fast, and frighten her away. Unfortunately, the next thought that occurred to him was that, though it might be difficult to make love atop a horse, it would be child's play to make love in a chair. His chair, in which Cara was sitting so relaxed.

Her eyes were heavy-lidded, her hair gleamed in the firelight, her bosom strained against the confines of that dratted dress. "The devil with Zoë," he murmured. "I don't want to talk about your niece tonight."

Nor did Cara, truth be told. Still, she had an auntly duty to perform. "Let her down easily, I beg you, Nicky. For the sake of the family."

"Your family spends entirely too much time pandering to the chit." Nick stroked Cara's calf. "Perhaps we might talk about Norwood instead. And about why you married him when I had just laid my own heart at your feet."

Because she had been as young and foolish as Zoë. Because Norwood had been steady and mature and safe. "Because you laid the rest of yourself elsewhere. In Lucasta Clitheroe's bed, to be precise."

He hadn't, actually. At least not then. But Nick didn't wish to ruin the rest of the evening with an argument that he could never win. "That was a long time ago."

Nine years, ten months, and three days, to be precise. Was Nick truly content that his nephew should be his heir? Unusual, if true. Perhaps the marquess was wise enough to realize that he would be miserable tied down to just one woman. Not that marriage had curtailed the amorous pursuits of any man she knew. With the exception of Norwood, of course, but Norwood had been of an age when the fires of youth had burned to embers, and he was content with her. Cara missed her husband. If not an ardent lover, he had been her friend. He had cherished her. And treated her rather as if she were a favorite grandchild.

But Cara was no child. She was a grown woman, and Nicky's hand had progressed up her calf to toy with the embroidered silk garter tied above her knee. Her skin tingled, pleasurably.

Beau feared the marquess would play fast and loose with his daughter. Would he mind if the marquess played fast and loose with his sister instead? Would Cara mind, herself? Well, of course she'd mind, but perhaps minding would be worth it in the end. Nicky had gone to great effort to bring her back to London if what he said was true.

His hand had moved to her knee, and gone no further. Perhaps, now that he had seen her, and spent time with her, he had changed his mind. It would be like Nicky, to politely try and spare her feelings.

He had not kissed her tonight. He had not kissed her again after the first time. Perhaps that kiss had disappointed him. Cara had not kissed anyone in such a manner in a very long time. Even her own brother told her she was dull and drab. Not that she had ever kissed Beau in such a manner—unlike Lord Byron and his half sister, apparently—but she hoped she could trust him to be truthful about her looks.

Cara wanted to be desirable. She wanted Nicky to find her so. Lord knew she found *him* desirable. Abruptly she said, "I am no longer a green girl."

Nicky had been waiting to see if she would box his ears for his various presumptions, although he was not especially worried, since her toes curled blissfully against his thigh. "And I thank God for it. If you won't tell me about Norwood, perhaps you would like to talk about Paul Anderley."

Cara didn't want to talk about anyone. She wanted to give herself up to the pleasure of Nicky's caress. If, that was, he could be induced to keep caressing her, instead of merely lounging there with his hand on her knee. "Squire Anderley is a neighbor. He has been kind to me, no more."

Squire Anderley hadn't struck Nick as the least bit kind, but rather as a man with a purpose. "Your neighbor who followed you to town."

Cara shrugged. "It is a hunter's strategy to block all the earths while the fox is going about her business. Paul wants Norwood's property. It marches next to his."

Nick knew damned well that property wasn't all Anderley wanted. Easy enough to recognize a dog-in-the-manger attitude when he was experiencing one himself. "And what do you want?"

She didn't want him to stop touching her, for one thing. "Freedom, I suppose. Paul seems to think that sheer persistence will eventually wear me down."

Nick had been about to untie her garter. Now he paused. Did Cara think that he also sought to wear her down? If so, it was unworthy. Wasn't it? His hand slid back down to her ankle, and then to her toes.

He had lost interest, Cara thought glumly. As Norwood used to do. It was true, then: she was too old for an *affaire*. Her companion, however, was not. The man looked positively pagan in the firelight. Any damsel threatened by this bold marauder would immediately immolate herself upon his chest.

Of course Nicky was destined to have an *amour*, as he had said himself. Or *amours*. Countless numbers of them, no doubt. Cara couldn't bear the thought.

If older now, she was surely also wiser than she once had been. Cara wrapped herself in dignity. "You don't have to try and pretend to want me, Nicky. It is very kind of you, but I know I am no longer in your style."

Pretend to want her? She thought he had to force himself? Could Cara not know how magnificent she was?

Nick felt like throttling someone. Norwood might have been a likely candidate, but he had already stuck his spoon in the wall. "What *is* my style?" he asked.

"I don't know." Cara folded her fingers together in her lap to keep from grabbing his hand and plopping it back down on her knee. "But I would think she should be young, at least."

Unaware that Zoë had inspired her elders with an acute awareness of their mortality, Nick regarded Cara with astonishment. "My love, you are an idiot," he said, and got up to tend the fire.

Her feet felt chilled without his warmth. Cara tucked them beneath her chair. Indeed, all of her felt chilled, despite the nearness of the fire. If only she might wrap Nicky around her like a warm blanket. His shirt strained over the muscles of his back as he knelt on the hearth. Her hand itched to stroke down his back, across his hips, his—Um. She licked her lips.

Nick glanced up and caught her wistful look. His own expression was unreadable. "What do you want, Cara?" he repeated quietly.

She didn't want to fall in love again, to feel that slow sweet stirring of the blood. She especially didn't want to fall in love with the scoundrel who had broken her heart the first time. Her pulse skittered. "In general? Or just now."

He moved toward her, as handsome and powerful and as irresistible as sin. "I'll settle for just now."

Cara was more of a Loversall than anyone, save

Nicky, had ever realized. Even as her head begged her
for caution, her heart urged the opposite. She whispered, "If you betray me again, I swear I'll cut out
your heart." And then he was kneeling before her, and
she was reaching out for him; and his arms were
warm around her body, and his lips against her throat.

13

It was a lovely London morning. Or if not precisely lovely, because the day was overcast and gray, still an especially fine specimen of a morning, with the Creator in His heaven, and all well with the world. Perhaps that also was a bit of an overstatement, considering the seemingly endless difficulties with the French and the equally unfriendly affairs of the Prince and Princess of Wales, but Lord Mannering refused to relinquish his good mood. Regardless of gray days and ongoing hostilities, he was in a splendid frame of mind.

He rode astride his great black horse through the city streets. The air was thick with the smell of animal dung and sea-coal smoke, noisy with the clatter of hooves and wheels, the shouts of street sellers with their baskets and barrows: orange girls and milkmaids, chairmen and chimney sweeps; purveyors of fresh hot tea and gingerbread and steak-and-kidney pies. Nick observed an altercation between a traveling chair repairman and the driver of a charcoal car with a benevolent smile.

Few members of the *ton* were out and about so early. Nick was banking that one member in particular hadn't yet packed up her belongings and set out for the Cotswolds. Not that it was all *that* early, but he hadn't managed to get out of bed as early as he'd meant to. He doubted that Cara had either, since it had been quite late when she'd finally gone home.

Ah, sweet Cara. She was as wonderfully passionate as he remembered her. And as contrary, he made no doubt. If only he could whisk her off to some secluded castle, and make love to her there for months, or years, until he determined the nature of her fears, and set them finally to rest.

He inhaled deeply, and coughed, and wished that the Creator in his heaven might be inspired to do something about the quality of London's air. Thusly ruminating, Lord Mannering arrived in Brook Street, and tossed his reins to a groom. Ah yes, it was a fine morning, if not lovely. He mounted the front steps.

Widdle opened the door. It was still sufficiently early that the daily deluge of posies and invitations and impassioned pleas of eternal devotion hadn't yet begun to arrive. However, the butler was ever on the alert lest some member of the household creep home in the wee hours of the morning, or a certain squire appear on the doorstep with an underhanded suggestion, and a bribe.

No bribe was forthcoming from this gentleman, however. He merely extended a visiting card and inquired if any of the family were yet astir. Widdle, who knew perfectly well that all the members of the family had arisen—the master, mistress, and lady were in the breakfast room, while the demoiselle was engaged in a game of hide-and-seek with the dog—accepted the card delicately between his thumb and index finger and said that he would ascertain.

The marquess was not accustomed to being left cooling his heels like a common tradesman who should more properly have gone to the servants' door. However, on this loveliest of mornings, he overlooked the snub. He strolled around the hallway, inspected its scant furnishings, which included a porcelain vase, a pair of uncomfortable-looking Egyptian chairs, a carved umbrella stand, and a handsome wooden staircase with barley-sugar-twisted balusters.

Alas, poor Nicky. Instead of basking—and yes, he had been basking, which should not be held against him, for he had waited a long time for the events of the previous night—he should perhaps instead have been contemplating hubris; or the fate of a gentleman named Icarus who donned wax wings and flew too close to the sun; or his Creator's tendency to give, and then take away; for of all the members of the household, it was Zoë who found him standing in the hallway, contemplating the porcelain urn.

Lord Mannering was lost in thought. Thoughts of her, of course; why else would the marquess have come here, and at such an unfashionable hour? If he didn't look like he was languishing, at least he looked like a man who had made up his mind. "Hello!" she said. He started. "Have you come to see me, then?"

Discourage her, Nick told himself. But gently, so she didn't fly into the boughs. "No, I have come to speak with your father. But it is always a pleasure to see you, Miss Loversall."

"La! So formal!" Zoë moved closer. "It is entirely unnecessary for you to speak to Beau—indeed I wish you wouldn't! And if you had *truly* wished to see me, you should have gone to Mrs. Yarrow's musical party last night! Baron Fitzrichard's cousin played the harp very prettily. The baron was wearing a blue cravat. I'd never seen anything like it." She giggled. "I don't think anyone else had either, from the way that people stared!"

Nick wished that he had brought the baron with him on this visit, blue cravat or no. He suspected that he'd made a grave mistake in coming unchaperoned to this house, as well as in mentioning the purpose of his visit. "I fear you've misunderstood," he said, as he backed away.

Zoë had misunderstood nothing. The man was besotted with her, was he not? Although perhaps she did fail to understand why so experienced a seducer failed to make an assault on her virtue when they found themselves so fortuitously alone. Indeed, he seemed to be retreating even as she advanced. "You said I was the most beautiful damsel in England, and that you awaited my pleasure, and that I'm yours to command." She dimpled. "You also said that you'd slay a dragon for me, but we needn't go that far!"

He'd said a great deal of nonsense, reflected Nick, as he edged toward the door. The blasted chit trailed after him as if he were a magnet, and she were iron. "That's the sort of nonsense one says when one is flattering a young woman. I also said you were a hardened flirt, if you'll recall."

Zoë trod close upon his heels, or toes, since he was progressing backward and she was not. She was changing her mind about the marquess never being dull. He was being dull right now. Perhaps he was not as manly as she'd thought. Or perhaps he was feeling his great age, which was very inconvenient of him, for this was the perfect moment to embark upon their *affaire de coeur*, and if to do so in the hallway of her papa's house was not what she had anticipated, it still gave the business a certain cachet.

"I'm a flirt, I admit it!" she said, as she deftly placed herself between the marquess and his only means of escape. "But I've also tumbled violently in love, just as you said I would, with *you*! You needn't get down on your knees if it is too painful because of your rheumatism; I quite understand. But in case you hadn't noticed, 'tis the perfect moment for you to ravish me, because we are quite alone."

Of course Nick had noticed they were alone. He deplored the circumstance. "I'm not going to ravish you, in this hallway or anywhere else." He moved sideways toward the stair.

A pity. Zoë had decided that to be ravished in the hallway of her papa's house would have been quite worthy of a Loversall. "So be it, if you're determined to be a gentleman about the thing. Not that I know why you should be when I don't wish you to, but we may talk about that another time." She summoned forth a blush. "You may kiss me now."

Nick had backed up as far as he could against the stairway. The carved banister dug into his back. "I don't want to kiss you."

Closer she drew, ever closer, narrowing the gap, a curly-headed moppet straight from the nether regions, with eyelashes atwitch and pretty lips aquiver and hands extended to clamp on to him. "Silly man!" she cooed. "Of course you do. Come now, there's no need to pretend."

There was nothing for it. He was going to have to do her physical damage. Nick had never hit a female in his life, but this one was inspiring him with a nigh irresistible urge to lay a stern hand on her backside.

Fate intervened, in the form of Daisy, who had grown tired of searching for Zoë in the drawing room and was

eager to resume their romp. Upon finding her playmate
in conversation with a stranger, the setter woofed and
wagged her tail. Aware by now of the dog's customary
behavior with newcomers, Zoë counted to five and
then put herself smack in Daisy's path. Daisy jumped
up, and knocked Zoë into Nick, and Nick onto the
stairs. Nick yelped as his head connected with the banister and his back with a sharp step. Zoë shrieked
prettily. Thinking this a much more interesting game
than hide-and-seek, Daisy leapt upon them both.

Nick groaned and opened his eyes to find himself
nose-to-nose with a tail-wagging, drooling setter, and
Zoë sprawled atop him, and a sharp breath-stealing
pain shooting up his spine. He wondered if he had
broken it. "Let me up," he said, and put his hands on
Zoë 's waist to move her away from him, or tried to;
the setter's enthusiastic participation made it hard to
get a grip.

Zoë had no intention of moving. She had the marquess exactly where she wanted him, and she meant
for him to go nowhere else until he'd ravished her a
little bit. "Have you damaged yourself?" she murmured, solicitously.

If he was damaged, which seemed likely in light of
the agonizing ache that had settled in his lower back,
Nick certainly had not done it to himself. "Kindly remove yourself from my person," he snapped, and
gave Zoë a shove. Instead of complying, she flung her
arms around his neck, and hitched herself further up
on his body, and pressed her lips to his.

Nick was horrified to be assaulted thus by a young
lady—the term "lady" being debatable—and even
more so when she tried to plunge her tongue into his
mouth. Clearly the chit had been practicing. Heaven

only knew where that tongue had been. "Stop that!" he said, through clenched teeth, and tried to turn his head away, a feat made nigh impossible by the dog sitting on his shoulder. Every time he moved, a flame of pain shot up his spine.

Zoë clutched the marquess in her grip like an ardent octopus, and pondered her next move. She had expected such an experienced gentleman to show a tad more polish than he had thus far done. Could his worldly reputation be a sham?

Perhaps he feared to offend her maidenly sensibilities. Perhaps instead of struggling to free himself he was writhing in the throes of ardor. "You can do better than that!" she said, and licked his nose.

"I don't want to do better!" snarled Nick, still through gritted teeth, lest she attack him again with her blasted tongue. "Will you please get *off*!"

No one thwarted Zoë with impunity. If Lord Mannering didn't want her now, he would. She clutched his ears and kissed him again, and then for good measure grabbed one of his hands and thrust it into the bosom of her dress. "Feel my heart! It is fluttering against my chest like the wings of an imprisoned bird struggling to be free!"

Nick couldn't help but feel Zoë 's heart beating, and her breast, which was very nice, but didn't interest him in the least because it was attached to her. He tried to free his hand, but couldn't, due to the combined squirming weight of both Zoë and the dog, which had decided this was a good moment in which to bathe his face.

Nick turned his head in a vain attempt to escape the dog's caress. "I don't know what the devil you've been reading, but the damned book should be banned. Take your elbow out of my ribs!"

Zoë obliged, but only so that she might take further liberties with Nick's person. Daisy, having thoroughly washed his left cheek, moved on to investigate his eyebrow. He could stop neither of them. The marquess sprawled upon the stairs like a man crucified. Beau strolled into the hallway, and stopped, and stared.

The master of the household was up earlier than once had been his habit; he had hardly any reason to pursue certain evening activities these days. Beau had already bathed and shaved and breakfasted, perused the newspaper and pondered the latest follies of the ministry; had read a political essay as well as accounts of recent social events, cockfights and a boxing match; had lingered over advertisements for wives, lottery tickets, and an intriguing patent nostrum guaranteed to revive manly vigor, the name of which he had carefully noted. It was with the notion of tracking down this miracle medicine that he had entered the hallway, expecting to have Widdle fetch his hat and walking stick. That Widdle wasn't in the hallway was hardly surprising, since the butler was seldom where one might expect him to be. What *was* surprising was the excessively bizarre *ménage à trios* being enacted on the stairway. Cara's dog, Beau recognized, and his own daughter, and— The devil, was that *Mannering*?

Here was a fine thing! Beau had heard his daughter shriek, and the dog barking, but since neither circumstance was unusual, he had thought it merely part of their current game. A game that had taken an unexpected turn. "Zoë! This isn't what I meant by bringing him up to scratch!"

Nick didn't like the sound of "up to scratch." He pushed feebly at the dog. "Loversall. I wish to talk to you about—"

"Me!" Zoë sighed as her papa grabbed her arm and hauled her upright. "But it is for naught, alas, because I'm too young to wed."

Beau was having none of this nonsense, not after the exhibition he'd just witnessed. "You're nothing of the sort. Daisy, remove yourself from the marquess. Now!"

Daisy gave Nick's face one last slobber, then flopped off him and onto the stair. Zoë pouted. "You said—"

"I've said a lot of things that later turned out to be cork-brained." Beau watched Lord Mannering wince as he attempted to sit up. "It's the devil getting older, isn't it? You should have known better than to attempt the business on the stair! I haven't done such a thing myself for—" He paused to consider how long it had been, and then recalled with whom Mannering had been going about the business. "You will make restitution for this, my lord!"

Nick achieved a sitting position, and paused. His back hurt like Hades, and his head wasn't far behind. "I didn't—"

Beau extended his hand and pulled the marquess to his feet. "No, but you would have. I know a compromising situation when I see one. If I hadn't walked in when I did, you'd have had her up against the wall!"

A brief silence ensued while Beau contemplated the last time he had had a lady up against a wall (which had been far longer ago than he liked), and Nick considered the same matter (only a few hours past, in his case), and Zoë pondered the mechanics of the thing. "Gracious! I don't know that I would care for that. It sounds most uncomfortable. Shall I walk on your back, Lord Mannering? I do it for Beau when he gets in a knot."

Nick had already been considerably closer to Zoë than he cared to be today, or ever. "No!" he said, and frowned at Beau. "Restitution for what?"

Beau folded his arms across his chest and attempted to look stern. "You've besmirched my daughter's reputation. Now you must make amends."

He was cast as the piece's villain? Nick drew in an indignant breath, and winced. "Your daughter has damn near broke my back. You should be grateful that I don't sue you. Indeed, I *may* sue you. That girl is an affliction, a misery, a blight! You should have drowned her at birth."

Drowned her? "Well!" huffed Zoë, more than a little bit dismayed to find her True Love so poor-spirited. Or if not her True Love, then the gentleman with whom she had decided to Experience Life. Perhaps she should have instead chosen a viscount or perhaps a Hussar, but definitely not the knight, for he was even more ancient than Lord Mannering. "He has insulted me, Beau! Are you going to fight a duel?"

Beau wasn't *that* cork-brained. Mannering was a crack shot, and he looked at the moment as if he could cheerfully dispatch any number of people without a second thought. "No, puss. I'm going to see you safely wed."

Nick started to protest. Zoë spoke first. "But I was only flirting!" she wailed.

Beau was not at all pleased to see this further evidence of the family nature in his daughter. "This is what comes of that sort of thing, my girl!"

Her beloved papa speaking to her as if she were a stranger! It surpassed belief. It also surpassed all patience, and Zoë flew into a tantrum, shrieking at the top of her lungs and flinging things about. Since there was so little furniture in the hallway, she had to content herself with hurling the chairs and decapitating the umbrella stand, kicking over and shattering the large urn that stood at the foot of the stair. Then she threw herself on the floor, kicking and flailing her feet and arms about. Daisy, thinking this a grand new game, and the best one yet, leapt into the fray, took Zoë 's skirt between her teeth, and dragged her around the hallway. Zoë disliked this development. Her face turned bright red. She shrieked one last time, and began to hold her breath.

Beau lowered his hands from his ears, where he had placed them during the worst of Zoë 's histrionics, and turned to the startled marquess. "It's almost over now. She'll either decide to breathe again, or turn blue or swoon."

The sooner the chit swooned, the better. If she stopped breathing altogether, it would be better yet. "I didn't come here to ask for your daughter's hand," Nick said.

"Can't say as I blame you," Beau admitted. "Still, I saw what I saw—speaking of hands and where they were and where they shouldn't have been!—and you'll marry her, my lord. Because you wouldn't like what the world would say of you if it became known that you ruined a lass's reputation and then turned your back on her, I think."

Do unto others . . . Nick pondered his own recent

use of blackmail. "I hardly ruined her. She threw herself on me—"

"I didn't!" protested Zoë , from her position on the floor.

Beau ignored her. So did Nick. "And I had no choice but to defend myself. You know, at some point in time, you should probably have turned her over your knee. Or locked her in her room." Or even better, pitched her off the roof.

Beau looked at his daughter, who was regaining her normal color, now that she had decided to again breathe. It might well be true that she had initiated matters, but the marquess would marry her nonetheless, because someone clearly had to marry her, and soon. Perhaps Mannering would be able to keep her in line. Although the episode on the stairway suggested otherwise. But then there was the title. And the extensive Mannering fortune. Beau could do far worse for his only chick.

Nick disliked that contemplative expression. "No one saw but you," he pointed out. "Your daughter misunderstood my purpose in coming here. I wished to talk to you about something else altogether. Perhaps we might just forget that this unfortunate incident ever took place."

Unfortunate incident? Too long ignored, Zoë got up from the floor. Lord Mannering didn't sound a bit like a man whose heart was engaged, which put her on her mettle, because if she was going to break his heart— which he richly deserved, pretending to not want to kiss her—then she must engage it first. When she *did* get around to breaking his heart, 'twould be all the more satisfying if the whole world knew she had brought London's most determined bachelor to heel before she had crushed him flat beneath her boot. And in the meantime she would be a marchioness.

Beau hadn't stopped talking. "Do you deny trying to entice my daughter into a squalid little intrigue?"

Not Beau's daughter, but his sister. And there had been nothing squalid about it. Nick touched the painful lump that was forming on the back of his head. "I do."

Beau knew more than a little about intrigues himself. He was beginning to suspect that his daughter also knew more about them than she should. "Nonetheless, you'll marry her, my lord."

Zoë tripped gracefully across the floor to slip her arm through Nick's. He attempted to remove it. She dug in her fingernails and smiled beatifically. "I shall become your marchioness with pleasure, Lord Mannering," she said, just as Widdle returned to the hallway with the other members of the family, and Lord Mannering's visiting card.

Both ladies gazed upon the scene with astonishment. "I see Zoë has been in her tantrums again." Ianthe sighed, as she knelt down to pick up the pieces of her prized vase. Daisy ran to her mistress, who stood still as a stone.

"I'll get you another!" said Beau, before Ianthe could start moaning over the damned vase. "More importantly, Mannering has come to make Zoë a declaration. She has accepted. With my blessing, of course."

Ianthe sank back on her heels and looked astonished. "In the front hallway?"

"He could wait no longer," Zoë said smugly, already half believing the fiction herself. "Passion overwhelmed us both, and he swept me right off my feet."

Lord Mannering might still have protested, had

indeed parted his lips to speak; but then he saw the contemptuous expression on Lady Norwood's lovely face, and his jaw snapped shut.

14

Baron Fitzrichard was not unfamiliar with the great old mansion so appreciated by members of the Mannering family who wished to seclude themselves from the world. However, he had never before visited the master bedchamber, where massive beams supported the ceiling, and tapestries featuring a procession of lions and dragons and unicorns marched across the walls, and bright rugs gleamed on the polished wooden floor. Chests and chairs were scattered about the room, along with various oddities, including ancient books, and a foot rule, and a gaily colored feathered fan. In one corner stood an ancient and somewhat battered suit of armor known fondly to the family as Ferdinand.

Scarlet velvet draperies adorned the square-paned windows and the enormous canopied four-poster bed. "You can't say I didn't warn you, Nicky!" Fitz said, as he regarded its occupant. "And you should have listened to me, because it's plain as the nose on your face that I knew what I was talking about!"

The nose on Lord Mannering's face was not plain at that moment, but buried in a pillow, for he was sprawled on his bed while Jacob rubbed a balsam containing white Spanish soap, opium, rectified spirits of wine, and camphor on his abused back. In addition to these measures, a fomentation of white poppy heads, elder flowers, and water had been applied to the lump on his head; and Mary had rushed to the apothecary for a draught composed of liquid laudanum, cinnamon water, and common syrup, which should prove marvelously efficacious if one subscribed to the dictum that the worse a medicine tasted the greater its curative powers. No matter how severe his discomfort, however, the marquess was adamant about not ingesting anything containing horses' hooves or wood lice, and furthermore had refused to let himself be cupped.

As result of all these measures—in particular the opium, poppy heads, and laudanum—Nick was not feeling as poorly as he had when he arrived here. "That will be sufficient abuse for the moment, Jacob," he muttered, into the pillow. Jacob replaced the lid on the jar of balsam and withdrew.

Fitz ventured further into the chamber and hauled a velvet-upholstered chair closer to the bed. "Insanity in the family!" he continued. "I suspected as much, and now I'm sure. You *do* want to be leg-shackled. You must! Although I'd think being leg-shackled to the little Loversall would be a fate worse than death!"

Nick gritted his teeth, rolled over on his back, and groaned. As result of the ministrations of his faithful servants, the pain in his head had settled down to aching dully like an abscessed tooth, unless he tried to move. His back, however, still felt as if some great unseen beast had sunk in its fangs and refused to let go. "I *don't* want to get leg-shackled," he ground out. "And I'm not *going* to get leg-shackled. I just haven't said so yet."

Fitz waved a lavender-scented handkerchief beneath his nose to combat the scent of camphor wafting from the bedstead. "The notice has already been sent to the *Gazette*! You told me so yourself."

Nick painfully pulled himself to a semi-sitting position. "I don't give a damn about the *Gazette*."

Fitz studied his friend over the lace edge of his handkerchief. The marquess looked positively decadent, propped up amidst his pillows in the ancient bed, wearing nothing more than a sheet draped casually across his lower half. Fitz felt positively drab in comparison, for Nicky's summons had interrupted his toilette, as result of which he was wearing the plainest of his waistcoats. Furthermore, there had been no time to tie his cravat in anything more intricate than the Mail Coach, which could be found gracing the necks of stage coachmen and guards, swells and ruffians alike; and he still had whiskers on his chin.

Considering the urgency of that summons, Fitz had at the very least expected to find Nicky on his deathbed, and was somewhat annoyed to discover he was not. "I thought you was supposed to be a regular out and outer! Here I leave you alone for a minute and you land in the suds. Why did you go and do such a beetle-headed thing as enter that house alone? Why *did* you go there, by the by? And at so uncivilized an hour?"

Nick wondered what had prompted him to desire Fitz's companionship in this, his hour of need. "I wanted to speak with Beau."

Despite his fondness for colored neck-cloths and the like, the baron was no greenhead. He fluttered the handkerchief. "But not, I'll wager, about Miss Zoë."

Nick developed a sudden interest in the edging on his sheets. "No."

Fitz's eyes narrowed. "Or Ianthe."

Nick moved, and twinged, and grimaced. "No, not Ianthe."

"Ha!" said Fitz, though not with disapproval. "You should have taken me with you. You've taken me everywhere else! Gunter's, if you will remember? Lady Miller's? Riding in the Park? Now look what's happened when you didn't. You're in the devil's own scrape."

"Tell me something I don't know. Although I doubt that it would have made a difference even had you been there. The little trollop was determined to have her way with me. You'd probably have ended up in the melee alongside the dog."

Fitz widened his eyes at the vision thus conjured. "Trollop? Ain't that a little strong?"

"Is it? The chit threw herself on me, and thrust my hand into the bosom of her dress, and tried to stick her tongue down my throat."

"Egad! And you *let* her do all this?"

"I hadn't much choice in the matter. She and the dog were both on top of me, and my back was broke."

Fitz inhaled more deeply of the handkerchief, and wished he'd brought along his hartshorn, not for the marquess but for himself. "I'd be all in a twitter if I was you. In point of fact, I *am* all in a twitter, and it ain't me as will be walking down the aisle, thank God. Maybe you can persuade her to cry off."

"Her father wouldn't let her, even if she could be persuaded to, which is doubtful, because now she fancies herself a marchioness." Gingerly, Nick touched his sore head. "I can't blame him for wishing to see her safely married. Not that I mean to oblige him! If I must, I'll cry off myself."

Fitz was so shocked that he dropped his

handkerchief. "If you was to cry off, it would make a dreadful scandal. You wouldn't do such a thing!"

Nick raised his eyebrows. "The little Loversall?"

Fitz reconsidered. "You would. I would myself, no matter how dastardly a thing it was. Not that *I* would have got myself in this pickle in the first place. You ain't thought this through, Nicky. You'd survive the business, because of who you are, but would she?"

Nick regarded his friend with disfavor. "I thought you didn't like the chit. If you *do* like her, perhaps you'd care to take her off my hands."

Fitz shuddered at the notion. "Of course I don't like the chit. She's a veritable curse—just look at you! As well as a brazen baggage, but still, does she deserve to have her reputation ruined? More to the point, even if she *does* deserve it, can you bear to be such a blackguard?"

Nick scowled. "I'd rather ruin her than murder her, and that's the only other choice."

It occurred to the baron that he was perhaps arguing the wrong side of the case. He certainly didn't wish to see the marquess stand trial for murder, although Nicky would probably be let off on the grounds that it had been justified. "She's bound to tie her garter in public sooner or later, being as she's a Loversall," Fitz said bracingly. "So it don't signify!"

Nick couldn't bring himself to comment. He leaned his throbbing head back among his pillows and pondered the predicament that he was in. Despite the aches and pains that assailed the various portions of his anatomy, his pride was perhaps damaged most of all, for he had got caught like the greenest lad. What Fitz had said was true, wish as he might to deny it: Once the notion of his impending nuptials was published—and nothing short of murder would prevent Beau from having the announcement published—there was no way Nick could honorably withdraw. The only consolation was that Zoë demanded an elaborate ceremony in St. George's, Hanover Square, which would take some time to prepare.

There must be some way out of this coil. If only Nick could think. His various aches and pains—combined with opium, poppy heads, and laudanum—made concentration difficult. Just hours ago he had been in the best of moods, and mere hours before that—Alas, the scent of camphor had overpowered any scent of Cara that might have lingered in his bed.

Silence descended on the bedchamber, broken only by the cheerful crackle of the fire that burned in the pretty carved fireplace, guarded there by andirons in the form of mythological beasts. Fitz picked up a book from the bedside table—Antonio de Torquemada's *The Spanish Mandevile of myracles: or, The garden of curious flowers : wherein are handled sundry points of humanity, philosophy, divinity, and geography, beautified with many strange and pleasant histories / first written in Spanish by Anthonio de Torquemeda, and translated out of that tongue into English,* 'imprinted by Bernard Alsop, by the assigne of Richard Hawkins, and are to be solde at his house by Saint Annes Church neere Aldersgate, 1618'—and leafed through the pages.

The bedroom door flew open, distracting Fitz from his *Miracles* (most notably the woman wrecked on an African shore who had mated with an ape and produced two sons) and the marquess from his nostalgic thoughts. Nick flinched, thinking that Jacob had returned to lay hands on him once again. Instead, Lady

Norwood stalked like some avenging fury into the bedchamber. Behind her, in the hallway, the little maidservant wrung her hands. "It's that sorry I am, my lord! I told her ladyship that you wasn't receiving visitors, but she said that wouldn't include her, and I didn't know but what she was right, considering— Hem! And then she pushed right past me as if I wasn't there!"

"It's all right, Mary." Nick wondered if the poor girl might like a swallow of his laudanum draught. "Her ladyship is welcome in my bedchamber at any hour of the day or night. Greetings, *cara mia*. Have you brought your knife?"

What she had brought was a temper worthy of Zoë. Cara walked over to the corner basin stand, picked up an ewer and threw it on the floor, where it shattered into bits. Then she gave the coat of armor a good hard kick. "I thought I'd find you hiding here, you coward. Tell me that this is all a bag of moonshine. Tell me that you weren't so bloody randy that you tried to ravish Zoë on the hall stairs!"

Nick was feeling far from randy at the moment, though Cara's eyes were sparkling, and her bosom was heaving, and her hair was a tempting tangle of red-gold ringlets sticking out every which way. Due to all his assorted aches, Nick was uncertain whether he would ever be able to engage in amorous congress again, which would be a great pity, but life would certainly be more peaceful in that case. "In point of fact, it was she who tried to ravish me," he retorted. Cara snorted and walked toward the fireplace. Nick took a firm grip on his sheet.

Fascinating, mused Fitz, for it was evident to the baron that Lady Norwood was no stranger to this house, which certainly gave lie to the notion that Lord Mannering conducted himself at all times like a perfect gentleman. For a lady to visit a gentleman in his quarters—let alone know her way around his bedchamber—was scandalous indeed, and if word of it got out Lady Norwood's reputation would be ruined. Not that Nicky had conducted himself like a perfect gentleman on the stairway with Zoë, either, but that was an entirely different matter, and one that understandably had her aunt in a high dudgeon. Lady Norwood picked up a porcelain vase and flung it on the hearth. Fitz winced. "Perhaps I should leave."

Cara spared him only the briefest of glances before she picked up the fireplace poker and returned her attention to the figure on the bed. That familiar bed with its labyrinthine carving of animals and flowers. That even more familiar half-naked gentleman. How dare he flaunt his bare chest at her as if one glance at that glorious expanse of skin muscle would blunt the force of her outrage? "You are going nowhere, Baron Fitzrichard! I've nothing to say to Lord Mannering that you shouldn't hear. Since you are his friend, you must already know that the man is a—a—"

Nick was growing increasingly annoyed to be so continuously maligned. Cara of all people should know the nature of her niece. As well as his own nature, which didn't include ravishing brazen misses on their papa's hall stair steps. Although Cara had never thought highly of his nature, now that he considered it. "Satyr? Goat? Toad?" he suggested, in a snit of his own. "Lying cur, perhaps? Or maybe a dastardly rat with no more morals than to amuse myself with both niece and aunt at the same time? Oh, and we must not forget my desire for revenge!"

The poker had a very satisfying weight. Cara brandished it and sent a book of Elizabethan riddles flying smack into the fireplace. "I was thinking more along the lines of pond scum."

Lord but she was beautiful, thought Nick, even if the only fruit she put him in mind of today was a lemon, because her expression was as sour as if she'd bit into one. Then he realized that she had called him pond scum.

So be it. He wriggled himself into a more provocative pose, and strove for a leer. "What would you have had me do, my love? The wench offered me *carte blanche*. I could hardly turn down so tempting an armful. Not that I'd meant to marry her, merely thought to set her up in a little house somewhere. But then your brother interfered."

Cara stared at the marquess in astonishment. As did Fitz. "I say, Nicky!" The baron gasped.

"You despicable man!" cried Cara, at almost the same moment. "I'm surprised you let Beau force you into offering for Zoë."

Nick wished he had a snuffbox so that he might flick it open, in the one-handed fashion so favored by Fitz, to further demonstrate his insouciance. "Had I made your niece an offer, it wouldn't have been of an honorable sort. Your brother blackmailed me into doing the right thing. I suppose I still might have refused him, vile seducer that I am. Apparently I still have a shred of conscience left, alas."

Cara went so rigid that she might have sat upon the poker. "You are insufferable!"

Nick donned his most knavish look. "That's not what you said last night! You can't delude yourself that you didn't know what I was like, *cara*. After what we once were to one another."

"God bless my soul!" interjected Fitz. "Nicky, don't you think—" He broke off, silenced by the combined weight of two glares.

Lady Norwood turned her fury back on the marquess. "*Once* you had rather more finesse. Now you are a nothing but a boorish knave. A lecherous wretch. A lustful libertine who is incapable of resisting any female who flings herself at you!"

"By George!" breathed Fitz. Lady Norwood scowled at him again, in a fashion that recalled the adage that it was wise to humor lunatics. Especially lunatics who were clutching fireplace pokers. "You've hit it on the nose! He's a curst loose fish!"

"How kind of you to defend me!" Lord Mannering said scathingly. "But unnecessary. The lady is a shrew."

"Coming it rather too strong," said Fitz, because the marquess appeared unaware of the correct manner in which to deal with madwomen. "She's merely taken a bit of a pet, which is understandable, all things considered."

Cara's eyes glittered. She stepped closer to the bed. Prudently, Fitz snatched the draught out of her reach, and removed himself from the chair. "Lustful slug," she said

Nick lounged on his pillows like a sultan awaiting the arrival of his harem. "I'm not sure that slugs experience lust. Take another shot."

Cara stood gazing down at the almost naked figure on the bed. Well did she remember how Nicky looked naked. Damn him. And how he'd felt. "Just what *would* it take to satisfy your salacious appetites?"

Nick stared back at her, and remembered how she

had looked sprawled naked in his bed. And what she'd done, damn her. "More than *you* can offer, clearly," he retorted, with every ounce of villainy at his command.

Cara blanched, then flushed, and hurled the fireplace poker straight at him. Nick ducked to avoid it, and yelped with the pain. She looked concerned. "You missed," he said.

That was the absolutely final straw, and it broke not only the camel's back but tweaked its tail as well. "You faithless, rake-helly *imbecile!*" shouted Cara, and punched him on the jaw. Nick collapsed back onto his pillows. Cara turned on her heel and stalked out of the room. Behind her, the door slammed.

Cautiously, Fitz ventured out from behind the chair where he'd been cowering, and tiptoed toward the bed, where he hoped to assure himself that it wasn't bellows to mend with his friend. Well, it clearly *was* bellows to mend, that was incontestable, but Fitz wished to make sure the facer that Lady Norwood had landed hadn't knocked the marquess out cold.

The marquess was very much awake. He lay back on his pillows, staring at the canopy, hand to his newly damaged jaw. "I'm not sure but what you deserved that," Fitz observed.

Nick knew damned well he deserved it, which put him in no better mood. Fitz was still clutching the draught. "Give me that damned glass," he said, and snatched it, and drained it dry.

Fitz perched cautiously on the edge of the bed. "That's a fine woman, Nicky. Even if she does have the devil of a temper. You shouldn't have provoked her like that."

Nick moved his jaw about to make certain that he could. "And she didn't provoke me, I suppose."

Fitz wasn't about to be drawn into a discussion of who had behaved more badly. He had leaned forward to inspect the abused jaw. "By Jove! A matched set of bruises. Maybe you'll set a new style."

In no mood for humor, Lord Mannering snarled. Fitz regarded him with unusual seriousness. "Nicky, you *are* going to cry off, are you not?"

The marquess closed his eyes. "I'm not going to do anything just yet. Go away and let me rest."

This was the thanks a fellow got for supporting his friend in adversity? Huffily, Fitz removed himself from the bed. "You must know your own business best, of course. But if you *don't* cry off, I shan't stand up for you, so don't even ask!"

15

One more fling of the dice, indeed. Cara should have known from bitter experience that she might fling the dice all she wished and never know other than a losing hand, unlike her Great-Great-Great Grandmother Alyce, who had parlayed a lucky tendency toward sevens and elevens into the proprietorship of an exclusive gaming house in Holborn, where she had surrounded herself with a curious assortment of foreign princes, barons, and ambassadors, children and grandchildren, as well as a menagerie that included several cats, an even dozen King Charles spaniels, an excessively fat rabbit, and a little Moorish page, until she died at age eighty-three in the arms of her favorite footman, of a spasm of the heart resulting from retrocedent gout.

"What flapdoodle!" Barrow interrupted these glum thoughts with a vigorously wielded hairbrush. "The whole household is on its ear. And where did you go this morning, I'd like to know? Not that I expect you to tell me, for I'm just a servant, and never mind that I've been at your side through thick and thin! Far be it from *me* to tell you that you shouldn't be going out alone, for you're in London, and not in the country now! With your hair looking like a bird's nest! And what's become of your green hair ribbon, pray?"

Cara bit her lip. The green ribbon was the least of the items she had left at Nicky's house. "I'm sure it will turn up. Stop fussing, Barrow. I look well enough."

So she did, due in no small measure to the abigail's clever fingers, which had persuaded the bird's nest into neat coils and braids, and the rest of her ladyship into a round dress of pale blue cambric. Barrow set down the hairbrush with a last disapproving sniff. "I know what I know! Take care, my lady, that Squire Anderley doesn't wash his hands of you, and then where would you be?"

Safely at home in the Cotswolds, with her lilacs and her roses and her kumquat tree, where she was now prevented from returning by Zoë's impending nuptials. "That will be enough, Barrow!" Cara said, with unaccustomed severity, and walked out of the room. The abigail dropped down on the dressing stool, and regarded her own reflection in the looking glass. If that green ribbon turned up anywhere in the vicinity, she'd eat it on toast.

Ianthe was in the drawing room, seated in a cabriole-legged wing chair, on the table in front of her a hand-engraved silver teapot made by Mr. Robert Hennell of London in 1782, along with her dainty-slippered feet. Scattered about the carpet were wads of paper, as well as a dejected Daisy, who was in disgrace for her part in this morning's contretemps, although no one except Zoë knew for certain exactly what Daisy's part had been. That ebullient young miss had gone riding with a party of her friends, whom she was entertaining with a lavishly embellished account of her romantic adventure with Lord Mannering in the front hallway of her papa's house, thereby shattering the dreams of several Hussars, both viscounts, the baronet, and the admiral, though the aged knight held out hope that it was early days yet. Ianthe wore a long-sleeved dress of figured chintz, and around her shoulder a fringed shawl.

She looked up as Cara walked into the room, followed by two footmen carrying a sorry-looking sapling in a wooden tub. Ianthe eyed it doubtfully. "What are you going to do with that?"

What Cara would have liked to do was bash a certain marquess over the head with it, if only she could figure how, not that she wished to damage the poor thing. The tree, that was, not Nicky. "'That' is a Sophora japonica, a Japanese pagoda tree. In time it will grow to as much as seventy-five feet tall, and equally as wide around, if given enough space. It flowers in the summer." Cara touched a leaf. "I'm told there is an especially fine specimen at Kew."

Doubtfully, Ianthe eyed the sapling, which didn't look as if it would achieve seven feet in height, let alone seventy-five. "But, Cara, there is hardly sufficient space for such a thing—lovely as it is!—in the drawing room," she said.

The Sophora japonica wasn't the least bit lovely, although it *was* heavy. Cara bade the footmen set it down. "I will tell you where to take it later," she said, and sent them from the room.

Ianthe was still staring at the tree. "Take it?" she said.

"I am going to return it to its rightful owner!" Cara stared at her cousin's feet, propped on the tea table in a posture sufficiently rag-mannered to be worthy of Zoë. "Ianthe, are you well?"

Ianthe poured a cup of tea for her cousin. "Beau says that this latest disaster is all my fault."

Cara watched Daisy crawl across the carpet on her

belly. She relented and gave the dog a pat. "Why is it your fault that N—Lord Mannering!—tried to seduce Zoë?"

Why was it that Lord Mannering had given Cara a Sophora japonica, sorry a specimen as it might have been? Ianthe had no doubt where the tree had come from. "Beau has gotten into the habit of thinking everything is my fault! For him to call me a wet goose was one thing, or even a watering pot, for I realize that I have had a tendency to be a little *damp*. But to call me a goose-cap was the outside of enough, and then to compound matters by accusing me of being an arch wife—" Ianthe lifted her teacup as if to propose a toast. "I have had an epiphany."

The family was prone to epiphanies, along with their adventures. "Beau is a sapskull," Cara soothed. "He's probably already sorry for what he said."

"I doubt it." Ianthe wrinkled her nose. "He will have gone to one of his clubs—or one of his mistresses—without giving the matter another thought. And that *is* my fault, for I have made him into every bit as great a monster as he has made Zoë." She looked at the wads of paper strewn about the floor. "Furthermore, I don't see why *I* should be the one to make up a list of wedding guests!"

Ianthe was in a temper. It didn't happen often, but she was, after all, a member of the same family as Cara and Zoë. "I have also been accused of being the reason that his daughter has a weakness for promiscuity," she added, before Cara could speak. "*Me!* After I have devoted myself to his interests all these years. With perhaps the exception of a few discreet escapades, but Zoë never knew about them, and neither did he!"

Nor did Cara wish to know, although she was glad her cousin had had some consolation for her doomed romance. "I am so sorry, Ianthe."

"Why? I'm not." And indeed, Ianthe's gaze was brighter than was usual, and her cheek more flushed, which was not entirely attributable to the brandy that she'd poured into her tea cup. "I have decided that once Zoë is safely married, I shall remove to Brighton, or perhaps to Bath. Perhaps Wilhelmina will have recovered by then from her disaster with that Frenchman. Gentlemen *are* the very devil, are they not? I wish I might leave right now. But I cannot, any more than you, lest we provide more fodder for the gossip mill." Ianthe waved her handkerchief. "However, I *shan't* arrange the wedding, and if you'll take my advice, you'll also refuse. Let Beau deal with his brat."

Mention of Zoë's marriage plunged Cara back into the dumps, which she had already visited as result of her decision to return the Sophora japonica, since a lady could hardly accept presents from gentlemen who went about seducing young women on stairways. "What if there were not to be a wedding?" she said.

Ianthe had her own notions about who had seduced whom on the stairway, or had attempted to. The marquess hadn't looked especially rapturous. Or even particularly comfortable. A pity Daisy couldn't speak.

With a deft diversionary maneuver of her handkerchief, Ianthe slipped more brandy into her teacup. "Of course there will be a wedding. All has worked out for the best."

Daisy looked as woebegone as Cara felt. Cara scratched her ears. "Worked out for the *best?*"

"Certainly! Zoë will be married, which will make

Beau happy, and you may return to your home, which will make Squire Anderley happy, and everyone will live happily forevermore!"

Cara wasn't certain she hadn't liked Ianthe better heartsore. "You failed to mention yourself."

Ianthe lifted her teacup, and inhaled its aroma. "I am not destined to be happy. Remember, I had my heart broke long ago."

"Hearts don't break! Or if they do, they heal," retorted Cara, though her own hadn't, or if it had, then she'd turned around and broken it open once again. "You neglected to mention Lord Mannering."

"Nicky," wasn't it? "Oh, well! How can he help but be happy when he has been favored by Zoë? After all, he *did* show her a marked partiality."

"All my eye! She laid siege to the poor man."

"You don't think he's smitten?"

"I know he isn't! Or I thought I knew. Oh, *drat!*"

"Have some more tea," said Ianthe.

Cara sighed. "You knew."

Ianthe removed her feet from the table and tucked them up beneath her in the chair. "I guessed. Part of it, at least. You referred to the marquess by his first name. And then there is the Sophora japonica."

Cara looked at the tree. "I have done some absurd things in that quarter, I fear."

"We have all done absurd things! It is part of being a Loversall. And now I am positively agog with curiosity, so pray tell me everything." Ianthe paused to reconsider. "Or not *everything*, perhaps. There is a limit to how many embarrassing revelations I can tolerate at what Zoë refers to as my advanced age. Come, Cara! I am awaiting your revelations with bated breath."

So she was, along with bright eyes and flushed

cheeks and not a tear in sight. Cara supposed she must confide in someone, and who better than her cousin? "Nicky and I—That is, we—Oh, he never had the least interest in Zoë! It was all a subterfuge to lure me back to town."

"How very enterprising of him! And how romantic."

"Yes, it was, wasn't it?" There came a brief, nostalgic pause. "And now the horrid child has compromised him, because it's sure as check he didn't wish to compromise *her*, although I accused him of it. As well as other things." She looked so unhappy that Ianthe extended the handkerchief. "Nick will never forgive me for the things I said. And if he does, I may never forgive *him* for what he said in return!"

Ianthe was fascinated. Drama had been going on all around her, and she had been oblivious to it, caught up in her own troubles, which in comparison seemed minor, save for the destruction of her favorite vase. "What *did* you say?"

"I accused him of being a complete knave."

Ianthe looked judicious. "That's not so very bad."

"I also called him a lecherous wretch, and a lustful slug. And pond scum. He called me a shrew."

Perhaps it was the brandy, or her sudden sense of liberation, but Ianthe wished to laugh. "Somehow I'm not surprised."

"Nor am I." Since Ianthe seemed so comfortable, Cara tucked up her own feet. "In one tiny corner of my brain I knew Nicky had deliberately set up my bristles, because he was angry that I'd think for a moment that he would try to do what he was accused of doing, let alone with Zoë; but the rest of my brain was consumed by a ferocious rage." Despite her melancholy, she smiled. "Baron Fitzrichard said Nicky was a loose fish. What's that you're pouring into your tea?"

Ianthe passed the brandy decanter. "Baron Fitzrichard was witness to all this?"

Cara poured a liberal splash of brandy into her cup, and set the decanter down on the table. "Oh, yes. By that time, I had already broken a ewer, and kicked a suit of armor, and flung a book into the fire at that point."

"A suit of armor?"

"Ferdinand stands in the corner of the bedroom. Ianthe, it is the most amazing old house."

"You were in Lord Mannering's bedroom."

And not for the first time. "Well, that's where *he* was. It appears that he has hurt his back. Baron Fitzrichard was also there, so it isn't as if I wasn't chaperoned."

As if a Loversall would care about such stuff! Ianthe gave her cousin a chiding glance. Cara added, "And then Nicky said it would take more than *I* could offer to satisfy his salacious appetites."

Ianthe was fascinated. "And then?"

"And then I threw the fireplace poker at him, and called him a rake-helly imbecile, and punched him in the jaw!"

Ianthe fell back in her chair. "Oh, my!"

"Just so." Cara stared into her teacup. Daisy laid her head in her mistress's lap. A teardrop splashed onto the dog's head.

Ianthe held out a second handkerchief. "Cara, why did you marry Norwood?"

Cara blew her nose. "Need you ask? To begin with, we have Great-Aunt Amelia and Grandmother Sophie, Great-Great-Great Grandmother Alyce and Third-Cousin Ermyntrude. Then there are Francesca and Gwyneth and Leda and Ariadne. Not to mention Romola and Odo and Casimir!"

"Drusilla," added Ianthe. "And don't forget Maria-Louise, who became so incensed with her husband for not coming home at night that she locked him in his own wine cellar and swallowed the key. In short, you were afraid."

Cara studied her teacup. "Perhaps. And then Lucasta Clitheroe told me that she and Nicky had been having an *affaire* at the same time he was pledging eternal devotion to me."

"Gracious! He pledged eternal devotion, Cara? Truly?"

"Truly, I don't recall exactly what was said, but it was heady stuff." Cara remembered what had been said afterward clearly enough, and it had been remarkably similar to what she had said early that very morning, with the substitution of "maw-worm" for "pond scum." Although she hadn't hurled a fireplace poker on the previous occasion. Cara dropped her face into her hands.

Suddenly Ianthe wished for no more brandy. "So it was Mannering even then."

"It's always been Mannering. And I am very much afraid that it always will be."

"Then there's only one thing to do," Ianthe said gently. "You must apologize."

Cara raised her head. "That's all well and good, but it doesn't solve the problem of Zoë. What if Nicky *does* want her?"

"No man with a grain of sense would want her!" retorted Ianthe. "She must have taken him by surprise."

"Nonetheless she is still betrothed to him."

"My dear," murmured Ianthe. "One muddle at a time."

There came a tapping at the door, and Widdle stepped into the room. "Squire Anderley," he announced. Daisy sprang to attention. The butler took a backward step.

"Daisy, no!" Ianthe said sternly, as Cara looked around the room in search of a hiding place. "You have already done enough damage for one day. Widdle, where have you put the squire?"

Widdle had gained a fair notion of how things worked in this household, and didn't think Lady Norwood much cared for Squire Anderley, who hadn't been inclined to offer a gratuity today, as result of which he'd left his squireship cooling his heels in the front hall. In point of fact, Widdle took considerable pleasure in leaving all manner of people cooling their heels in the front hallway, as discovered earlier by Lord Mannering.

"A pity," mused Ianthe, "that Zoë didn't try and play off her tricks on your squire."

"He's not *my* squire!" Cara untangled herself quickly from her skirts and the chair. "You talk to him, Ianthe! Tell him I have gone shopping, or taken to my bed with a fatal fever, or anything you like!"

Ianthe couldn't look at Squire Anderley without thinking of the ceremony in which the huntsmaster smeared the blood of the quarry onto the cheek of a newly initiated hunt follower. No wonder Cara wished to run away. "Where are you going?" she inquired.

Cara shook out her skirts. "To apologize."

Ianthe snatched up the brandy decanter and hid it behind her chair. "Don't forget your tree."

16

Lord Mannering was awakened from a fretful slumber by a commotion in the hallway. He opened one wary eye to see Lady Norwood walk into the room. Flanking her were his servants, both of whom looked wary, and an orange-speckled dog. At the sight of him, Daisy woofed and wagged her tail. "Keep that creature away from me," he said, and scooted, painfully, to the far side of the bed.

Cara paused on the threshold. This would all be simpler if the marquess wore something other than a sheet. A sheet, moreover, which had slipped down around his lean hips. She forced her gaze back to his face. "I have hold of her collar, as you would see if you cared to look. Daisy has come to apologize." She paused. He waited. "Oh, very well! As have I. I had to swear to Mary that I wouldn't hit you again before she let me through the door."

The maidservant looked embarrassed, but resolute. As did Jacob, who said, "The lady returned the Sophora japonica. Shall I take it to the conservatory, my lord?"

Since it appeared no mayhem was to be enacted on his person in the immediate future, Nick edged back across the bed, an act which not only angered his un-

happy back, but also further discomposed his sheet, as
he was well aware. Cara was equally aware, judging
from the effort she appeared to experience keeping her
gaze where it belonged. "Do nothing with the tree just
yet. The lady has a habit of changing her mind. Would
you care for tea, Lady Norwood? Sherry? I would offer
to share my laudanum, but I appear to have drunk it
all."

That would explain his somewhat rakish aspect.
Laudanum, and the sheet which came close to covering nothing that it should. Not that Cara hadn't
already seen that nothing, although it was unfair to
call it nothing when it was something indeed. And not
only had she seen it, she had touched it, and felt it,
and—

Goodness, but the room was warm. Naturally,
Nicky wouldn't notice; the damned man had precious
little on.

He was watching her, somewhat smugly. "Ah—
Thank you, no sheet. That is, no tea!"

She looked mouth-watering, as always, even with her
hair ruthlessly subdued into coils and braids, and her
bosom in a pale blue dress. "That will be all, Mary,
Jacob. I don't believe the lady has any murderous intent." Cara frowned, and he added, "Of course, I could
be wrong. No, it's all right, Mary! I spoke in jest. You
may leave us alone." The door closed behind the servants, and Nick eyed Cara. "I *did* speak in jest, I trust?"

Cara approached the bed, Daisy's collar still firmly
in hand. "Cousin Fenella shot her lover, then herself.
I merely brought back your tree."

Nick knew better than to say he had expected her.
Warily, he looked to see if she had also brought a gun.

"Boorish knave? Lecherous wretch? Although I believe you hit your peak with 'lustful slug.'"

Cara cleared her throat. "I may have been a little carried away by the violence of my feelings, perhaps."

"A little?" Nick touched his sore jaw.

"Very well, a lot! I apologize for hitting you." Cara looked around the room, but saw no sign of the earlier destruction. "And for breaking your ewer, and your vase."

Nick was not feeling especially magnanimous. He folded his arms across his chest. "And for burning my book of Elizabethan riddles? Not to mention denting poor Ferdinand."

Cara glanced guiltily at the suit of armor. Nicky was still angry with her, and she could hardly blame him. "I'm also sorry I called you an imbecile," she murmured.

A faithless, rake-helly imbecile, if Nick recalled correctly, and he was certain that he did. "I don't think," he retorted, "that I'm sorry I called you a shrew."

She returned her brooding gaze to him. "You're not going to make this easy, are you?"

"Is there some reason why I should?"

"Why *did* you come to the house?"

"I wished to speak to your brother."

Cara could no longer bear the sight of all that splendid flesh. "Sit!" she said to Daisy, and to her tormentor, "Why?"

Nick watched her wander aimlessly around the chamber. She paused to touch the backgammon board. He hoped she wouldn't take it in her head to throw it at him. "I fear that's a moot point now."

Cara moved away from the backgammon set, lest she succumb to an impulse to damage him with it. "*Did* you have your hand down Zoë's dress? If you didn't, you might as well have, because she is a prattle box."

"I didn't *want* to have my hand anywhere near the dratted chit." Nick gazed without favor on Daisy, who was lying on the hearth. "That blasted hound made it impossible for me to escape. You needn't point out that a gentleman wouldn't tattle on a lady. Your niece is no lady." He moved, and winced. "And it's becoming more and more clear that I am no gentleman."

Having maligned the marquess to the best of her ability, Cara now felt the need to play devil's advocate. She moved closer to the bed. "If you weren't a gentleman, you wouldn't have agreed to marry her. She truly did try to seduce you, didn't she?"

Nick looked up at her lovely face. Cara's expression was utterly serious, as if she placed a great deal of importance on his words. "Your niece hasn't the least notion of what seduction is. However, she *has* been practicing kissing, in case you want to know. Not that she's very good at it." His gaze lingered on her lips. "Not a fraction as good as you are."

Lady Norwood didn't trust this change of mood. Mistrust didn't stop her, however, from sitting down on the bed. "Is that the truth, Nicky?"

"Truth is what one believes at the moment. What do *you* believe, Cara?"

Cara didn't know what she believed. "You're bruised," she said, and touched his cheek.

"Bruises aren't the least of it," retorted Lord Mannering, and brushed his lips against her fingers.

"Are you hurt so very badly?"

"I am." Neither of them was talking about bruises, he thought, as he moved his mouth to her wrist.

Cara touched her fingers to his other bruise. "I fear

I displayed an unbecoming tendency toward temper, my lord."

He drew her closer. "Tumultuous passions," he murmured, against her throat.

"A dreadful lack of self-control," she whispered. "The family has a tendency toward melodrama, alas. And remarkable wrong-headedness."

Nick's skilled fingers worked the buttons of her dress. "And to enjoy the pleasures of the flesh."

He pushed the gown aside. His lips were warm against her throat, her shoulder, the hollow of her neck. Cara was ablaze with sensation. Disjointed fragments drifted through her brain. *Creatures of the senses . . . Love unwisely and too well . . . Tormented by unrequited love . . .*

Nick drew back, and broke the mood. "I may never leave this room again. Perhaps your niece wouldn't wish to have a bedridden spouse."

Zoë wouldn't mind at all if she'd ever shared a bed with Nicky. "Turn over," Cara said, and reached for the jar of basalm on the bedside table.

Nick was nothing loath. He rolled over on his belly—not without a groan—and the sheet slid lower still. Cara feasted her eyes upon that mouthwatering expanse of muscular male back, and took refuge in the familiar obfuscation. "It is a common belief in Gloucestershire that wood and coal ashes applied after lawn-mowing will kill caterpillars and slugs. The combination is particularly efficacious if well watered with the contents of a chamber pot."

Nick wondered first if Cara intended to smear him with wood and coal ashes, and secondly if the chamber pot was tucked safely out of reach. Cara dipped her fingers into the ointment, and began to rub, and kept to herself the additional snippet that in Gloucestershire, parsley wine was esteemed as a powerful aphrodisiac.

Parsley be damned, one only needed the sight of an almost-naked Nicky. Cara stroked her hands over his back. His skin was warm and smooth and spicy-smelling, although the latter was only a memory, because the scent of camphor was heavy in the air. *Concentrate,* she told herself, as her hands slid smoothly over his skin, applying light pressure here, and heavier pressure there, making light, slow, circular motions with her fingertips, or a heavier motion with the heel of her hand. The trapezius received her attentions first, the broad triangular muscle that lay just below the skin, covering the upper back, part of the neck, and the shoulders; then the levator scapula, the rhomboids, the latissimus dorsi and the external obliques; and the erector spinae, or sacrospinalis, those several combined muscles that ran from the neck to the small of the back.

Nick groaned with pleasure as she ran her fingers over and between his ribs, then rubbed with the heel of her hand. "Where did you learn to do that?"

"Norwood." Cara pressed a gentle fingertip into an abused muscle, moved her fingers in tiny circles over the spot.

Norwood had been of an advanced age when he might expect to get a little stiff. Although Nick was a little stiff himself, and he was nowhere near Norwood's age. Uncomfortable as it was, he was glad he lay facedown. Cara was paying particular attention to his gluteus maximus. He moaned.

Cara recalled herself to her business, which was not stroking the marquess's exceedingly fine rump. "A pre-ride massage will help your horse limber up;

a post-ride rubdown will help restore muscles that may have been abused. My mare gets the most absurd expressions when I find her pleasure spot."

She'd found his pleasure spot, and he was going to react in an absurd fashion also if she didn't stop. Nick reached up and caught her hand. She frowned. "Am I hurting you?"

"More than you can imagine." Nick pulled her down beside him. When she halfheartedly protested, he rolled her under him, imprisoning her hands above her head. "A forfeit is required, I think."

Cara was incapable of further objection. The heat of his body seared through her layers of clothing. His strong and very hard body. She couldn't have spoken at that moment to save her life. At that moment, she didn't *wish* to save her life. Smiling slightly, he lowered his lips to hers.

Several moments later—how many Cara couldn't say, but her bodice was thoroughly unbuttoned, and her hair as thoroughly unpinned—Nick released her and leaned back on his pillows. "You *do* kiss better than your niece. I don't suppose you'd allow me to set you up in a little house somewhere?"

"Like you intended for Zoë? Don't provoke me, Nicky, lest I damage your lovely backgammon board. Come back and finish what you started, you wretch."

He propped himself up on one elbow and regarded her. "No," he said.

She stared at him. "*No?* Nicky, are you mad?"

Cara's bristles may have subsided, but Nick's were far from lying flat. "Yes, I'm mad. Furious. Incensed. You *might* have thought it a damned odd thing that I made love to you in one hour and betrothed myself to your niece in the next!"

She burned, she throbbed, she ached. She threw a pillow at him. "Nicky, you are a beast!"

"Are you in affliction, darling? Alas, despite your low opinion of me, I cannot slake my salacious appetites with you while I am betrothed to someone else." He looked diabolic. "It would be *dishonorable*."

Cara eyed him askance. He added, "Lucasta Clitheroe? I didn't, and we weren't. Although I wished to be. You were shilly-shallying."

So he had insisted at the time, and she hadn't believed him. Yes, and why should she believe him now? Cara perceived a pattern. Nick had seduced her, and at the same time amused himself with Lucasta Clitheroe. Now he had seduced her again, and betrothed himself to Zoë. To complete her chagrin, he said, "You see, I *am* capable of resisting a woman who wants me."

She might well have throttled him, or wept with vexation, or screamed until she was purple in the face; definitely she would have damaged him had he not grasped her arms. "The devil fly away with you!" she snapped.

The wretch smiled at her. "We begin to understand one another better, I think. And if you hit me again, I swear I'll hit you back!"

Cara might have done so nonetheless, had not the door flown open. Daisy leapt up from the hearth. Cara scrambled into the corner of the bed, behind the velvet draperies, and tried to restore order to her dress.

Zoë burst into the room, followed by Mary and Jacob and another manservant, whom Nick recognized as his valet. "I'm that sorry, my lord, she was threatening to go to your club. I thought you'd rather she came here. She *says* that she's your fiancée."

Lord Mannering wished that his fiancée had gone to Hades. She was simultaneously pouting, trying to move out of range of the servants, and looking curiously around the room. "Where did you find her?"

The valet dripped disapproval. "She called in Bedford Square. We bundled her off before she could make more of a rumpus. Few of the servants saw her there."

Nick wondered if his faithful valet might be persuaded to bundle up the young woman and toss her into the river. "James, you are a treasure. Remind me to increase your wage."

Zoë stomped her foot. "I don't see why everyone is making such a fuss because I wish to inquire about my fiancé's health. What a strange room this is! What's that awful smell? Is that a suit of armor? What an ugly bed!" She walked closer to it. "Why, Lord Mannering, you aren't wearing any clothes!"

The marquess disliked the look in his fiancée's eye. "No!" he said, and yanked the sheet up to his chin. On hearing that stern tone, Daisy—who had all this while been trying to get Zoë's attention—sat down on her skirt.

Zoë looked down at the setter, which she had noticed in a peripheral fashion, because she was accustomed to the creature's jumps and barks. About Daisy in this setting, however, there was something very queer. Whatever was she doing here?

Again, Zoë glanced at the ugly bed. Rumpled sheets, half-naked marquess—

Zoë was not short of understanding. Her fiancé had not rumpled those sheets all by himself. No timorous maiden, she marched toward the bed, and grabbed hold of the velvet drapery, and twitched it aside. Her jaw dropped open at sight of her aunt scrunched up in a corner, disheveled and not entirely dressed. Cara looked embarrassed. The marquess looked as if he was trying not to laugh.

What there was to laugh about in such a moment, Zoë couldn't begin to imagine. "You betrayed me!" she yelled.

"Alas, you have found me out," said Lord Mannering, with a wonderfully wicked sneer. "I am a vile seducer. Your aunt will tell you so." He grasped Cara's wrist and pulled her across the bed toward him. "*Won't* you, my pet?"

17

A vile seducer? Lord Mannering? Zoë stared. Granted, he was handling Cara in a very familiar manner, dragging her across the bed and up against his pillows, but still—

Cara shot the marquess a stern look, not without difficulty, because he held her so close, and proximity to Nicky, as has already been demonstrated, wreaked havoc with the workings of her otherwise excellent mind. She did recall, however, that she had been brought to London with a purpose other than snuggling with Nicky. "What are you doing here, Zoë? For a young woman to visit a gentleman in his lodging is a truly shocking thing."

"Really!" The ribbons on Zoë's pretty bonnet fluttered, and the roses trembled. "And for an *old* woman it is not? Better that I should ask what *you* are doing here? And with my fiancé!"

Understandable, if regrettable, that Zoë should be in a tweak. Cara tried to adjust her bodice, which had gotten disarranged again in her slide across the sheets. "This isn't what it seems."

"What a clanker!" Zoë clucked disapprovingly as Lord Mannering prevented Cara's further struggles with her uncooperative bodice by clamping his hand around her wrist. "You must think that I'm a flat. There's nothing wrong with my eyes! I know what I see."

The marquess arched an eyebrow. "Ah, but appearances can be deceiving, can they not?"

A hit, a palpable hit, but to say that Zoë experienced a twinge of remorse would be to overstate the case. However, she did wrinkle her pretty nose. "You had your hand down the bosom of my dress!"

"Perhaps, but I'm not the one who put it there."

"Lawks!" breathed Mary, recalling Nick to the presence of his owl-eyed servants. He sent all three of them off to fetch some tea. "Since you were kind enough to inquire, Miss Loversall, I feel like the very devil. It is uncertain if I will ever walk again. Now that you have ascertained the state of my health, perhaps you will go away. And take that dog with you!" Guiltily, Daisy slunk back to the hearth.

Lord Mannering *looked* like the devil, not ill but diabolical. And Zoë's aunt looked devilishly comfortable, cuddled up against him like that. Cara's bodice was clearly unbuttoned—she could barely keep it on her shoulders—and her hair was as tousled and tangled as if it had never seen a brush. "Whether you can walk or not, my lord, it is evident that you are well enough to engage in certain other activities!" There was a marked dearth of breakable items in the chamber. Zoë eyed the backgammon board.

"Touch that board and you risk your life," said the marquess. He sounded as though he meant every word.

Zoë picked up the brightly colored fan instead, and wondered what such a thing was doing in a gentleman's bedroom, a question her aunt might have answered, though not without giggling. "I have a very delicate constitution, and this outrage must surely be a great shock to my heart." Languidly, she fanned herself. "Perhaps I may even swoon."

"If you must," said the marquess. "Do it by the hearth, where you can't damage anything."

Zoë straightened—it wasn't very *comfortable* to wilt—and gazed sternly at the figures on the bed. Lord Mannering looked as comfortable as any oriental pasha with one of his houris clutched to his side. "I think very poorly of you, my lord!"

Why did that not surprise him? Nick might have been more annoyed about the low esteem in which so many people seemed to hold him had not Cara been pressed up as close against him as if she wished to crawl inside and hide. "Why, I wonder, should you think I care?"

"Insufferable!" Zoë gasped, and took a turn about the chamber, much as her aunt had done before her, although without the resultant breakage, and uttering such dramatic phrases as, "I won't trust myself to ex- ➝press," and "Things have come to a sorry pass," and "I do think it very hard," a phrase that caused Cara to snicker, despite her embarrassment.

"Brava! A performance worthy of Mrs. Siddons," said Lord Mannering, when he had listened to as much nonsense as he could tolerate, "fleshpots" having been the deciding word. "Now, if you can stop emoting for a moment, perhaps we might put our heads together and discover some way out of this predicament."

"It is more than a predicament!" Zoë put her hands on her slender hips. "You are supposed to seduce me, Lord Mannering, and here I find you seducing my Aunt Cara instead. You should be ashamed."

Nick regarded her with the interest he might have accorded a particularly repulsive insect. "Why is that?"

"It should be obvious! Unless you are so great a rogue that you don't care if Aunt Cara gets her heart broken and sinks into a decline, which very well might prove fatal at her age. Because I must tell you, my lord, that though I mean to be an understanding sort of wife—after all, I shall be having *affaires* of my own—I do not intend that you should have an *affaire* with my own aunt!"

Cara might well have spoken, had not Nick put a hand behind her head and pressed her face back down against his chest. "Too late. And whatever sort of wife you make—which I suspect will be dreadful— you won't be mine, so I don't care."

Zoë wafted the fan. "Don't be absurd, my lord. Of course you're going to marry me. You haven't any choice."

Cara struggled. Nick held her all the tighter. "You really are a limb of Satan, aren't you, Zoë? If you start shrieking again, I shall have you thrown out of the house, so you had much better not."

Zoë opened her mouth and closed it, and opened it again. "You cannot mean that you prefer Aunt Cara! You said I was the most beautiful damsel in all of England! I remember it quite well."

The marquess recalled what his life had been before Cara had returned to town, his days filled with the usual gentlemanly pursuits, as were his evenings, all uniformly pleasant and unprovocative—and bland. "Your aunt is no longer a damsel, for which I am immensely grateful, and I prefer her above anyone of any age, even when she's angry with me, as she is at the moment. Will you behave yourself, *cara,* if I let you go?"

Cara nodded. He allowed her to raise her head. However, he still held her against his side, so that she couldn't scoot off the bed.

Not that she wanted to go anywhere. Nicky's hand was soothing, and his body warm. His gorgeous, almost naked body. He was behaving outrageously. Cara hoped he knew what he was about. "So," said the marquess. "You see why this farce of a betrothal must come to an end."

Zoë saw nothing of the sort. Now more than ever she meant to crush Lord Mannering's black heart beneath her heel. "You'll forget about Aunt Cara soon enough, once you're married to me. And then she will wither away like Cousin Ianthe, which will serve her right."

Since she was prevented from removing herself to a safer distance by Nick's strong arm, and since he had just said such very nice things about her, even if they *had* been said merely in an effort to put off Zoë, Cara relaxed back against his broad chest. "I left Ianthe entertaining Squire Anderley and drinking brandy and planning to remove to Bath or Brighton. I think she's got over her broken heart. *And* she refuses to plan your wedding, and I certainly won't, so you and Beau are on your own."

Zoë frowned. "Beau doesn't know anything about weddings."

"Except how to avoid them," observed Nick.

Zoë had wanted St. George's, Hanover Square, but she was an adaptable miss. "Very well, we'll be wed by special license, then. Or even better yet, elope! And we will do it soon, before you make any further assault on Aunt Cara's virtue!"

Cara roused from the blissful stupor induced by Nicky's lazy fingers drawing circles on her arm. "If I don't give a fig about my virtue, I don't see why anyone else should, particularly since that horse has long since left the gate."

A Loversall was seldom shocked, but Zoë was so much so at that moment that she plopped down on the bed. "No virtue?" she gasped.

"None." Cara snapped her fingers. "Gone. Poof. Like a dandelion in the wind."

Zoë was impressed. "You've only just come to town!"

Nick smiled. "It doesn't take long."

They were interrupted at this juncture by Mary with the tea tray—a task the male servants decided she could handle on her own, although she had promised to report back to them each and every detail of what was going on. It quickly being established that Lord Mannering was either unable to leave his bed, or in no mood to do so, and additionally that he wasn't willing to let Lady Norwood do so either, the tray was set down carefully on the counterpane. Nick would have preferred brandy to tea, but had been told that he may not have it, and so Mary thoughtfully fetched some more of the laudanum draught. Since Zoë felt in need of refreshment, and Daisy in need of company, all four ended up snug as bugs in the great carved bed—or like a pasha surrounded by two houris and a hound.

Zoë's desire to pitch a fit was temporarily superseded by her amazement regarding her aunt's behavior. She leaned against a carved bedpost. "I know we Loversalls are victims of our tumultuous passions, but this seems a little *fast*."

Nick lifted one of Cara's hands to his lips and gazed soulfully at her. "You refer to the abruptness of our, ah, connection. A mere moment can seem a lifetime when one is in the grasp of a fatal passion."

Cara gazed soulfully back at him. "Ah, but what signifies a lifetime when one's senses are overwhelmed?"

Zoë munched on a biscuit and pondered the queer circumstance that Lord Mannering was looking at her aunt the way she'd wished him to look at her. "Isn't it unusual that a gentleman should have a fan in his bedroom?"

Cara smiled. Lord Mannering looked wolfish. "Not at all," he said.

Zoë dropped her gaze to the fan, and contemplated the many uses to which such a thing might be put. Daisy crawled closer and poked at it with her nose.

"No!" said Nick, and reached for the fan, and groaned from the resultant pain. Cara placed her hand on his bare back and rubbed. He purred.

It was a very nice bare back, as Zoë had already noted, as was his front, not that she had viewed a great number of nude male torsos, but she was sufficiently her father's daughter to appreciate the aesthetics of the thing. "I am still willing to walk on you, my lord. Beau says I have gifted feet."

"No!" snapped Cara, wearied with the game. "Keep your feet right where they are. Just so you know it, Zoë, I'm not going to let you marry Nicky even if I have to elope with him myself!"

The marquess looked intrigued. "*Would* you elope with me?"

"No!" said Zoë. "Because then you would abandon

her and break her heart, because it's clear to me now, my lord, that you are a swine!"

"Swine," mused Nick. "There's a new one for the list."

Zoë was still ruminating. "You must have known Aunt Cara before, because even a female of our family wouldn't give her all so quickly as this."

As Cara recalled, it hadn't taken her very long to give her all after she'd first set eyes on Nicky. She glanced at him. He winked.

Zoë tsk'd. "But then you came upon me alone in the front hallway, and couldn't help yourself, and made a dead-set at me, which was a very shabby thing to do. Don't elope with him, Aunt Cara. He'll just cast you aside."

Perhaps it was the laudanum that made this conversation so damned difficult to follow. "Why should you think I would cast Cara aside?"

Zoë knew what she knew. This *was* the same man who had accosted her in Papa's front hall. Or allowed her to accost him, which was practically the same thing. Although she had to regard her aunt with a new respect, for thinking about a thing (as Zoë had), and doing it (as Cara *clearly* had), were two entirely different things. "I shan't allow you to be cruel to Aunt Cara. It's perfectly all right if you're cruel to *me*, because I don't care. I was going to break your heart anyway."

Lord Mannering looked sardonic. "You were."

"I was." Zoë rubbed against the carved bedpost, which made an excellent back-scratcher. "And I probably still will, so you shouldn't fall in love with me, because I wish to have a child someday, and you are—"

"Too old." Nick picked up the fan and trailed it

along Cara's arm, which gave Zoë a notion of what else he might have done with it, the naughty man. A less self-centered miss might have found herself embarrassingly *de trop*. Zoë merely nibbled on a scone.

The laudanum was working its magic. As was the realization that Cara hadn't removed herself from the bed, though she could have done so easily enough, had she truly tried. The marquess decided he *would* be able to engage in amorous congress again, aches and pains be damned. But first he must manage to get himself unbetrothed, because he had been so cockle-brained as to tell Cara that he wouldn't quench his appetites with her while he was betrothed to another, and if he didn't quench said appetites soon, he would surely go mad; and were he to go mad, she would say he deserved it for the way he had treated her earlier, which had indeed been shabby, not to mention cockle-brained. He didn't doubt for an instant she would have her revenge.

Nick wound a tendril of Cara's hair around his finger and wondered what form that revenge might take. Perhaps she would tie him to the bed and torture him with the fan. She glanced quizzically at him as he groaned.

Poor Aunt Cara! She was smiling at the marquess in a positively addled fashion, although every damsel learned from the cradle the folly of exposing her heart on her sleeve. Aunt Cara had exposed a great deal more than her heart, as anyone with half an eye could see. Clandestine meetings, assignations—but when had there been an opportunity for matters to progress so far?

Oho! All those headaches. Zoë's eyes narrowed as she filed this information away. "Lord Mannering is your True Love! This changes everything.

Poor Aunt Cara. For your True Love to turn out to be such a—a—"

"Slug," supplied Lord Mannering. "Toad. Maw-worm."

Cara winced. He had remembered. "What makes you think that Lord Mannering is my True Love?" she inquired, thus distracting the marquess from his musing about which amatory position might be most suitable for a gentleman with a damaged back.

"Why else would you have married Norwood?" Zoë said reasonably. "Unless you were in love with someone else? I'm glad to have the business explained. Although I don't suppose you would wish me to tell that to the people who keep asking me."

"I would much prefer that you did not." Cara refused to look at Nick, who took her hand nonetheless and raised it to his lips.

"I don't think you should do that," Zoë said sternly. "It's me you're going to marry, if you will recall."

The marquess frowned at her over Cara's finger-tips. "You really are the most tiresome chit. The truth is, I don't even like you much."

"Oh!" Zoë clasped her hands to her breast, not the wisest of reactions, since she was still clutching the scone, and consequently smeared crumbs and butter all over her carriage dress, as well as her white collar. After Daisy leapt up to lend her assistance, not even the pink roses and ribbons on Zoë's bonnet remained unscathed.

Zoë took off that item and set it on the floor, out of the dog's sight. "Are you saying that you *didn't* come to my papa's house to make me an offer, my lord?"

Nick had certainly tried to say so, several times. "I did not."

"But you said—"

"I *said* I wished to speak with your father. I didn't say what about."

Zoë watched as Lord Mannering pressed his lips to Cara's fingers, and she raised her other hand to touch his bruised cheek, and leapt to a conclusion that might have smote her sooner, had she not been so self-involved and young: Zoë hadn't been able to engage the marquess's heart because it had already been engaged elsewhere. "It was all a sham, wasn't it? You only pretended to be interested in me, Lord Mannering, so that Beau would bully Aunt Cara into coming to town."

The marquess glanced at her. "Well, yes."

A terrible blow to a damsel's pride to find out in so rude a manner that her fiancé preferred someone else. Zoë snatched up the fan and fluttered it. "You needn't think that I shall fall into the dumps!"

"Nothing so extreme," soothed Nick. "You are merely going to decide that we wouldn't suit, and cry off."

Wouldn't suit? The most elusive bachelor in London wouldn't suit her? A marquess, to boot? No one would believe such a silly thing. Besides, Zoë wasn't entirely convinced that she wished to cry off, and thereby forfeit her chance of becoming a marchioness.

Lord Mannering and her aunt were still making sheep's eyes at each other, which was hardly what Zoë had anticipated regarding the Experiencing of Life. She consoled herself that any step along life's pathway was probably better than none. Even if it meant she had to temporarily give up her dream of being wed in St. George's, Hanover Square. "I've made a muddle, haven't I?" She sighed.

Zoë was at her most appealing in this rare moment

of self-doubt. Cara leaned forward to touch her hand. Even Nick regarded her with slightly less disfavor. "You didn't make a muddle all by yourself. I *am* guilty of using you in an attempt to lure your aunt to town. Since you've made no secret of your opinion that I'm bordering on decrepitude, no one will think it odd of you to cry off."

Zoë wondered if the marquess *was* in his dotage. It would explain many things. "I can't cry off now, for the whole world knows we were caught in a compromising situation, and I don't wish to look like bachelor's fare, thank you very much! Not that *I* care about such stuff, but you may be sure Beau does. He has become positively prudish of late!" She pushed away Daisy, who wished to lick her face. "I don't suppose you'd care to shoot each other, or drink poison, or fall upon a sword?"

"Odo, Fenella, and Drusilla," said Cara, in response to Nick's puzzled look. "And no, we would not."

A pity. Zoë had rather fancied such a dramatic end to her proposal. "Then I see nothing else for it. I shall simply tell Beau the truth, and ask him to find a way out of this coil! However, Lord Mannering, you must promise me that you will reform. Beau wouldn't wish to see Aunt Cara hurl herself off the battlements, or be eaten by a bear, because she found you in the throes of ardor with someone else." Zoë paused and looked thoughtful. "Well, Beau might not mind so much, but Cousin Ianthe almost certainly would!"

18

The various members of the Loversall household were gathered in the drawing room, Ianthe in her usual position behind the tea tray, which on this occasion held a coffee urn in Pontypool Japan, decorated with a rustic landscape featuring sheep. Cara perched on the sofa near the fireplace, and Beau lounged in a deep-seated chair, with Daisy leaning against his knee. All were watching Zoë pace the carpet, gesturing and de-claiming dramatically. "And so," she concluded, "you see that it was all a great misunderstanding! It isn't me who Lord Mannering wants, but Aunt Cara!" She clasped her hands to her bosom. "True Love will have its way!"

Beau eyed his sister. "This exceeds all belief."

Cara was growing annoyed with so many people—well, actually just two of them, if she didn't include herself—expressing surprise that the marquess should want her. "What exceeds belief?" she snapped. "That someone should think I wasn't an antidote?"

Beau recalled that his sister had a temper of her own, though thankfully not equal to his daughter's. "That's not what I meant." He looked at his daughter. "You aren't going to try and tell me Mannering didn't make you flattering overtures."

Zoë noticed a butter stain on her sleeve, and rubbed absently at it. "Well, yes, he did. But that was only because he wished for you to send for Aunt Cara to show me the error of my ways. She is *his* True Love, you see, but then she went and married Norwood."

Ah. There was one mystery explained. For a woman who loved one man to abruptly marry another made perfect sense for, and to, a Loversall. Beau turned back to Cara. "You and Mannering."

"He *did* give her the Sophora japonica," Ianthe pointed out. "A very romantic gesture, don't you think?" Beau eyed the sapling, drooping in its wooden pot before a tall window. The tree had taken a marked dislike to being dragged all about the town. "You're not planting that thing in *my* garden! It looks like something the dog dragged in," he said.

Cara thought she might plant itch-weed in her brother's garden, and train it to climb up the wall at night, and creep into his window, and invade his bed. "I wouldn't dream of it. I shall take my Sophora japonica home with me to the Cotswolds when I leave, which may be very soon!"

Beau didn't wish his sister to leave just yet. There was a wedding to plan. "No need to get on your high ropes. I was merely a bit surprised." He gazed sternly upon his daughter. "I don't know what rig you think you're running, miss, but I'm here to tell you that you shan't!"

Zoë stamped her little foot. "You're not listening, Beau, and it makes me very cross! Surely you don't wish Aunt Cara to turn out like Casimir, or Drusilla, or Odo!"

Casimir and Odo, Beau recollected. Both had been sapskulls. "Drusilla?" he inquired.

"The sword," offered Ianthe. "Such a *final* step, I've always thought. After all, one never knows what may happen on the morrow."

Beau had a notion that the morrow would prove depressingly like today, and the day before it. His little soldier—which hadn't been so little in its prime, but certainly was a sorry specimen in its current state— would march no more, alas. Yes, and why the devil was Ianthe so cheerful? It was most unlike her.

Beau needed some brandy. Where was the blasted decanter? There it sat, empty, by the coffeepot.

Empty? His good smuggled French brandy all drunk up? Beau realized then that the ladies of his household looked a little odd, and furthermore that all three were sipping coffee instead of tea. He hoped the thieves had appreciated the quality of their tipple, and wondered if they were foxed.

This suspicion was not unfounded. Although Cara's bodice was no longer buttoned crooked, thanks to Zoë, she still had a rumpled look. Zoë's carriage dress was speckled with what looked like butter stains. While Ianthe—Difficult to say exactly was different about Ianthe, save that she wasn't crying. She looked a little fuzzy around the edges somehow.

Beau was disregarding her. It made Zoë cross. She would have to try a little harder to get across her point. Perhaps he would be more understanding if he were brought to understand how shocking it had been for his daughter to find his sister in her own fiancé's bed. Delicately Zoë hinted, "Aunt Cara is no stranger to the pleasures of the flesh."

Cara blushed red as a ripe apple. "Zoë!"

Beau didn't care to know about his sister's pleasures, especially when he was currently enjoying no pleasures of his own. "I didn't bring you to town to indulge Zoë in such nonsense, Cara! I am very disappointed in you."

Dangerously, Cara's eyes sparkled. "Are you, then?"

Matters would not be advanced were Cara to throw a tantrum. "Mannering is absolutely enraptured," Ianthe interrupted. "Look at the tree."

Beau didn't want to look at the damned tree. "Never have I heard such a bag of moonshine!" he snapped. He waited for Ianthe to burst into a flood of tears, and was startled when she merely gazed at him, and shook her head.

Zoë's papa was proving to be very stubborn. She sat down on a striped stool at his feet and gazed beseechingly up at him. "I *do* wish you would pay attention, Beau! I've had the matter explained to me most clearly—as I'm trying to explain it to you, if only you would listen!—and now that I see how things are, I quite agree that the betrothal must end."

Beau turned his frown on his daughter. "Can you deny that Mannering was underneath you on the stairway, miss?"

Zoë fluttered her long lashes. "Daisy knocked us over. He just happened to be what I landed on."

Beau looked at the dog. Daisy wagged her tail. "I suppose you're going to tell me next that his hand *wasn't* in the bodice of your dress?"

Zoë squirmed. "Well, yes. But I don't think he *wanted* it to be there, so that shouldn't count."

Beau knew from experience about men's hands and damsels' breasts, which there was little sweeter than, unless it was a damsel's bottom, or perhaps her thigh. A man's hand didn't find itself in the vicinity of a damsel's breast, etcetera, without a certain amount of forethought and planning on its owner's part. The owner of the hand, that was, not the owner of the breast.

In Zoë's case, he conceded that she may have had a few forethoughts herself. "I shouldn't think he really wishes to marry me," she added. "He called me a limb of Satan, among other things."

Beau touched one of his daughter's glowing curls. "You don't really expect me to believe Mannering wished to speak to me about Cara, puss."

Zoë rubbed her cheek against his hand. "Queer in him, isn't it? We can only hope he doesn't come to repent his choice."

Beau glanced from his daughter to his sister, who was looking at him as if she wished to give him a good shake. "Whatever Mannering may be he's not such a mooncalf as all that! I can't imagine what has possessed your aunt to lend her credence to such a Canterbury tale."

Cara definitely wanted to shake her brother. First he's called her dull and drab, and now he insisted that no man would want her hand. "It's all true!" she protested. "Every word of it, and more."

More, was there? Definitely, Beau didn't want to know. "Then Mannering must be a damned rake-helly fellow, that's all I can say! You'd do much better to have your squire."

"Squire Anderley is very knowledgeable," remarked Ianthe. "He explained to me today that hounds have sterns, not tails, where a fox's tail is called a brush. Furthermore, hounds do not bark, they speak, and while they are running on the line of a fox they are said to throw tongue. It was all most interesting. I see perfectly why Cara doesn't want him. Perhaps Zoë would like to marry him instead."

"No!" said Zoë, and her father, simultaneously. Then Zoë looked thoughtful. "But perhaps *you*—"

"No," Ianthe said firmly. "I could never marry a man who murders rabbits." Beau stared at her, astonished by the notion that Ianthe might marry anyone.

"Rabbits?" echoed Cara.

"Rabbits," insisted Ianthe. "You must know how it is with gentlemen like that. First a rabbit, and then a fox, and the next thing you know they're being hanged for murdering a magistrate."

Zoë could have cared less about murdered magistrates. She fixed her papa with a gimlet eye and returned to the attack. "You said Lord Mannering is a rakehell. Surely you wouldn't wish me to marry a rakehell, Beau!"

Beau regarded his daughter with exasperation. He hadn't been born yesterday. Thought of how many yesterdays had passed since his birth, and his resultant flagging powers, not to mention his empty brandy decanter, left him further annoyed. His daughter had been compromised, with or without her cooperation, and he meant to see her safely wed, so that his life could then hopefully return to what it once had been. "I didn't say Mannering was a rakehell. I said he had behaved in a rake-helly manner, which is quite a different thing. We shall go on much better if you cease trying to flimflam me, miss!"

Zoë sprang up from the stool to again pace the floor. She picked up a two-branched fashion of Sheffield plate. "Not the candelabrum, please," Ianthe protested. "You have already broken my favorite vase."

Zoë set down the candelabrum. Beau reflected again that there was something damned queer today about his womenfolk. "I shan't change my mind, even if you break everything in the house," he said sternly, then turned to Ianthe. "Where's the wedding list?"

Ianthe lifted the coffeepot. "I threw it in the fire."

Beau looked at the fireplace, where a merry blaze was burning. "But we must have a wedding list!"

Ianthe poured coffee into her cup. "Then you may make it up yourself, because I shan't."

"Don't look at me," said Cara, as he turned to her. "I'm about to have my heart broken by this business, if you will recall."

Zoë arched her delicate eyebrows at her papa. "You know no one can read my writing! Heaven knows who might turn up were I to make out the list." She looked thoughtful. "Maybe even the Prince of Wales."

Beau stared at the women. They stared back at him. Beau was unaccustomed to being the focus of such unified feminine opprobrium, though he might well have expected it from his mistresses, were they ever to meet.

He didn't crumble under the weight of the ladies' disapproval, nor did he even quail, but instead got up from the chair. "You'll marry Mannering and there's an end to it!" Daisy rose also, and trailed after him toward the door.

"Papa!" Looking her most woeful, Zoë clutched at his arm. Without the merest glance, Beau brushed her aside. She stepped back, tripped over Daisy, and sat down abruptly on her *derrière*. Zoë shrieked. Beau fled. He knew damned well there was some good smuggled French brandy at his club.

The door slammed shut behind him. Zoë flopped on her back, still wailing, and drummed her heels and fists on the floor. Daisy licked her face. Ianthe set down the coffeepot. "Damnation!" Cara said.

Zoë pushed Daisy off her and sat up. "That certainly went well. Do you know, I may be young and selfish and wrapped up in my own concerns, but it occurs to me that Beau seems a little preoccupied."

Ianthe and Cara exchanged glances. Zoë scowled at them. "Did you think I wasn't listening? I am hardly deaf. 'Vain' and 'spoilt' and 'shameless' come to mind. For a start."

Best Zoë was distracted before she got to brooding on this topic. "Your father has good reason to be preoccupied," pointed out Ianthe.

Zoë snorted, delicately, and climbed to her feet. "If it was *me* he was preoccupied about, he would have paid more attention to my feelings, which is hardly the case. No, Beau must be thinking about something of monstrous importance, perhaps to do with government, or the ongoing hostilities with the French, for he wouldn't otherwise be so cruel to his only chick!"

"If your father had paid *less* attention to his only chick in the past, we might not now find ourselves in this pickle," retorted Cara. She broke off, "pickle" having put her in mind of a certain largely naked marquess, who had treated her abominably. She was looking forward very much to treating him abominably in turn, to taking him to the height of passion and leaving him dangling there while she took a stroll around the block. Perhaps to prevent him from following her, she would tie him to the bedposts. Although, were Nicky tied to the bedposts, it was highly unlikely that she would be going anywhere. To have that magnificent body vulnerable to mistreatment from her hands, her lips, the feather fan—

Daisy wandered over to Ianthe, and flopped down in front of her chair. Ianthe rested her feet on the setter's back. She couldn't think where her slippers had gotten to. Not that she particularly cared. "We must think of something else."

"You *might* think of my position!" sulked Zoë. "I appeared so clever as to have brought Mannering up to scratch. To cry off now——I shall look like the worst nitwit. And you needn't point out that I have brought this upon myself, because I am very aware of it!"

Valiantly, Ianthe refrained from comment. Zoë dropped down beside her on the sofa. "I didn't wish to marry anyone! At least, not yet! Oh, I *did* think it would be nice to be a marchioness, but not if it breaks Aunt Cara's heart. No, and so I shan't, even though Beau drags me to the altar, because he can't force me to speak." She nibbled on her thumbnail. "Or maybe he can, because I don't like being locked up in my room. Maybe I'll wed Lord Mannering, and then run off with someone else. After I've had the wedding night, of course, because there's no point in missing that. I *was* thinking of having an *affaire de coeur* with Lord Mannering, after all, although I didn't anticipate marrying him." Gustily, she sighed. "It is a great pity! I would make a lovely bride."

Cara was distracted from contemplation of what torture she might inflict upon Lord Mannering. "How long has it been since someone boxed your pretty ears?"

Zoë grinned. "That got your attention! I understand that you are positively betwattled, Aunt Cara, but pray try and concentrate. Cousin Ianthe is right. Since Beau has proven himself immune to reason, we must put our heads together and *think!*"

19

"I wouldn't wish to be accused of vulgar curiosity."
Fitz raised his quizzing glass. "But *both* of them?
There? In that very bed?"

Lord Mannering was in the process of tying his cravat, his chin pointed toward the ceiling, while James
stood at the ready, holding a spare length of starched
white cloth. "You forgot the dog."

Fitz stared at the great carved bed. "I knew I
shouldn't have left."

Nick lowered his chin. "Ah. You are suggesting a
ménage à cinq. I didn't realize you favored that sort
of thing."

"I ain't suggesting anything of the sort. Don't try
and change the subject." Fitz turned the quizzing
glass on his friend. "You look like the devil, Nicky, if
you don't mind me saying so."

If the marquess didn't mind, his valet felt otherwise. James had already shaved his master and
brushed his hair, persuaded him into fresh body linen,
breeches and waistcoat. Nothing could be done to
dispel the aroma of camphor that clung to his person,
alas, save to plunge him into a hip bath, a venture
that, considering the condition of his poor back, it
was unlikely either of them would survive. The valet's

lip trembled. "Shame on you, Fitz," said Nick. "You've upset James."

The baron was stricken with remorse. He knew, none better, the value of a good valet, his own incomparable Françoise having made no small contribution to the vision that was Fitz this afternoon. His chin was smoothly shaven now, if not his upper lip, the growth there at this stage in its evolution rather resembling a fuzzy caterpillar; the rest of him clad nattily in a purple coat with large plated buttons, a chequered waistcoat, kerseymere inexpressibles, gleaming boots, and a stunningly violet cravat. "No offense, James! You're a dashed good fellow, and I'm sure no one could have made Nicky look better than you have! It's the little Loversall as is responsible for him not being able to stand up straight, and Lady Norwood for the bruises on his face."

"I can too stand up straight," said the marquess, and attempted to, and groaned.

Fitz had had the foresight to bring along his vinaigrette. He uncapped the bottle and waved it under his friend's nose. "You don't have to do this."

Lord Mannering pushed away the bottle. "Yes, I do. My blasted fiancée was going to explain everything to her papa, and ask him for his advice. Therefore, we are going to the Park, and discover what she accomplished, if anything at all."

As well as set tongues to wagging, thought Fitz, especially if Lady Norwood was also present to punch the marquess, or whatever else she'd done to inspire the besotted expression that occasionally crossed his face. Fitz glanced at the suit of armor that stood in the corner. What amazing things Ferdinand must have seen not only in the past few hours, but during his lifetime. Although perhaps "lifetime" was not the right word.

As Fitz was thus speculating, James assisted his master to don an excellently tailored dark green coat, designed to fit its owner like a glove. Since the garment's owner was at the moment none too supple, by the time the jacket was smoothed across his broad shoulders, both he and his valet were perspiring gently, and Nick was as white as his bedsheets.

"You don't—" Fitz said again.

"Yes, I do!" snarled Nick.

James rang for Jacob, and together they assisted the marquess down the stair. By the time they reached the bottom, Lord Mannering was perspiring rather more profusely, and both James and Jacob were looking pale. Mary waited in the hallway, bearing cane and gloves and tall beaver hat, the latter well brushed on the outside with a soft cloth, and wiped inside with a clean handkerchief. Fitz held out the vinaigrette. Nick swore.

The front door opened. A young gentleman with chestnut hair and hazel eyes walked into the hall, and stopped, and stared. "Hello, Unc! This is a surprise. I was going to go to ground, and here you're hiding here first."

"Don't call me Unc." Sourly, Nick regarded his nephew and heir. "Your mother thinks you've fallen in with bad company. And I'm not hiding here."

"No, he's just having assignations," observed Fitz. "Hello, Colin. I like your coat. The paisley mixture, ain't it? You have a piece of lint there, on your sleeve."

Colin flicked away the lint. "Assignations, Nicky? Maybe it's time we had a little uncle-nephew talk. I *am* nineteen."

Lord Mannering put on his hat and picked up his

cane. "To what happy accident do we owe so unexpected a visit, Colin?"

Fascinated, Colin gazed upon his uncle's bruises. "Speaking of accidents, what's happened to you?"

"I told you he was having assignations!" said Fitz. "And I'll talk to you about them, if your uncle won't. What would you like to know?"

At the thought of Fitz expounding upon assignations, Colin lost his powers of speech. Fitz patted his shoulder. "You think about it. My vast storehouse of knowledge is at your disposal whenever you wish. Colin's got sent down from university again, Nicky. It's plain as the nose on your face. What was it this time, performing monkeys? Short-sheeting the don's bed? Boxing the watch?"

"No, it was a pig. In the chapel." Colin grinned. "A large, rather smelly pig, which furthermore had been greased."

Nick tried not to laugh, not because he had any desire to set an example for his nephew, but because laughing hurt. "Cabbage head."

Colin was still staring at his uncle. "Nicky, what *did* happen to you?"

"Lady Norwood," explained Fitz, before Nick could formulate a response. "She has a handy bunch of fives."

Colin blinked. "She *hit* Nicky?"

Fitz took Colin's arm. "That ain't all she's done to him. Come along, I'll tell you about it on the way to the Park."

Waiting in the street was an open barouche, drawn by two pair of white horses, the driver perched on his seat outside. Inside, two seats faced each other. The collapsible hood that extended over the back seat was folded down.

Nick was ashen by the time he settled on the dark leather. "I'm not sure this is a good idea," said Fitz.

Gingerly, Nick stretched out his legs. "Since I don't recall the last time I *had* a good idea, we might as well proceed."

The driver flicked his reins, and the barouche moved forward. Colin settled down beside his uncle, with a vague notion of being handy in case of some catastrophe, such as Nicky's fainting and being pitched off the seat. He inhaled and his nostrils twitched. "What's that smell?"

Fitz had come equipped not only with his vinai-grette, but also with a lavender-soaked handkerchief and, just in case, a spare. This, he graciously extended to Colin. "Camphor. Among your uncle's other mis-fortunes is a damaged back. As well as a fiancée."

Gingerly, Colin accepted the handkerchief, which was edged daintily with lace. "Wish you joy and all that, but isn't it a little sudden, Unc?" Conversation paused then, as the barouche swerved to avoid col-liding with a pedestrian. The marquess groaned. Fitz offered his vinaigrette. Nick glared at him.

It was that rarest of occasions, a sunny London day, and a great proportion of the populace was taking ad-vantage of the weather to crowd into the streets: town criers in cocked hats and flaxen wigs; postmen in red and gold; ruddy-faced countrymen and porters with their loads; housewives on their way home from mar-ket; bowlegged ostlers; sharp-eyed lads in dirty salt-and-pepper coats and battered low-brimmed hats. As Lord Mannering's barouche wound its way through hackney coaches and fine carriages, carts drawn by donkeys and others by small boys, past a heavy dray laden with beer barrels, and around a bailiff's wagon piled so high with household furnishings that it looked like it would at any moment collapse, Fitz explained to Colin how his uncle had been accused of attempting to ravish a damsel on her papa's hall stair steps, although as it turned out she was trying to ravish him instead; and about the older woman whom he *had* ravished; and how the two of them had ended up together with him in a bed, along with a dog. Fitz considered it time Colin knew about such things. Nick gritted his teeth against the swaying of the cart, and tried not to groan.

"Are you trying to humbug me?" Colin inquired.

Fitz snorted. "I'd come up with a better tale than this if I was! Unfortunately, it's all true. He's in love with her, else he wouldn't be behaving like a jackass. And she's in love with him. Lady Norwood, that is."

Despite himself, for he was quite out of charity with both his companions, Nick asked, "How do you know that?"

Fitz leaned forward, the better to speak to the fascinated Colin. "She called him a satyr, toad, goat, lying cur, dastardly rat, and lustful slug. Not to mention pond scum. In my experience, only true affection inspires a woman to such heights."

"You forgot maw-worm."

Fitz ruminated. "I don't remember her calling you a maw-worm."

Nick sighed. "That was the time before."

"I say!" said Fitz. "You don't mean to tell me that you and Lady Norwood, ah—"

"Several times. Both then and now."

"One hesitates to ask"—Fitz didn't—"but when was *then?*"

"Before she married Norwood."

"In that case, why *did* she marry Norwood?"

Nick looked his most sardonic. "My dear Fitz, the lady is a Loversall." He clasped his hands on the handle of his cane and leaned slightly forward in the hope that this change of position might ease the strain on his back. "I hesitate to mention this, but Zoë called me a swine."

Fitz shrugged. "That don't signify. She ain't in love with anyone but herself."

"Narcissus!" Colin was pleased to make a contribution to the conversation. "Narcissus was punished by Nemesis for his cruelty to Echo and the other nymphs, and fell in love with his own reflection in a pond, and pined away, and died."

Said Fitz, disapprovingly, "Sounds like a blasted Loversall."

"Hera took away Echo's ability to speak after Echo kept her distracted while the nymphs Zeus had been dallying with escaped. See, I have been tending to my studies, Nicky," Colin concluded. "What's a Loversall?"

"I believe you!" protested Nick. "It's your mother who thinks you're preoccupied with things such as greased pigs. More to the point is me escaping from the nymph with whom I *didn't* dally, I think."

Colin shook his head. "And you called me a cabbage head! I may have got sent down, but I'm not a penny the worse for it, which is more than can be said of you! I am sadly disillusioned, Nicky! Here I thought you were up to all the rigs, and it turns out you're as great a jingle-brain as anyone else."

"Maybe worse," mused Fitz. "Remember that dog in his bed."

Colin snickered. Fitz grinned. "I'm glad the two of you are finding such amusement in my predicament!" Nick snapped.

"Never mind!" soothed Fitz. "We're going to stick as close as court plasters lest you tumble into worse trouble yet!" He regarded his friend's pale, set features, and decided a diversion was in order. The remainder of their journey to the Park was enlivened by his explanation of the intricacies of the violet cloth wound around his throat, which had been laid first on the back of the neck, the ends brought forward and tied in a large knot, the ends then being carried under the arms and tied in the back, thereby making a very pretty appearance, and giving the wearer a languishingly amorous look.

All the beau monde promenaded in Hyde Park on this fine day, as a result of which the ducks had retreated to the safety of their shelters, as had the cows and deer. The Prince Regent and the Duke of York; Georgiana, Duchess of Devonshire; the Ladies Cowper, Foley, Hertford, and Mountjoy; the Earl of Sefton and the Ladies of Molyneux—all these worthies were known to Lord Mannering, as he was to them, and all were eager to say hello, and to comment on his upcoming nuptials—although only Prinny dared chuckle and chide him for getting caught—and then to murmur among themselves that the marquess looked less like a man about to contract a marriage than one who'd just been told he'd got a case of the pox.

On the pathway just ahead, a young lady held court. She was dressed in a pale brown riding habit, and a hat with a jaunty plume, and mounted on a pretty chestnut horse. Flocked around her were admiring gentlemen of various ages, as well as several women whose noses appeared to have been put out of joint.

She shimmered, and sparkled, and shot out rays brighter than the sun. "*That,*" said Fitz, "is a Loversall."

Zoë rode over to the barouche, causing her abandoned admirers to glower and mutter among themselves. "Hello, Lord Mannering! I'm glad to see that you can walk. Or sit, anyway! You look especially fine today, Baron Fitzrichard. I have a gown the same color as your cravat." Her curious gaze moved to Colin. Her eyelashes fluttered. "And who is *this*?"

"My nephew, Colin Kennet. Colin, this is Miss Zoë Loversall."

"The heir!" said Zoë, and dimpled. "You poor thing! I am so sorry to cut up your hopes. But it may not come to that, you know, for your uncle is quite old."

She was vivid, luminous. She had dimples. She was terrifying. Colin looked at his uncle. "Old?"

"She refers to the siring of children," Nick said sourly. "Heirs. That sort of thing."

Fitz flicked his handkerchief. "Should you require further enlightenment, Colin, you need only ask."

Zoë regarded the baron's handkerchief, and then one that Colin clutched forgotten in his hand. She sniffed the air. "Lavender-scented handkerchiefs? Is that the new rage?" Fitz contemplated his handkerchief, and gave it an experimental twitch.

Nick had wondered how Colin might react to Zoë. He supposed he shouldn't be surprised that the boy looked thunderstruck. "Your aunt isn't with you?"

"When I last saw Aunt Cara she was having that ugly tree of yours carried out into the garden." Zoë moved her flirtatious gaze from Colin to his uncle.

"I wonder if it would be possible to speak with you privately, my lord."

"No!" Not for all the tea in China. "I have no secrets from Colin and Fitz."

"Very well, then!" Zoë urged her horse closer, and leaned forward confidingly. "Beau is deaf to reason. He's being obstinate. Unless we are very clever, it *will* be St. George's, Hanover Square, with or without a wedding list—we have all refused to make one up, you see, but that won't stop Beau!—and Aunt Cara will have her heart broke. I think you should elope. Then *I* can be the one to nurse a broken heart."

On general principles, Lord Mannering didn't care to do anything his fiancée wished. "Thereby destroying both your aunt's reputation and my own. I think not. Perhaps I'll just cry off instead."

"You can't!" cried Zoë, loud enough to cause several curious glances to be cast in their direction. She lowered her voice. "I won't let you! I'd look the veriest pig-widgeon if you did."

"You'd look the veriest pig-widgeon if he eloped with your aunt," Fitz pointed out.

"That's different!" protested Zoë, with a pretty pout. "If he eloped with Aunt Cara, everyone would assume her tumultuous passions had got the better of them both." She dimpled at Colin. "It's a family trait. And if Aunt Cara won't agree, he'll just have to carry her off."

"With *his* back?" interjected Fitz. "Not that Lady Norwood ain't a fine figure of a woman. I wouldn't mind carrying her off myself, if I were inclined toward that sort of thing, which I ain't, but it wouldn't resolve this fix." The marquess clenched his teeth, due not to any unease caused by the baron's suggestion, but to the agony that this excursion was causing his abused spine.

"I wish you *would* elope," said Colin. "Because I've decided I don't want to be your heir. What if you were to pop off tomorrow? I never thought of it before, but look at the condition you're in. I'm only nineteen! That's too young to become a marquess. Come to think of it, I may *always* be too young to become a marquess."

Zoë stared at him in astonishment. "How very ungrateful of you!" she said.

"Oh?" inquired Colin. "And it's not ungrateful of you to entangle my uncle in this muddle when it's clear as noonday that who he really wants is your aunt?"

Zoë could hardly stamp her foot since she was on horseback, and there was nothing throwable within her reach. She had to settle for a sneer. It was a masterful sneer, of course, complete with twitched nose and curled lip. "You, sir, are very rude!" she said.

Colin shrugged. "And you're a flirt. Uncle Nicky *should* cry off. He can hardly make you look a greater pig-widgeon than you make yourself."

Zoë stared at him with open-mouthed astonishment. Nick twisted painfully sideways on the seat to regard his nephew and heir. Elegantly, Baron Fitzrichard wafted his handkerchief—the Fitz flourish, he would style it—and said: "I believe I've just hit upon a scheme."

20

While Lord Mannering and Miss Loversall were rendezvousing in Hyde Park, Lady Norwood was wandering along the crushed stone pathways of her brother's garden and contemplating the very real possibility that she might be a goose. Daisy kept close to her side. The setter was less ebullient than usual, in deference to her mistress's mood.

Late afternoon shadows crept through the overgrown garden. Cara paused by the old mulberry tree. She had run away from Nicky once because she feared the intensity of her feelings, and now what had she done but practically fling herself back into his bed? Yes, and she would probably run away again, this very moment, if not that if by so doing she would abandon him to Zoë. *Moon-madness*, she told herself, and walked farther along the path. If she couldn't think clearly in Nicky's presence, she was doing little better out of it.

Ah, but the world was a different place with Nicky in it, colors brighter, textures more complex, the air itself sweeter to breathe, as if only in his presence did all her senses come alive. When Cara had first known him, and loved him, she had been so giddy with the wonder of it that her feet had scarcely touched the ground. Then, with the suspicion of his betrayal, she'd landed with a thump, and taken refuge with a kindly, elderly gentleman who would never do her harm. Fortunate for Nicky that she had done so. Cara wasn't the type of Loversall to fall upon her lover's sword, but rather—like Great-Aunt Judith—to take a sharp weapon to his more vulnerable parts. At least that was said to have been Judith's intention before Reynaldo took her in his arms and subdued her with a rapier of a different sort.

Odd to equate love with weapons, mused Cara, as she paused by the neglected pond where a single daffodil poked its head through the weeds. But love was a struggle, was it not? If not with one's lover, then with oneself, for it was so intoxicating to surrender to another, and yet so dangerous. Despite all her dramatic posturing, Zoë had no notion what it truly meant to have one's heart crushed underfoot. Yet if Nicky spoke the truth, he had been guilty of no betrayal, and all the pain Cara had suffered she had caused herself. She bent down and pulled away the weeds from around the daffodil so that it might breathe. Since no one had known about her feelings for Nicky—they had been too new, too precious, to share—there had been no one to whom she could turn for consolation or advice. Beau had been, as always, wrapped up in his own concerns, and Ianthe preoccupied with Beau and Zoë. If Norwood had suspected that her heart belonged to another, he had never said a word.

Her heart! How melodramatic. *Was* she a ninnyhammer, given a second chance, and still to hesitate? Yet if Nicky made the world brighter, he also made it infinitely less safe. Could he be faithful? Could she? Odds weren't in their favor, given her family history, and if Cara had never wanted anyone else, she wasn't so naïve as to delude herself that Nicky had waited for her all these years. A gentleman didn't become so skilled a lover by simply thinking about the thing.

If only Beau weren't so deaf to reason. Were Zoë truly forced to marry Nicky, Cara might well visit the Temple and make her brother a present of Casimir's bear. She knelt down in the dirt and attacked a particularly stubborn patch of broad-leafed spurge with her trowel, and wondered about the length of an ursine life span. Daisy sprawled, dozing, by her side.

In the shadows of the mulberry tree, Paul Anderley stood watching. Never had he known a woman who could look so desirable while yet so rumpled, her dress wrinkled and grass-stained, a streak of dirt across her cheek. Underhanded tactics, to bribe the butler to reveal her whereabouts, but one could never underestimate the element of surprise. "Cara," he said.

Cara roused from her reverie, realized she was kneading the dirt as if it were a certain marquess, and rose hastily to her feet. "Paul. What are you doing here? No, Daisy! No jumping, if you please."

The setter ignored this poor-spirited request. She ran toward the squire, tail wagging in greeting. "Sit!" he said sternly, and she flopped at his feet.

If only Cara were as obedient. "I apologize for disturbing your solitude, but it's damned difficult to speak privately with you. You'll be returning to the country soon, after your niece is wed. Perhaps you will allow me to oversee the arrangements. And then we may pick up where we left off." Paul had had quite enough of London. Nothing that had happened here thus far had changed his opinion of the blasted place.

Cara wondered guiltily if she had encouraged the squire to think things that he shouldn't. This sojourn in London had enabled her to clarify her feelings about him, even if it had left her even more confused about everything else. "My niece isn't going to get married. At least not to Lord Mannering."

Paul wasn't pleased to hear this, for his suspicion that Cara might fancy Mannering herself had been temporarily set to rest by the newspaper account of her niece's impending nuptials. "They're betrothed. I read it in the *Gazette*."

"One cannot believe everything one reads." Cara gestured vaguely with the trowel. "I was thinking of planting lilies here. Did you know that Elizabethans laid red vermilion or cinnabar and blue azure of the yellow mineral orpiment at the roots of lilies to modify the color of the flowers? Roman gardeners soaked lily bulbs in purple wine to induce purple tints."

Paul was accustomed to her efforts to throw him off the scent. "Elizabethans also steeped cloves in rose water, bruised them, and bound them about the roots of gillyflowers in the hope of producing clove-scented flowers. You see that I've read up on the subject. Are you telling me Mannering *isn't* betrothed to your niece?"

"No, but he isn't going to marry her. Have you seen the rose garden?" Cara pointed out an Alba rose with its pale pink buds and gray-green foliage, used as a hedge plant; Banksea roses of white and yellow, vigorous climbers with virtually no thorns; China roses and Damask; Centifolia with its hundred petals; red Gallicas with their green button eyes. Paul broke off a Rose du Roi and handed it to her. Cara regarded the flower and recalled that out-of-season blooming betokened a disaster in the family. "I do not plan to return to Norwood House soon."

Paul looked around, in search of patience. Lady Norwood was being particularly annoying today. His gaze fell upon the Sophora japonica drooping in a shaft of sunlight. "What the devil is *that*?" he said.

Cara touched a leaf. "My Sophora japonica. Also known as a Chinese scholar or Japanese pagoda tree. It will bear yellow flowers in late summer. Lord Mannering gave it to me." She raised her gaze to his face. "In regard to his lordship, there is something I must tell you, Paul."

"I didn't come here to talk about Mannering!" Nor did Paul want to hear what he suspected Lady Norwood was going to say. "Be done with this nonsense. I'll take you back to Norwood House, and—"

"It's you who's talking nonsense!" Cara interrupted crossly. "I've already said that I'm not going back to Norwood House! I mean, of course I'm going back to Norwood House, but not with you. How many times have I told you that I don't mean to marry, Paul!"

Numerous times. Times beyond counting. Paul had chosen to ignore them all. "I'm beginning to think myself trifled with!" he said, in an effort to lighten the mood.

Cara turned away. That the man cared for her, she knew. She wondered if he realized himself that he cared more for her property. "Yes, well, perhaps you were," she said, and walked farther down the path.

Daisy followed, her tail wagging. Paul trailed after them. "This isn't like you."

Cara glanced back over her shoulder. "I don't know

why you should think you know what I'm like. You've never made any effort to find out."

Paul stared at her in astonishment. "How can you say that? I thought we were friends."

Absently, Cara pulled up a cornflower. "A friend wouldn't be plaguing me like this."

Plaguing her? "I've formed a lasting passion for you!" Paul protested.

"Fiddle!" Cara yanked away a vine that was creeping along up the old stone wall. "The only lasting passion you have formed is for Norwood's property, and I'm not going to give it up."

Paul was stunned by so sharp a dismissal. "Cara—"

"Not another word!" snapped Cara. "I'm all out of patience with you." Yes, and so she looked it, with her hands on her hips, and on her lovely face a scowl.

She was out of patience? He had been so careful not to rush his fences, had even put aside all his other business to follow her to town. "Your niece isn't the only member of the family who's a flirt. She is, don't deny it! I've seen the chit in action. She even tried to flirt with me. Not that I don't consider your brother entirely to blame."

Cara could not help remarking the difference between Nicky and the squire in this telling moment. Both were handsome men. Where Paul looked like he very much wished to lay violent hands on her, however, given similar provocation, Nicky would simply walk away. Although he hadn't walked away, had he, when she'd hit him, and thrown a poker at him, and called him names.

Paul was staring at her. He deserved some explanation. "Zoë flirted with you. I flirted with you. So, probably, did Ianthe. What of it? Have you forgotten that we are all Loversalls?"

Beau was also a Loversall. At least *he* hadn't flirted with Paul. Unless provoking a person fell in the same category, perish the thought.

He must regroup. The huntsman must think like a fox, or in this case a female, which was considerably more difficult. "You encouraged me—"

"I did nothing of the sort." Cara regarded him, an uprooted snapdragon dangling from her hand. "You're making too much of this, Paul. You never even kissed me."

Paul knew he hadn't kissed her. He hadn't wished to frighten her with the degree of his passion. Now he realized that he should have followed his instincts long ago, thrown Cara over his shoulder and carried her off to his lair, there to have his wicked way with her, whether she wanted it or not, for if he couldn't overwhelm her senses, he would frighten her into submission. He was not an unskilled lover. She would forgive him after the *fait accompli*. And if she didn't forgive him right away, he would keep her prisoner in his turret room, and make love to her until she did. Not that he *had* a turret room, but he could have one built. "That omission can be remedied," he said.

The squire stood as still as one of the old garden statues, a disturbing gleam in his hazel eyes, a strange expression on his face. A wolfish expression, perhaps. Or if not a wolf, some other predator with sharp claws and fangs. Perhaps even a preternatural creature that could only be repelled with holy water and a cross. Lacking either of these items, Cara raised the trowel and took a backward step. "No, it can't." Daisy dropped down among the snapdragons, looking back and forth between the two of them, perplexed.

Cara held the damned trowel as if it were a weapon. As if a mere woman, no matter how magnificent, could be any match for a man's strength. Quick as a snake, Paul reached out and caught her arm, tossed aside the trowel, and pulled her into his embrace.

Once Cara had wondered if she wished to kiss him. Now she knew that she did not. Paul, at least, seemed to be enjoying the embrace, judging from the manner in which one hand held her pressed against his body, and the other tangled in her hair. He seemed to be under the impression that she was also enjoying it, for he grasped a handful of her skirt, and murmured unintelligibly against her throat.

Cara stomped down, hard, on his foot. He flinched. She put her palms against his chest and shoved. Still he didn't release her, but pulled away enough to look down into her face. Cara drew back her fist and punched him in the nose. Paul staggered backward, tripped over Daisy, and fell flat on his back.

Cara's hands flew to her mouth. Was this some new permutation of the family nature, that she went about assaulting all her admirers? She hadn't meant to harm the squire, merely to discourage him. His nose was bleeding profusely. "Oh, Paul! I'm so sorry!" she cried, and dropped to her knees to dab at his face with her skirts. Not wishing to be left out, Daisy lent her own efforts to the affair.

A soil-smudged skirt, a dog's damp tongue—Paul pushed them both away, and staggered to his feet. Cara rose also, still attempting to staunch the flow of blood with her skirts, thereby displaying neat pink stockings and white petticoats, a sight Paul might have enjoyed under circumstances other than these. His nose hurt like the devil. He wondered if it was broken.

Ianthe rounded the corner to see Paul Anderley bleeding profusely from a battered nose, and Cara holding her skirts almost above her head. "Angels defend us!" She gasped.

Blasted interruptions! The squire grabbed Cara's arm and dragged her closer. "I fear I've sullied your reputation, my dear Lady Norwood. To be discovered alone together like this—Of course I'll provide you with the protection of my name."

"Ballocks!" retorted Cara, and shoved at him.

Ianthe wasn't one to lose her head in a crisis, which was fortunate, in light of the perennial crises indulged in by various members of her family. This crisis, at least, was in part her doing, because she had been so caught up in her own plans that Paul had slipped past her guard. Fortunately, Widdle had confessed.

She glanced back down the pathway. Only seconds left. Ianthe hurried to the squire, and none too gently tweaked his bloody nose. He yelped and released Cara, who moved quickly out of reach.

"What the devil!" moaned Paul.

"You poor, poor man! All that nasty blood! Oh, heaven, I feel faint!" Judging the distance nicely, Ianthe swooned gracefully into his arms.

Paul reacted as would any gentleman, and caught her, although he gazed upon his burden with an expression akin to a fisherman who had unexpectedly been struck by a wet boot. Daisy leapt up, and attempted to lick Ianthe's face. "No!" said Cara, and pulled the dog away.

Footsteps crunched on the pathway. Baron Fitzrichard and Zoë rounded the corner, trailed by

Lord Mannering, who was leaning on the arm of another young man Cara didn't know. Nor did Daisy recognize him. The dog raced toward them, barking. Fitz quelled her enthusiasm with a single stern glance through his quizzing glass. The setter sat down and looked perplexed. Nick stood stock still, staring. Colin bent down to scratch the setter's ears.

Fitz turned his quizzing glass on the squire. "Not especially scientific, but effective nonetheless. Should you ever wish to turn professional, Lady Norwood, I would consider it a privilege to have the handling of you in the ring. Yes, Nicky, we know you wish to have Anderley's guts for grilling, but perhaps he's already suffered punishment enough. His valet ain't ever going to save that coat. Although damned if I ain't tempted to call him out myself for dripping blood on Miss Ianthe!"

Paul scowled and clutched at his burden, who was a great deal heavier than she looked. He could hardly lay her down among the weeds. "Call me out if you will!" he snapped. "But not on Miss Ianthe's sake. Lady Norwood and I have been discovered in a compromising situation. I have offered her the protection of my good name."

Lord Mannering knew what *he'd* done to Lady Norwood, and it had only earned him bruises. All too easy to imagine what misbehavior might have earned the squire his bloody nose. He started forward. Colin took firmer hold of the wriggling dog.

Quickly, Cara moved to the marquess, and grasped his arm. "And I have already told you, Paul, that I have a perfectly good name of my own. It was nothing, Nicky. Remember your back."

Paul objected to his embrace being referred to in

such terms. If he hadn't been as polished as he'd like, it was because pent-up passion had turned his mind to mush. Then Lady Norwood had taken advantage of his weakened state of mind, and hit him in the nose. "The devil it was nothing!" he said.

Zoë had been waiting to see if the gentlemen would come to blows. When it appeared to her disappointment that they would not, largely because Cara was clutching Lord Mannering, and Squire Anderley was burdened with Ianthe, she plucked the lavender-scented handkerchief from Fitz's fingers and dabbed at the squire's nose. "That's what you get, Squire Anderley, for putting yourself in the pathway of True Love! Come along back to the house and we'll get you a nice cold compress. Oh, you're still holding Cousin Ianthe. I've never known her to swoon before. Usually she just cries. Perhaps she's shamming it."

Paul looked down at the lady who rested so gracefully in his arms. She opened one apologetic blue eye. Abruptly, he released her. Ianthe staggered. Fitz stepped forward and caught her before she could fall among the snapdragons, and waved his vinaigrette under her nose. "Figured chintz provides an excellent opportunity for the interplay of predominate and subordinate colors. I especially like the orange. A pity about the blood."

Ianthe pushed away the vinaigrette, and cast a wary glance around. Squire Anderley held the sodden handkerchief to his nose, while Zoë clung to his arm and cooed, and Lord Mannering applied his own handkerchief to the dirt on Lady Norwood's cheek. The young gentleman was hugging Daisy, and looking bewildered. "Thank you, Baron Fitzrichard. I've tried to keep your advice in mind. Shall we adjourn to the house? I believe that must be another new style of tying your cravat. What do you call it, other than superb?"

Fitz made an elegant leg, and offered her his arm. "I hadn't decided until just this moment, but Squire Anderley has inspired me: I shall call it the Point Non Plus. Now tell me about your cousin. I don't suppose she's had sparring lessons. What do you think, Nicky, shall I arrange an exhibition match at the Castle Tavern? After all, I *am* a member of the Pugilistic Club!"

21

To say that these events set the household on its ear might be an exaggeration, for this was an establishment accustomed to the fits and foibles of numerous Loversalls, but there was no little reaction to the blood-spattered condition of the ladies—Barrow in particular had a great deal to say about missed opportunities while she tidied up Lady Norwood—and Squire Anderley's damaged nose. Various remedies were suggested for his condition, from brown paper stuck under the upper lip to a cold compress on the back of the neck, head tilted forward or leaned back, the bridge of the nose pinched five minutes or ten. In this latter effort, Baron Fitzrichard offered his assistance. The squire refused. When at length all these matters had reached a resolution, various refreshments of an alcoholic nature were served in the drawing room, brandy for the gentlemen, sherry for the ladies, and ratafia for Zoë, who had a sweet tooth, tea being considered of far too prosaic a nature for an occasion such as this.

Lord Mannering and his nephew sat on one of the sofas that flanked the chimney, Ianthe on the other, and Zoë on the confidante. Lady Norwood had removed herself a discreet distance from both the squire and the marquess, and sat in a stuffed chair with Daisy sprawled at her feet. Baron Fitzrichard was pacing the floor, the fireplace poker in his hand, demonstrating for the captive audience his knowledge of swordplay.

He assumed the *en garde* position, feet at right angles, sword arm extended, left arm raised in a graceful arc. "To seek for a true defense with an untrue weapon is to angle on the earth for fish, and to hunt in the sea for hares. Naturally I wouldn't wish my great friend Nicky to stand his trial for murder, as surely he must if forced to marry Miss Zoë, although *were* such an unhappy event to take place, I wonder what I'd wear. Mourning black, of course, for we shall not see the likes of him again. Maybe I'll create a new tying of my cravat for the occasion and name it the Exécuteur. Around the neck once, I believe; no indentures or creases, like a noose. Or perhaps the very opposite. One crease coming down from each ear, and a third in a horizontal direction, stretching from one of the side indentures to the other all the way to the ear. Or perhaps two collateral dents, and two horizontal ones, and maybe a large knot. Or perhaps no knot at all, but the two ends joined as a chain link . . ."

Zoë thunked down her ratafia glass on the table. "There's no time for this silliness! Beau will be home soon for dinner. Unless you've decided I'm *not* to become unbetrothed, which is fine with me, because even though Cara wouldn't like it if I married Lord Mannering, *I* would like to be a marchioness." She licked the sweet syrup off her lips. "Perhaps I shall be the first Loversall to ever become divorced."

At mention of the time, everyone glanced at the grandfather clock, save Nick, who looked at Cara.

She steadfastly refused to meet his eye, which made him wonder if perhaps there had been more to the episode in the garden than he knew. Perhaps she *did* fancy Anderley a little bit. Enough so that the man had considered himself justified in taking liberties. God knew Cara was a splendid woman to take liberties with. The two of them *had* been living in the country together. Or if not together, side by side.

Cara had said she didn't want the squire, and that he had wanted only Norwood's property. She had certainly given every indication of wanting Nick herself. Yes, and he'd been such a gudgeon as to refuse her. Were not his back bound up so tightly that he could hardly move, he would have kicked himself.

If only she would look at him. If only she'd get out of that bloody distant chair and come rub his back. Somehow it seemed Paul Anderley's fault that she did neither. Nick glowered at that gentleman. One of the numerous remedies for nosebleed having proven efficacious, the squire had finally left off pinching the bridge of his nose.

Damned if he wasn't jealous! Nick didn't recall that he'd ever felt this way before, not even over Norwood, but Norwood had been as old as Methuselah, and Cara hadn't popped him in the nose. At least so far as Nick knew. Now he had a notion of how Cara had felt about his betrothal to Zoë. And that old business with Lucasta Clitheroe. He was surprised she hadn't shot him. He certainly felt like shooting the squire.

"A single blow cuts off the head, the arm, the head!" said Fitz, with a nicely executed lunge. "You're not paying attention, Nicky. Zoë has suggested that she marry you, and Lady Norwood marry Squire Anderley, and then you can *all* get divorced. Lady Norwood don't like the notion. What do *you* think?"

Lord Mannering thought he would cut out the squire's liver and fry it if he so much as looked at Lady Norwood, and so he said. Squire Anderley suggested that the marquess might like to try, or so the others assumed he meant; his speech had deteriorated sadly in the past half hour.

Fitz made a pretty step backward. "Is it valorous for a man to go naked against his enemy? Chop and change, turn and return."

Nick turned his scowl on his friend. "I'm not sure you're taking this business seriously enough."

"My dear Nicky, you don't understand the paradoxes of trial by combat!" Fitz performed a *balestra,* and a *flèche.* "Moreover, it is unsportsmanlike to give a man his bastings when someone has already drawn his cork." He pointed the poker at the squire. "And *you* can't sport your canvas when your opponent's back is already broke. Are you all right, Nicky? You're looking a little green."

Scant wonder. Nick wished that he might take off his coat and stretch out on the floor while Cara made slow circular motions with her fingers along his aching spine. "I'm fine. Never better. You said you had a plan. When do you think you might tell us what it is?"

"The eye is deceived by the swift motion of the hand!" After a last practiced flourish, Fitz set the poker on the floor and leaned on it as if it were a cane. "My plan is brilliant in its utter simplicity, if I do say so myself. Zoë is betrothed to Nicky because she was caught with him in a compromising position. To get them *un*betrothed, she must simply get caught in a compromising position with someone else."

Some damsels might have fainted dead away at the shocking notion of being caught in compromising positions twice in as many days. Zoë clapped her hands. "Baron Fitzrichard, you are a genius!" she cried.

The others were less certain. Although Lord Mannering was willing to try anything, both Cara and Ianthe nurtured doubts. Colin was still struggling to grasp the complexities of the situation. Squire Anderley was more interested in the bloodied condition of his coat.

Fitz paced around the chamber. "The only question is, by whom? Nicky has already compromised her, and no one would believe it of me." He studied Paul.

That worthy felt the weight of several gazes, and looked up. "I be dabbed"—sniff—"ib *I* comprabise da berdicious liddle twid."

Zoë huffed. Fitz shrugged. "Suit yourself. I just thought that since you seemed wishful of compromising *someone*, you should be given the chance."

There came a brief digression while the squire mentioned such terms as "fribbery fripple" and "Bawd Stweet bow" and "shaw-be-bed," and Fitz in turn chided him for being an old sobersides. Irritably, Zoë reminded the gentlemen of the minutes ticking away on the old grandfather clock.

"That's it, then." Fitz turned to Colin. "You're our only hope."

Colin gaped at him. "*Me?* But I just got here!"

"Don't you want to help your uncle avoid standing trial for murder?" Fitz grasped the young man by the arm and dragged him toward the fireplace. "Nicky will be grateful to you for it. Maybe he'll even give you a reward."

Colin dug in his heels. "Are you *bribing* me?"

"It's that or blackmail," said Fitz. "I doubt your mother would be amused by an account of the greased pig."

The marquess took his cue. "Poor Maria would take to her bed. On the other hand, *I* might be inspired to double your allowance. Starting the moment I am again a free man."

Colin knew his mama worried about him. She worried about everything. He'd come to the conclusion, from conversations with his mates, that worrying was simply what mothers *did*.

She'd probably worry all the more, however, were Nicky entrapped in a marriage with Miss Tumultuous Passions. Colin muttered, "I should have never touched that pig."

Fitz kept firm hold of Colin's arm, just in case he took a notion to bolt. "Come here, Zoë. When Beau enters the room, he'll find the two of you locked in an embrace."

Zoë tripped forward, willingly enough. "What sort of embrace?" Colin inquired suspiciously, "Where will the rest of you be?"

"In the garden, waiting to make our own entrance, so that Beau won't be able to pretend he didn't see what he saw," answered Ianthe. "I shall inform Widdle to alert us immediately Beau steps through the front door." She rang for the butler, who was happy to lend his assistance, on the promise of a generous gratuity. Widdle was also happy to see that Squire Anderley's nose was swelling like a toad. It was Widdle's opinion that the squire had come by his just desserts when the lady popped his cork, being as he'd been going around bribing servants, and Gawd knew what else.

"One arm around her waist," suggested Fitz. "The other—"

"I'm not going to practice," Colin protested. "It's too much to ask."

"But we must make it look real or Beau won't believe us, and then we'll be back where we started." Zoë clutched at Colin. "There's nothing wrong with practicing a little bit. I *need* to practice if I'm going to have an *affaire de coeur.*"

Colin snatched his sleeve away. "You're no more capable of passion than a gnat."

Zoë's blue eyes widened. "Oh!" she said.

"On second thought, a gnat might be *more* capable, because it isn't likely to fall in love with its own reflection." Ianthe cleared her throat, and Colin recalled their audience. "I beg your pardon. I shouldn't have said that."

Zoë was hardly in a position to hold grudges against people who said things they shouldn't. She regarded Colin curiously. "You don't like me much, do you?"

He frowned at her. "Why should I?"

Zoë wasn't used to introspection. She wrinkled her brow. "Why shouldn't you? I am accomplished, beautiful of course, and quite amiable!"

Suddenly, she found herself the cynosure of all eyes. "Well I am!" she insisted.

"No you ain't!" said Fitz. "You're the devil's spawn. Nicky said so, and he should know."

Nick stirred, uncomfortably. "I don't think I was quite that severe."

Zoë awarded him her most melting look. "You *don't* think I'm the devil's spawn?"

Nick grimaced. "I believe 'limb of Satan' was the phrase I used."

Zoë stamped her foot. "This exceeds belief! You must have maggots in your heads."

She looked as if she wished to throw something. Colin drew her fire. "Better maggots than windmills. Fitz said how you're determined to toss your bonnet over one."

Zoë cast a smouldering glance at that traitor. But what else could one expect from a man who wore a lilac cravat? "We Loversall women cannot resist the call of passion. Look at Aunt Cara. And Cousin Ianthe."

Cara had been wishing that the chair might swallow her up, so ashamed was she of her behavior. At this injustice, however, she roused. "Some of us don't openly defy the conventions, Zoë. We merely ignore them in private."

"Or *almost* private. Friends don't count." Fitz grinned at her. The squire frowned.

"A fig for privacy!" Zoë clasped her hands to her breast. "*I* shall know my own True Love immediately our eyes meet across a room. He will be bold and brave and dashing." She paused. "I wonder if I would prefer that he be light or dark. No matter! Waves of desire will sweep over me, stealing my breath, turning my bones to jelly, and causing my heart to go pit-a-pat. Overset with passion, I shall indulge my baser nature until we both are spent."

Paul Anderley looked revolted. "Good Lord," murmured Ianthe.

Cara said nothing at all, being deep in the contemplation of True Love, as was Lord Mannering. Colin voiced a hope that he might not get totty-headed for a great many more years.

"Totty-headed!" Zoë gasped.

"What else would you call it? Sighing and dying and running about knocking things around like a bunch of insane rabbits. No offense, Lady Norwood!" Cara glanced at Nicky. He winked.

"I don't believe a member of the family has been clapped in Bedlam yet," Ianthe remarked. "Although Great-Uncle Ambrose spent a fair amount of time locked in an attic room because he couldn't be trusted around the maidservants." Paul wondered if everyone in the room, save himself, was lunatic.

Widdle popped his head into the room. "Psst!" he hissed, and disappeared. "Take your places, ladies and gentlemen!" demanded Fitz.

Zoë regarded her prospective compromiser, who looked singularly unenthusiastic. Although it was highly improper for a young lady to be alone with a gentleman, she doubted that a single circumstance would be sufficient to *re*compromise her in her papa's eyes. After all, she had been plopped on top of a gentleman the first time. Some effort was required of Colin. "You may kiss me," she said, and puckered up.

No one had explained to Colin that kissing might be required. "I don't want to." He backed up a step.

How could any gentleman not want to kiss her? Zoë eyed him shrewdly. "You've never kissed anyone, have you? You're a—"

Colin blushed bright red. "Don't say it!"

"You are! Well, what of it? So am I. Although I'm *supposed* to be, and I don't think you are. As for kissing, there's nothing to it. I'll show you!"

Colin backed farther away from her. "No you won't!"

"This is no time to be missish!" snapped Zoë, and grabbed Colin by the lapels of his coat.

Fitz took in the situation at a glance. Nick was rising from the sofa with difficulty, assisted by Cara and Ianthe. Paul was getting to his feet with little less effort, for the movement had made his nose start again to bleed, and he seemed confused as to whether he should tip his head forward or back. Colin was attempting to draw away from Zoë.

Although this was no scene to undo a betrothal, Fitz did not abandon hope. All the participants needed was a little push. He thrust out the poker, so that the squire tripped over it, then gave the startled Colin a brisk shove. Zoë toppled sideways along with him. Daisy, who had been very restrained throughout all this, succumbed to her canine nature, and leapt upon the pile.

Beau walked into the room, then, to find his daughter rolling around the floor with two gentlemen and a dog, in front of an audience which included his sister and his cousin, both of whom were draped about Zoë's own fiancé, as well as Baron Fitzrichard, who raised his quizzing glass and said, "Shocking! I've never seen such a thing. I believe—yes, I am almost certain of it!—that I feel a spasm coming on!"

22

With an elegant flourish, Fitz swooned onto a sofa. Daisy disengaged herself from the tangle of bodies on the floor to run, barking, to Beau. "Down!" he snapped at her, then bellowed, "What the devil is going on here?"

"Alas!" cried Zoë. "We are caught *en flagrante delicto*! My good name is ruined!" Just in case it wasn't yet, she hooked a leg around one gentleman's knee, and an arm around the other's neck, and never mind that he was bleeding on her dress.

"I believe," remarked Lord Mannering, "that my heart is broken. Perhaps I shall retire to the country while it mends."

Beside him, Cara stirred and murmured, "Not to mention your back." She placed a hand on the small of his spine, and rubbed. He groaned. Ianthe drifted across the room to drape Baron Fitzrichard's lavender-scented handkerchief across his brow, and wave his vinaigrette beneath his nose. Fitz winked at her, and whispered, "Not as graceful a swoon as yours, I admit it! But effective, don't you think?"

Beau pushed Daisy aside. "*What* good name?" he inquired, as he grasped Zoë's arms and hauled her to her feet. "You're a Loversall. But that doesn't mean you can go around acting like a Paphian miss! The devil with St. George's. You'll be married straightaway."

"No, I won't!" Zoë thrust out her chin. "I don't wish to stand in the way of True Love, Beau."

"I don't care what you wish!" Beau stared at the two bodies on the floor, one of which was climbing to its feet, while the other lay bleeding on the carpet. "Is that *Anderley?* He looks queer as Dick's hatband. Have you killed him, puss?"

Zoë also looked at the squire, who *was* a little pale, perhaps because of all the blood he'd lost. "No, that was Aunt Cara. We think she might have broken his nose."

"The fox up and nipped you, squire?" Beau extended his hand. "You should stick a wad of paper under your lip and pinch your nose. I'd appreciate it if you tried not to drip on the rug."

With Beau's help, Paul stood up. "Wad I should hab is some branby!" he said.

"Excellent notion. So should I." Once the masculine ritual of decanter and glasses was completed, Beau gazed around the room, and found his sister rubbing Lord Mannering's back. The congratulations he had meant to give her on the excellence of her aim—it was Beau who had taught Cara to use her fists, a very long time ago—died in his throat. "Unhand the marquess!" he said instead. "He's going to marry Zoë at once."

Cara stiffened. Nick caught her wrist before she could move away. "No, I think I will not marry her at all. One week in your daughter's company and I would be fit to strangle her."

That's what came of these long betrothals. The

marquess sounded like a man who'd made up his mind, alas. Beau contemplated his daughter's two latest conquests. Paul Anderley was sprawled on the second sofa. "Don' book a' be. *I* bot boing do barry her!" The paper stuck beneath his upper lip, and the grip he had on the bridge of his nose, had an even more unfortunate effect on the clarity of his speech.

"Of course he isn't going to marry me!" Zoë draped herself over the back of Baron Fitzrichard's couch. "No one's going to marry me, and the sooner you accept that, the better it will be for everyone, Beau!"

Beau was a long way from acceptance. "Someone *is* going to marry you!" His gaze moved to Colin, who had retreated to the hearth along with the dog. "Who's *this*?"

"Colin Kennet, my nephew and heir," said Nick. "He won't marry her either, because I'll disinherit him if he does."

"I'm not going to marry anyone until I reach the age of reason," volunteered Colin. "Which from the way things are going looks to be a long way off. And even then I wouldn't marry *her*."

Zoë turned up her little nose. "You should be so fortunate."

Colin snorted. "I should be so cursed."

Stung, Zoë pushed out her lower lip. "I suppose you'd prefer a *biddable* female."

Colin petted Daisy, who was inspired by these raised voices to snuggle closer to him for protection. "Anybody would."

Zoë sniffed. "That shows all *you* know! Lord Mannering fancies Aunt Cara and she's not biddable by any means."

Colin glanced at his uncle, seated now in a walnut

wing chair. Lady Norwood remained by his side, perhaps because he held her wrist in a grasp that didn't look especially loverlike. Did Nicky think she might hit him again? These nuances of romantic behavior were too much for Colin to grasp.

While Zoë and Colin quarreled, the gentlemen followed suit, a disagreement that rapidly accelerated until mention was made of a duel. Fitz roused sufficiently to debate who was going to fight whom, Nicky being up to no such strenuous activities, although he himself would be happy to stand in. Or, alternately, to second someone. Fitz had already demonstrated his prowess with a fireplace poker, which it was a pity Beau had missed.

Beau rather thought it was a blessing. He stared at the baron's lilac cravat. "Nice necktie!" he said.

Fitz preened. "I call it the Point Non Plus. After Anderley there." Paul glowered. Ianthe thrust the vinaigrette under the baron's nose. "Stop it, all of you!"

Patience was not Zoë's long suit. She eyed the grandfather clock. When the babble of voices failed to abate, she walked over and gave it a great shove. The clock toppled sideways, and hit the floor with a great crash. In the sudden silence, she announced, "I cannot think I would be the right wife for you, Lord Mannering! There, I have cried off."

Beau stared from the shattered clock to his wayward daughter. "Great-Uncle Percival brought that clock with him when he fled Austria!"

Zoë plopped her hands on her hips. "If you don't start paying attention to me, I *will* break everything in the house! What's more important, Beau, your own daughter or some silly French spy?"

Beau wondered if he'd drunk too much of his

brandy. Else how had French spies got involved in this mess? "You can't cry off!"

"I already have." Zoë picked up the fireplace poker. "And everyone heard me. Isn't that right?"

"Right as a trivet!" Fitz decided it was safe to sit up. Safer than lying down, at any rate, when the spawn of Satan had a fireplace poker in her hand. "We all heard you cry off. Nicky's betrothal is at an end."

Beau glared impotently at his daughter, and then at his sister. "Blast it, Cara! I brought you to town so that Zoë might profit from your good sense!"

All eyes turned to Cara, who lowered her gaze to the hand that so firmly clasped her wrist. "How selfish of you, Lady Norwood," scolded Fitz, "to wish a little happiness of your own. Not that you look especially happy at the moment, but Nicky will make it up to you."

Cara bit her lip. "Don't tease her," said Ianthe. "We all know that the path of True Love is often beset with difficulties."

"Briars, brambles and banes!" agreed Fitz.

"It will only be a nine days' wonder." Zoë twirled the fireplace poker on her shoulder as if it were a parasol. "Perhaps I am one of those Loversall females who isn't meant to marry, like Gwyneth and Ariadne. If you try to force me, Beau, I'll just run away and wind up in a brothel, or perhaps victim of a white slavery ring."

Beau frowned at his daughter. "You aren't supposed to know about such things."

"Well, I do! And I shan't let you break Aunt Cara's heart, because although *you* might not mind if she flings herself off the battlements, Cousin Ianthe and I do! Anyway, Lord Mannering will cry off if I don't."

Fortunately the family battlements had long since passed into other hands. Beau turned his astonished gaze on the marquess. "You wouldn't."

Nick shifted in the chair and winced. He felt as though five hundred devils were sticking their pitchforks in his back. Cara's cool hand moved to touch his cheek. He looked up at her. "Oh yes I would."

"Lord Mannering prefers Aunt Cara," explained Zoë. "He told me so himself. As we tried to tell you!"

So they had, but he hadn't believed them. "You're been frolicking with my *sister?*" said Beau.

Nick didn't think that "frolicking" quite described what he'd been doing, but he didn't quibble. "I have."

Cara glanced at her brother. "Contrary to your expectations, Beau, as well as your daughter's, even people in their declining years can still enjoy *amour.*"

Beau disliked the fire in his sister's eye. There were still things in the room that could be broken. "I never said—"

"You said I was dull and drab and dreary and I don't even remember what else."

"Dwabble!" interjected the squire. "She bo sush ding."

"I'm sure I never meant—"

"Of course you did," put in Ianthe. "You always mean what you say. At least in the moment of saying it."

Beau raised his hands in defeat. "We'll just have to hold up our heads and pretend nothing untoward has happened. Ianthe will—"

"No, Ianthe won't. I am removing with Cousin Wilhelmina to Brighton."

Fitz brightened. "Excellent choice! I was planning

on going there myself. Prinny requires my advice about some additions to his Pavilion."

Ianthe met her cousin's gaze. "Zoë is *your* daughter, Beau. Perhaps one of your female friends might have some suggestions as to what you might do with her."

Beau had some notions of his own, but unfortunately the dungeons had departed the family along with the battlements. "I don't think I have any more female friends," he said.

Zoë moved to her papa's side. "No mistresses? Poor Beau! Aunt Cara isn't the only one who is growing old."

Beau might have taken exception with this comment, had he been listening. Instead, he was looking at Ianthe. "You are leaving me."

Ianthe smiled, a little wistfully. "It's time, don't you think?"

Beau was uncertain what he thought, save that the notion of Ianthe's departure was having a strange effect on parts of his person that hadn't perked up for some time, even during a visit to the Temple of Health in the Adelphi, where he had sat upon a magnetic throne, and taken a crackling electrical bath, and been prescribed a course of treatment that included Nervous Ætherial Balsam and Imperial Pills. And if he had foregone the fifty pounds that would have purchased him a romp in the Celestial Bed, he had still learned some bawdy lyrics, most memorably "he kneaded her dough with his long rolling-pin."

Beau was visited, then, by his own epiphany. Perhaps not Zoë's antics had quenched his ardor, but Ianthe's reproachful presence in the background of his life. "Yes, my love, I suppose it is."

Zoë didn't see why anyone should care if Ianthe

went to Brighton. "If I contrived to make it look like Lord Mannering had compromised me, he *truly* compromised Aunt Cara, because I found her hiding in his bed. So you should make him marry her instead."

Cara interrupted. "No one is making anyone marry anyone! Forget it, Beau."

Beau studied his sister. "Do I want to know why you were in Mannering's bed?"

Cara touched Nick's hand, locked so firmly around her wrist. "No."

Zoë played her trump card. "*And* he wasn't wearing any clothes."

Ianthe arched her eyebrows. "You didn't tell me he was naked, Cara!"

"He wasn't."

"Yes, I was."

"You were wearing a sheet."

"I'll vouch for it!" volunteered Fitz. "I saw them both myself."

Beau didn't care to imagine what Fitz might have been doing in the marquess's bedroom at that particular moment. Colin decided it was definitely time for an uncle-nephew talk.

"Cara wasn't naked," admitted Zoë. "But she was all rumpled, and I had to button her bodice myself. Did I mention that they were both in his bed? With a feather fan? Which was very poorly done of him, because he was supposed to be seducing me."

"What kind of feathers?" inquired Beau.

"I thought it was rather *well* done myself." Nick turned over Cara's hand and pressed a kiss on her palm. "So did your aunt, at the time, although she won't admit it, because right now I'm not in her good books."

Zoë lowered the poker. There was a wedding to

be planned. "You won't wish to tie the knot at St. George's. Perhaps you should get a special license instead. Or better yet, run off to Gretna Green! Aunt Cara, you *did* say you would elope with him."

Cara tried, ineffectively, to withdraw from Nicky's grasp. "Only to prevent him marrying you. Which we already know he isn't going to do."

Beau gave up musing about feathers to fix Nick with a stern eye. "It's clear to me, Mannering, that you haven't dealt well with the females of my family!"

"Oh, I don't know!" snickered Fitz. "Seems to me he's dealt prodigious well with one of them!"

Cara blushed. "None of this was his fault," protested Zoë. "Lord Mannering wished to speak to Beau about Aunt Cara when he met me in the hall."

Beau was growing short of temper. "Well, he can't have Cara now! Think of the scandal it would make."

Everybody stared at him, including Colin and the dog. Ianthe spoke for them all. "Don't be absurd!"

But Nicky had never said he wished to marry her. He could have come to speak to Beau about anything from horseflesh to the price of wheat. "Has it occurred to anyone to wonder what *I* want?" Cara asked.

Nick rubbed his thumb over the palm of her hand. "What do you want, *cara mia?*"

She wanted that clever thumb to rub certain other places. Which was something she wasn't prepared to announce in the middle of her brother's drawing room. "I don't know! But I'm *not* going to get married because I've been compromised!"

Cautiously, favoring his injured nose, Paul Anderley got up from his couch. "Do you bish be do bake you home?"

Did she? It was peaceful in the Cotswolds. Cara

decided she had already experienced enough peace for a lifetime. "I'm sorry, Paul. I don't."

It was over, then. Paul could only comport himself with the dignity of a Master of Hounds at the end of a long and unsuccessful hunt. At least his damned nose had stopped bleeding. He bowed, and turned toward the door.

Widdle waited in the hallway. The butler tutted at his appearance. Paul plopped his hat on his head and snatched up his cane.

Zoë nibbled on a fingernail. "I wouldn't think that you're suited for a nunnery, Aunt Cara. Like Francesca was. Although she *did* get snatched by pirates, and ended up in a harem, so perhaps it wouldn't be too bad."

Fitz rose from the sofa. "It's the very devil, isn't it, to cut up someone's hopes? Nicky's not plump current, you know. He needs to be treated gently. Come, Loversall, show me those gardens of which you're so proud."

Beau stared at him in astonishment. "I'm not—"

"Yes, you are!" said Ianthe, and gave him a frown.

"Ah, the gardens! Yes, indeed!" Beau ushered in his various guests around the broken clock and out through the French doors, along with Zoë and the dog, neither of whom especially wished to go. Zoë fluttered her eyelashes at her father. "Forgive me, Papa! I have behaved very badly. You will be cross with me."

Beau slid his arm around her shoulders. "Nonsense! Loversalls cannot help our bad behavior, puss. It is our wild blood." Ianthe rolled her eyes. Fitz took hold of Daisy's collar, and said, "Everyone makes mistakes, Lady Norwood. Only a fool makes the same one twice." He dragged the dog outside, and firmly closed the door.

Cara looked down at the marquess, and hoped she wasn't making the most monumental of mistakes. "Are you in pain?"

"Not so much as I'm going to be." He tugged on her wrist, and she plopped into his lap. He winced. She stiffened. "Nicky, your back!"

"My back is feeling better by the moment." He drew her close against his chest.

Cara inhaled the scent of camphor. Nothing had ever smelled so good to her. His heart beat strongly against her cheek. "I can't think when I'm near you, Nicky."

Her hair had escaped its pins to tangle on her shoulders. He wound a ringlet around his finger. "I don't want you to think. That's what got us in trouble before. Just trust your feelings. Trust me."

Cara leaned away just a little bit, so she could look into his eyes. "There was a note delivered earlier today. From Lucasta Clitheroe. Or Lady Fenton, I suppose I should say. She heard I'd returned to town, and she wanted me to know—Oh, Nicky, she admitted that she'd lied!"

Damned right her ladyship had lied, although she'd been reluctant to confess until Nick pointed out that Lord Fenton might not be best pleased to learn about their one-time affair. Let alone the other affairs she had enjoyed during the course of her marriage. "I am, of course, far too much the gentleman to say I told you so."

"You're not a gentleman at all." However, Cara made no attempt to move the hand that was stroking up her calf. "I married Norwood because I was afraid, Nicky." She took a deep breath. "I still am."

His hand on her calf stilled. "Of me? Don't be. Cara, I love you."

He loved her? Well, of course he loved her. Tears filled her eyes. "No, of myself. I *hit* you, Nicky. Twice."

"Perhaps I deserved it." He tugged on her ringlet. "I have not behaved especially well."

And she had? Cara shook her head. "You didn't deserve it, and I knew it. *And* I bloodied Paul Anderley's nose as well, even though I don't care about him one little bit."

Nick wondered where this was going. "Are you telling me you wish to bloody my nose?"

"I'm trying to tell you that I *don't*! Nicky, if we were truly together, and some other woman caught your eye, I might well murder you!"

Nick caught an errant teardrop on his fingertip. "You may murder me with my blessing, *cara,* if some other woman ever takes my eye."

Cara regarded him dubiously. "Gentlemen are known to have their mistresses. Look at Beau."

She had relaxed a little bit. Nick's hand continued its lazy journey toward her knee. "Loversalls have mistresses. I am not a Loversall. The shoe should be on the other foot. I should be worrying about you."

"As if I would ever—" She leaned her forehead against his. "I take your point. I am being a ninny, am I not?"

"You are being adorable." Past the knee now, to the thigh. "What *do* you want, Cara?"

The blasted man knew what she wanted. Her skin trembled beneath his touch. Trembled and twitched and grew prodigiously warm. That the marquess was suffering similar symptoms was apparent. She *was* sitting on his lap.

Cara leaned forward, and loosened his neck-cloth. "I want all I've ever wanted. Just to be with you." She brushed her lips across his. "And it occurs to me that you are no longer betrothed."

First his neck-cloth, then his waistcoat. Now Cara was making quick work of the buttons on his shirt. "Not that I would want to stop you, but the others are just outside in the garden," Nick murmured.

"The devil with the others!" retorted Cara. "As everyone keeps reminding me, I am a Loversall." Then her fingers moved to the fastenings of his breeches, and Nick decided he didn't care if they had the entire British Navy with them in the room. He slid his hand up past Cara's thigh to clasp her fine *derrière*.

Cara shifted her weight until she was straddling him. He caught her by the waist and held her there. "Much as I dislike to admit it," he murmured, "Zoë did have a good idea."

"What idea?" Cara's hands moved to the buttons of her bodice. "Ravishment, perhaps?"

How the devil could she think he'd ever want another woman? Cantalope. Grapefruit. Plump casaba melons topped with luscious berries. "Um. That, too. But I meant the special license. We might retire to the country for a time until another scandal takes the place of ours." He lowered her, just a little bit. "I have several gardens that you might like to tend."

She wriggled, she pouted, she nibbled at his ear. He refused to release her. "Are you blackmailing me, my lord?"

"I am." And damned hard it was on a man. "Marry me, my love."

"I suppose I must if you are going to be so cruel. I do love you, Nicky. Madly. Passionately. With all my soul. And—mercy, you're killing me! No, no, don't ever stop!"

Lord Mannering and Lady Norwood were married soon thereafter, by means of a special license, which his lordship obtained, through his considerable influence, in an amazingly short time. Although some spiteful comments were inevitably made about the marquess's recent betrothal to his marchioness's niece, this minor detail was largely overlooked in light of the family to which both ladies belonged. In no time at all Lord and Lady Mannering's gardening efforts produced not one heir but two, putting to rest any question of his lordship's virility, despite his advanced age, and causing his nephew Colin considerable relief.

Following the wedding ceremony, Colin returned gratefully to his studies; Baron Fitzrichard escorted Ianthe and her Cousin Wilhelmina to Brighton, where he set a trend for colored cravats and matching scented handkerchiefs, and Ianthe soon became a favorite of the Prince Regent's set, most especially a pair of dashing Georgian dukes; and Beau set out with his daughter and three of his favorite mistresses on an extended inspection of the war-torn Continent, which they all enjoyed very much.

The Sophora japonica, despite all expectations, thrived, and in time grew to be a most impressive seventy-five feet tall.

And yes, it *is* possible to make love on horseback, though not advisable to attempt the business in Hyde Park.

<u>BOOK YOUR PLACE ON OUR WEBSITE</u> <u>AND MAKE THE</u> <u>READING CONNECTION!</u>

We've created a customized website just for our very special readers, where you can get the inside scoop on everything that's going on with Zebra, Pinnacle and Kensington books.

When you come online, you'll have the exciting opportunity to:

- View covers of upcoming books
- Read sample chapters
- Learn about our future publishing schedule (listed by publication month *and author*)
- Find out when your favorite authors will be visiting a city near you
- Search for and order backlist books from our online catalog
- Check out author bios and background information
- Send e-mail to your favorite authors
- Meet the Kensington staff online
- Join us in weekly chats with authors, readers and other guests
- Get writing guidelines
- AND MUCH MORE!

Visit our website at
http://www.kensingtonbooks.com

More Historical Romance From
Jo Ann Ferguson

Available Wherever Books Are Sold!

Visit our website at **www.kensingtonbooks.com**.

More Regency Romance
From Zebra

Embrace the Romance of
Shannon Drake